A TAINTED
LIGHT

BEE DOUGLAS

For information contact:

Beedouglasbooks@gmail.com

Cover design by Clarise Tan from CT Cover Creations

ISBN: 978-1-7328365-2-5

First Edition: August 2019

10 9 8 7 6 5 4 3 2 1

To my rock –
Through the storms, you've kept me grounded. In tranquil times,
you've calmed my racing mind. You've steered me clear from
treacherous falls, but allowed me to explore at a reasonable pace.
For that, I will never be able to thank you. For that, you always be
my person.

Part One

Orpheus weeped and cried out, "Love is dead!"

1

"Turn right on the next street," I tell Willow. The lights of the old Chevy illuminate the development. Rows and rows of houses line the street with perfectly manicured lawns. Any cars in the drives are brand new, lacking any dents or rust. It took me a good half an hour to think of somewhere to go. With the Devil's Playground now reduced to ruins, there will be a lookout for any sight of me. We can't go to Kane or Royce's. My own home is too far out of the question. We need not only a safe place to hide out for the time being, but also somewhere that I can get Briggs help. He desperately needs medical attention.

Six months ago, I never thought my life would be this way. Being taken against my will and told that I'm a harbinger of Death was never on my bucket list. And yet, here we are. My name is Nora McKinley and I am a Banshee. It still has me reeling. Fuck, it sounds like I'm in some supernatural AA meeting. Decades ago, my family somehow got tangled up in the after life world. A power has been passed through the bloodline, trickling down to me. Instead of planning for another shift at the nursing home, I'm on the run from demons and the hands of Death.

Briggs lets out a shaky breath. I run my hand over the top of his head where it lays in my lap.

"We're almost there," I promise him.

As Willow turns, I tell her to look for a house with a black SUV in the driveway. It's halfway down the road and stands between two expansive brick homes. Willow cuts off the headlights as she pulls in.

"And this is safe?" she asks, leaning forward to look through the windshield. The living room window flickers on and off from the television. The climbing plants that decorate her trellis in the summer have turned brown with the changing weather. Pretty soon, snow will cover the flowerbeds and the world will become a much darker and colder place.

I nod, even though she can't see. "I'll be right back," I tell them. I go to move, sliding little by little to not cause Briggs more pain, but I stop. I can guarantee that she's pissed. Showing up alone wouldn't be the best thing to do in this situation. It'll be better if I take him with me. She can't exactly say no to a wounded man. "Help me get him out, Will."

She moves quickly, shutting the driver door and opening mine. It takes us several tries, but we finally get Briggs out. He uses what little strength he has left to stand while we support him. We creep slowly up the cement sidewalk. I knock on the front door, leaving a smear of blood. My stomach churns. It's probably Briggs', but it could be mine. Hell, it could belong to any number of people. Willow tosses me an incredulous look as time passes. Finally, after what seems like forever, the door opens.

She stands in pajama shorts and a hoodie with a pint of Ben & Jerry's ice cream in her hand. Shock fades quickly into a glare as recognition sinks in.

"Hey, Aggie," I say weakly. I deserve the way her eyes pierce through me. She's probably mentally sorting through all the different ways to murder me. And, honestly, I don't blame her.

She sighs, placing her free hand on her hip. "What do you want, Nora?"

I gesture to the man I'm holding up. "I need your help." Aggie reluctantly turns her attention away from me and her face pales when she sets eyes on Briggs. Apprehension shadows her expression.

"Please," I beg.

She glances at me with a suspicious look on her face. Nevertheless, she steps aside and holds open the door. "Take him to the spare bedroom. I'll grab my bag."

"Thank you," Willow sighs. The relief in her tone has me sneaking a glance in her direction.

We move inside and I direct us over to the stairs. With one of us in front and the other behind, we manage to get him up the stairs. He lets out a deep, agonizing groan as we lay him down on the bed.

Aggie's there, handing me a pair of scissors to cut open the front of his shirt. Briggs is a boar of a man, made up of pure muscle and testosterone. Even in his current state, I can make out the indents of abs as I pull his shirt off.

"What the hell have you gotten yourself into?" Aggie asks quietly, eyeing the deep stab wound that takes up a large portion of his lower abdomen. I give her a look, mentally promising her that I'll explain later. Shaking her head, Aggie sighs and, thankfully, gets to work.

We allow the medical instinct to take over. Neither of us are doctors, but that doesn't hinder us. We clean the area and prep it to be stitched up. Out of the corner of my eye, I see Willow step away to give us room to work. I don't miss the tears rolling down her cheeks as she watches.

"Willow," I call, "go in the bathroom and grab me towels. It's just across the hall."

She stands there in a form completely foreign to me. She's more than just distraught. She always has her emotions locked down tight. But these past few hours have been Hell - not just for me, but for her as well. When she pulls herself together, she slips out the door, following instructions.

"I don't see anything broken off in the wound," Aggie observes. She takes one of the towels Willow brings back and drops in the entire thing in a bowl of water. Once it's soaked, she places it directly over the area. Briggs lets out a loud bellow. The sound makes me jump, but Aggie is calm and collected. She doesn't falter and continues soaking up as much excess blood as possible.

It takes over an hour to get the wound closed. It's not our best work. There's going to be a terrible scar. Several areas that didn't hold the first time, needed to be restitched over again. But we were able to get him closed up enough that we can tape over it with gauze. My first instinct is to get him morphine to help with the pain, but the best Aggie has is generic Tylenol.

"It'll do," I tell her.

After we get him some type of pain relief, it's not long before he gives in to sleep. His chest moves with each uneasy breath he takes. His face has lost all of its natural olive skin tone; faded away from all the blood loss. In its place, a pained expression has taken over, tensing every muscle in his handsome face.

"I don't have another bed," Aggie tells Willow, "but I do have an air mattress. I can get it ready down in the living room."

Willow shakes her head. "I don't want to leave him."

"Understandable. Let me get it. There should be enough room in here."

"You can't tell her anything," she says to me once Aggie's out of earshot.

I roll my eyes. "How do you expect me to explain this? She's going to ask questions."

"It's none of her business."

"Will," I say, hardening my voice, "she's my best friend. I haven't spoken to her in months. I have to tell her something." She goes to open her mouth, but I cut her off. "She opened her home to us. Without that, Briggs would be dead by the time the sun comes up."

Her jaw clamps shut, nostrils flaring at my comment. I understand where she's coming from. Mortals aren't supposed to know about the world after life. It's a different level of stress they don't need. Plus, it would cause an offset in the balance if humans knew exactly what can condemn them.

When Aggie returns, Willow narrows her eyes. "Fine," she mutters, taking the blanket and pillow from my friend.

They make quick work of airing up the mattress. I do my best to clean up all the towels and gauze, trying not to make a bigger mess.

"We'll be down in the kitchen," Aggie tells Willow as she unfolds the blanket.

I pull the door shut and let Aggie take everything out of my hands. Following her down the stairs, I start thinking of all the possible excuses I could give her. This wouldn't be nearly as bad if I had been given the chance to say goodbye. But, after Raina smashed my phone into pieces, there was no going back. Unless it involved Reapers, demons, singing, or witchy training, I had no part in it. The outside world had been completely cut off.

"What are you doing?" I exclaim.

Aggie piles all the mess into the sink and tosses a couple of matches on top of them. She rolls her eyes. "I don't want the garbage man thinking I'm some type of serial killer."

Makes sense, I tell myself. The smell of burnt cloth fills the room. After the towels and gauze have turned to ash, she runs water and sprays the air with Febreze.

I take a seat at the little dinette table. She clasps her hands together, placing them on the tabletop as she sits across from me. Her brown eyes lock onto mine. Her face is stern, but also laced with a sense of calm, as if the last hour or so didn't happen. Was its relief? Sadness? Or was she just overwhelmed to the point that she couldn't convey any emotion through her facial expressions?

"Hi," I say meekly. She rolls her eyes. Letting out a sigh, I run my hands over my face. "Ag, you won't believe anything I'm about to tell you."

"Probably not."

"And you're not going to forgive me, even after I tell you what I've been going through these past months."

"Again," she repeats, "probably not."

Swallowing hard, I look her dead in the eyes. Remembering the way Kane had surfaced all of this with a simple question, I ask, "Do you know what a Banshee is?"

. . .

The clock above the stove has rolled over to the four o'clock hour by the time I'm done telling her my story. It wasn't a story though; it was the truth, every word I spoke. She didn't ask as many questions as I anticipated. Only the occasional definition or a "Who's that?" came from her mouth. Other than that, she paid close attention.

"Yeah," I shrug. There's nothing else I can say. I can't exactly apologize for being taken hostage. There's honestly not much I can apologize for. I didn't have control over much. Even the clothes I wore each night to sing weren't my choosing. Luna, a demon that had mastered the sin of lust, had purchased every garment that hung in the dressing room.

She narrows her eyes, placing me under her scrutinizing stare. I suck in my bottom lip, chewing on it while I let her process the bomb I just dropped on her.

"So... you can kill people?" I give a halfhearted nod. "With your voice?" Another nod. "And those people in my spare bedroom are basically reincarnated dead people?" Nod. She leans back and runs a hand through her blonde hair. "What the fuck, Nora? What the actual fuck?"

I stare at her, not able to tell if she believes anything I just said. If I hadn't just spent the last several months living through it, I doubt I would believe it either. Hell, it took me long enough to accept that I'm a Banshee, which isn't saying that I'm not still thrown off by the fact. It's a lot to take it. I just hope that having Briggs and Willow with me helps to solidify things.

"You've been cooped up with some guy that steals people's souls?" Yet another nod. "Where's he at?"

Swallowing hard, I try to calm the tears starting to blur my vision. "He's dead," I tell her in a raspy voice.

Her eyes soften. "You love him, don't you? Not a twisted Stockholm syndrome love, but actual love."

I wipe at the traitorous tears. "Yes."

Aggie stands up and practically runs around the little table. She wraps her arms around me. The hold I have over my emotions breaks; my shoulders sag and I give in to the tears. She squeezes me harder. A hug - a genuine hug. I didn't know I needed this type of connection. But I'd be lying if I said it didn't give me comfort.

After catching my breath, Aggie finally lets me go. She climbs back in her chair and takes my hand in hers.

"I'm sorry." I dry the wetness on my cheeks. "I didn't know where else to go. There's no way I could have taken him to my house."

"That's completely understandable."

I let the meek smirk play on my lips. "I can't thank you enough for helping us. Briggs," I gesture up the stairs, "is in bad shape."

"I'm glad I could help." She applies gentle pressure on my hand. "What are you guys going to do now?"

A sardonic laugh escapes and I shake my head. "I have no fucking clue. Briggs is in no condition to move. And if he were, I don't know where we could go."

"You're welcome here as long as you need." I thank her once more. Lightening the situation, she says, "Don't thank me. I have a hot man upstairs and I get to play his nurse. What more could a girl want?"

A laugh bubbles up from somewhere deep in my chest. She smiles, pleased with my reaction. I don't have the heart to tell her that his heart is set on Willow. Regardless, we're safe for the time being. Briggs has a bed and is able to take time to heal. I let out the breath I've been holding in for hours. This is the first time I've been able to relax in I don't know how long. But it won't last - it can't. I have to get with Willow and come up with a plan. But just for tonight, we're safe.

2

I didn't sleep. Between tossing around and the steady stream of thoughts, I wasn't able to keep my eyes shut long enough to even attempt to sleep. As exhausted as I was, I hoped I would've been able to get at least five minutes. And yet, I don't even think I got five seconds.

Once the sun starts peeking in through the blinds, I call it quits. I fold up the blanket Aggie gave and place it on the couch. The house is quiet. I do my best not to make any noise. The last thing I want to do is wake anyone up. Being friends with Aggie for as long as I have, I know my way through the house. I know what setting on her coffee maker gives the best tasting coffee. I even know where she keeps the good creamer, which are two necessities for nurses. I make a large pot for when everyone else wakes up, but take my cup once it's done and sit at her little table.

Aggie doesn't have much of a backyard, let alone a view. There's a small little shed tucked away in the corner and a tree that was planted before she bought the house. It's nothing like Kane's sky-high loft. There are no rooftops or streetlights; just a white wooden fence.

Just the thought of him makes my heart pull. It's a surreal feeling knowing that I will never see him again. That just yesterday morning we were tangled up in the sheets. I can still feel the pressure on my lips from the kiss he stole before leaving with Royce. If I'd known that I'd be waking up this morning without him, I would've treasured those last moments. More than that, I would've begged him not to go.

A lump starts to form in my throat. Everything about this is unfair. He finally gave in to his feelings. He finally accepted the connection between us. He shouldn't be gone. He should be here, kissing me in the morning light. A silent sob wracks through my body as tears spill down my cheeks. Covering my face with my hands, I let the pain of losing him wash over me. Adding to that, I let the pain of losing two other people take over.

Yvette and I had developed an odd sort of friendship. She pushed me, trusting that I could handle whatever she threw my way. No matter the tension that would build between us during our sessions together, she was there if I needed reassurance. But she walked out on us sometime yesterday morning.

And Royce? I wish I had known him longer. He was a hysterical person, taking charge of all the positive things life offered. But he's gone now too. Not gone - dead. Royce is dead. Kane is dead.

Another sob takes over, shaking my shoulders.

Arms wrap around me. I look up, coming face to face with Aggie. She squeezes me in her arms and kissing the top of my head. "It will be okay."

"How?" I ask, my voice raspy.

She wipes at the wet mess my face has turned into. "Because you're Nora McKinley. You are the strongest person I know."

I shake my head as another burst of tears rush down my cheeks. She shushes me, running her hand through my hair.

"You need to go shower," she tells me, holding me out at arm's length. "Get cleaned up. I did a little online shopping last night and have to pick a few things up." I go to open my mouth and offer my help, but she shakes her head. "You need to get yourself together. Shower. Eat something. I'll leave some clothes out for you. I won't be long."

"Okay." She kisses my head once more before disappearing to get herself ready for the day.

I will forever be thankful for her. It takes a special kind of person to care the way she does. Bringing in strays isn't something most people do, but Aggie does.

Once I finish my cup of coffee, I climb the stairs up to the main bathroom. Aggie set out a pair of leggings and a hoodie for me. Looking down, I take in the dirty and ripped clothes I still have on. I didn't have the energy to change last night. I slide my pants down my legs along with my underwear, then toss my sweater on the floor with them.

I don't even recognize the woman staring back at me in the mirror. Her hair is wild with knots. A mixture of dried blood and dirt coats her skin. Bruises splotch her sides and arms. The remnants of tears stain her cheeks. Her usual bright eyes are dark and sad. *"...you are Nora McKinley. You are the strongest person I know."* That's what Aggie had said. But I don't look it, let alone feel it.

Turning the shower faucet on, I let the steam fog up the

mirror before stepping in. I stay under the stream of water for what feels like forever. I wash my hair twice, making sure to comb my fingers through it to get all the tangles out. By the time I step out, the water runs clear, free from the grime that had been caked on.

A knock comes to the door, startling me. "Hurry up," Aggie's voice says. "You've been in there for over an hour. And I have something for you."

I dry off and put on the clothes she gave me. There's no denying they don't fit me properly, but they're a fuck ton better than my other war worn option that now lays in a heap on the floor. I'm still running the towel through my hair when I walk down to the kitchen. Aggie stands there with a smile on her face. Despite having her house overrun by a Banshee and two Accursed, she doesn't even have a hair out of place. That's Aggie for you - perfection.

She holds out a box in her hand. I take it, looking at her confused. "It's a present," she explains. Pulling the lid off, I find a cell phone inside. "It's to replace the broken one. You need it, especially with everything you have going on."

"You didn't have to do this."

She shrugs. "I know."

I wrap her in a hug, thanking her. Taking it out of the box, I turn it on and find that she not only has her number already programmed in, but she set the wallpaper to a picture of the two of us singing drunken karaoke at Etta's. A sense of sadness washes over me.

"This seems like a lifetime ago." I press the side button and darken the screen. "I need to go talk to Willow."

Aggie starts pulling out groceries from bags she has sitting on the counter. "She's showering in the downstairs bathroom." I grab the jug of milk she bought and put it in the fridge. "She's a bit testy, isn't she?"

I let out a breathy laugh. "Just a bit."

Aggie nods. "I like her."

Hearing that causes the corner of my mouth to quiver with a timid smile. Being plucked from one life and forced into another, I found comfort in Willow. She reminded me so much of my human friend. Both are extremely willful and stand their ground. She helped make my situation not seem as bad.

As if she heard us talking about her, Willow comes up the stairs. She's wearing one of the million pink shirts Aggie owns. She's probably as uncomfortable as she looks. This is a complete contrast from her norm. I haven't seen Willow in anything other than black.

"You wear that better than I do!" Aggie exclaims.

Willow gives me a *you've got to be shitting me* look. I have to put a hand over my mouth to hide my smile. No matter how similar these two are, Aggie is as light as Willow is dark. Seeing them together is amusing. Well... at least for me it is.

"We have to talk," Willow snaps. I nod in agreement, helping Aggie put the last few things she bought away.

Once all the bags are empty, Aggie looks awkwardly between us. "I'll just, uhm... go check on our patient."

Willow stares at her as she walks away, climbing up the stairs to the spare bedroom. When she was out of earshot, my Accursed friend sneers down at the shirt. "Really?"

"It's not that bad."

She rolls her eyes. Crossing her arms over her chest, she leans against the door jam. "We need to leave."

"Briggs can't move," I gesture upstairs. It hits me that I haven't checked in on him all morning. But then again, there were an issue, I would've known. I let that lone thought overshadow the rising guilt.

Her hard expression cracks just the slightest when I mention his name. "We can't stay here, Nora."

"I don't think you understand how bad he is. He almost died last night." I run a hand through my damp hair. "He could still die."

"And I don't think you understand that Death won't stop until they get their hands on you, especially after what happened last night."

Last night, after Kane had been... killed, a bout of sonic waves had erupted from somewhere deep inside of me. They were stronger than anything I ever felt before. In the middle of their rippling effect, a relieving power had taken over my body, making me even more connected to the vibrations. The Playground had been brought down to ruins; my voice caused the foundation crumbled.

"That wasn't normal. You had to have tapped into your Banshee more. Hell, you could've unleashed it." I scoff at her comment. "That's the only other explanation I can think of."

I shake my head. "I was just really distraught. I was riding on more emotion than power. That's it."

"Nora," she bites out, "how many times did getting upset only fuel your power? I've seen it in person a good handful of times. Kane was killed. Royce was," she swallows hard, "killed. You haven't experienced that kind of grief since you've been aware of what you are. That's what Yvette was pushing for: a major power rush to bring the Banshee out."

I want to argue with her and tell her that she's wrong. But I can't. Everything she just said is true. Aside from getting extremely pissed off or frustrated, I haven't felt that much emotion when I worked with the witch.

A quiet banging noise startles the both of us. We move for the stairs, adrenaline kicking in. Willow is faster to react than I am, hitting the top of the steps before I can.

Aggie lets out a piercing scream as she rounds the corner and is pushed against the wall by Willow. "What the fuck are you doing?!"

Willow pushes her aside, not giving her the time of day, and barges into the spare bedroom. Irritation and concern ooze from her pores. I pat Aggie's shoulder and peer into the room. Briggs is still asleep. He wears a tight grimace. Sweat coats his face. But despite his discomfort, he's breathing - he's alive.

"I'm sorry," I whisper to my friend.

Aggie rolls her eyes. "I dropped something. Did she really think I'd kill him?"

"Yes," Willow hisses, stepping back out into the hall. "This isn't your world. I have no clue who you are, which means I don't trust you."

Aggie's face turns bright red. "Excuse me? How dare you insinuate I'd do such a thing. You are a guest in my home. I didn't have to let you in."

"I told you this was a bad idea," she sneers at me.

"Stop it," I bite out. "She's a friend. She isn't going to hurt him or sell out information. Why can't you get that through your head?"

"She's not supposed to be a part of this."

"Neither was I."

"And look where that put us." Her words are like a verbal strike, leaving a stinging sensation across my face. Her face falls when she realizes what she said, complexion paling. "Nora, I'm sorry."

My mouth forms into a tight line. I don't respond. Beside me, Aggie crosses her arms across her chest, glancing between the both of us.

I didn't intend for any of this to happen. Willow knows that. She seemed to accept that I was unwillingly thrown into this mess. And yet, after her own case of word vomit, I can't help but wonder if she truly believes it. Or, after last night, if she blames me for Royce's death.

She lets out a sigh. "We need to leave. We're sitting ducks if we stay here."

I gesture to the room Briggs currently occupied. "He can't be moved. He needs to heal."

"We can't stay here. The Cathedral is the only safe place for us to go."

The Cathedral. Kane told me about that place. It's supposedly this huge church that houses Changelings and those seeking their protection. It was the only place Reapers wouldn't dare step foot in.

I open my mouth, but Aggie cuts to the chase. "You go. He can stay. I'll take care of him until he's able to be on his own." She turns to me. "If you're not here, those people might not have much cause to stick around."

That's the last thing I want to do. I don't want to drag her into this more than I already have, but she's right. Anywhere I go, they'll follow. If I stay here, it's only a matter of time before they sniff out my location.

I turn to Willow as she runs a hand through her thick black hair. "I guess that could work."

"Alright," I concede. "Then we have a plan."

3

Willow pulls the car along a sidewalk, joining all the other sedans that line the street. She cuts off the engine and we both get out. It's a quiet area, not far from where from Aggie and I went to college. Brownstones act as walls on either side of the street. Wrought iron fences separate yards barely big enough for one person to stand in. And yet, it's a rich neighborhood. It's not the type of rich like Aggie's development. This neighborhood stinks of old money.

"Where are we?" I ask.

A sigh escapes her. "The Cathedral is a couple blocks from here."

"Why did we park this far away?"

Her forehead crinkles. "They don't exactly approve of stolen vehicles."

She doesn't wait for me. I grab my bag from the back seat and follow her.

Aggie hadn't been too keen on me leaving again, but

there's nothing else I can do. Willow's right. I have to keep moving. Staying in one place for too long, even if it's my friend's house, would not only put me in danger, but her as well. With that being said, she had loaded up a duffle bag with some necessities: clothes, deodorant, toothbrush, paste. I didn't expect her to forgive me as quickly as she did, let alone go out and make sure I had everything I could ever need. And then offering to care for Briggs? She's gone above and beyond the call of friendship.

Willow is dead set on turning to the Changelings for help. She said they'd know what to do. We'd be safe there. But, after Kane and I were both attacked by them, I'm leery about this. For all I know, they'll want to use me against the hands of Death. Another pawn in their fucked-up game. Nevertheless, it's worth a shot.

"They're angels," Aggie had said. "How bad could they be?"

I didn't go into full detail about the raging war between Reapers and Changelings. I told her what she needed to know. Nothing more. Nothing less. She didn't see all the scars that covered Kane's body. She didn't gaze at a Changeling with pure hatred burning in its eyes. I'll let her keep believing what she needs to keep her spirits up.

When Willow told me we were going to the Cathedral, I expected to see just a big church. And yet, after we walk down a few blocks, the houses give way to an enormous concrete wall. Vines and moss cover every inch of it. A wrought iron gate sits in the middle. Even though the bars, I can't see anything aside from a long, winding drive and pillar topiaries.

Before I can ask one of the questions swarming around my mind, the sound of crackling comes from an intercom. "What is your business?"

She steps up to an old school system that I hadn't seen before. I look around, trying to find a camera or motion detector. Nothing.

"We need to speak to the Council."

"Her kind is not welcomed in these walls." Static muffles every word.

"Excuse me?"

Willow shoots me an irritated look over her shoulder. "She means no harm or ill will."

The person at the other end doesn't answer. White noise is the only thing that comes from the speaker. Running a hand through her mane of black hair, she lets out a frustrated sigh and mutters something under her breath.

A woman pushing a stroller jogs past, casting us a look. I shuffle my weight from one foot to another. I don't blame the girl for looking at us the way she does. Two women standing in the front of these gates in this neighborhood? It's probably more suspicious than I can even imagine.

Willow reaches out and angrily presses the button on the intercom over and over again. "Fuck! I didn't want to do this."

I wrap my arms around myself as a breeze blows through. Even through my jacket, a shiver races down my spine. The weather has dropped drastically since I had gone into my Banshee induced coma.

She takes a deep breath and hollers out, "Sanctuary!"

I glance around, hoping there aren't any other people around. The last thing we need is for someone to call the police. When the gates finally open, the hinges make a horrific creak. Willow walks through them without hesitation. Her head is held high and she pulls her shoulders back as if ready to face a battle.

I scurry in after her like a timid mouse. I keep close to her, even though her determined stride is hard to keep up with.

After what seems like miles, the drive opens up into a massive circle centered around an intricate fountain. My feet stop moving and my jaw drops as I take in the aged mansion. It looks more like a high-end private school than anything. Well, aside from the stained-glass windows and extravagant wooden cross on the steeple.

A loud whistle catches my attention. Willow stands yards away with an amused look on her face. She motions her head toward the doors. I set my awe aside and catch up.

Before her knuckles make contact with the ancient doors, both sides of the French style door are pulled inward. At this point, my mouth is permanently transfixed into an "O" shape. The stone architecture inside is designed perfectly. Standing in the center of the room is a man dressed in white robes. He's older, reminding me a lot of Bernie, Aggie's grandfather who had passed away months ago. Kane had been sent to collect his soul, which started our hellish spiral.

The thought of Kane and Bernie punches me right in the gut, making it hard to breath. I blink back the forming tears and fight to keep myself from crumbling on the marble floor.

Looking back at the man, I focus on the way his hands are clasped delicately together as he stares us down. "You have requested sanctuary." Willow goes to speak, but the man abruptly holds up his hand, cutting her off. He then continues in a gravelly voice. "Under the protection of sanctuary, there are mandatory rules and protocols in place that will be followed. We will not tolerate any infractions." I don't miss the way his eyes graze over me as he says this. "Your bags will be searched and then taken to assigned rooms. Meanwhile, I will take you to the

Council."

He turns on his heel and walks away from us. A man appears out of nowhere. He's dressed in fitted gray combat clothes. It's a shocking sight inside a supposed holy place. He extends his hand and I give him my bag. I contemplate thanking him, but Willow grabs my arm after tossing her own bag at him. We have to jog slightly to meet up with the robed man. He remains silent as we follow him down a hallway, heading toward another set of large doors that are guarded by two more combat-prepped men. Their pale skin and matching hair pegs them as Changelings. My jaw instinctively clamps down. With a snap of the older man's fingers, they pull open either door.

"They await you," he says, extending an arm into the dark room.

I turn to Willow, but she stares straight ahead, her expression set. She takes in a deep breath and steps inside. I look at the men for any sort of guidance, but they don't even flinch. Pushing aside my nerves, I walk inside. The doors slam shut, causing me to jump. The pits of Hell may be a scary place, but this place isn't exactly Disneyland.

Nearing the center of the room, a young boy sits directly under a stream of light. It stems from a stained-glass dome high above our heads. Despite being midday, the rest of the room is encased in darkness. Willow kneels down and bows her head. The boy can't be much older than Hannah. He looks at her with a face free of emotion. When his eyes turn to me, my cheeks start to burn.

I offer him a weak smile and a slight wave of my hand. "Hello."

"You've called upon sanctuary," he states. For being a child, he speaks in a hardened tone, articulating every word that comes out of his mouth. Standing, Willow nods her head. "Who seeks the protection of the Cathedral?"

"Willow Alder." My nose instinctively scrunches at how her voice changes, falling in line to the child.

The boy turns to me with his intense blue eyes. I pull my tongue from the roof of dry mouth. "Nora." Willow reaches over and pinches my side. "Ow! Eleanor McKinley."

He stares on in the space between the two of us. I can't help but notice that his hands still have that chubby shape. They probably are soft and unblemished from calluses, just like Hannah's.

After several minutes, he asks, "To what purpose does a member of the Accursed and a Banshee have inside these walls?"

Well, fuck, creepy little boy knows his shit.

"We seek the protection and aid of the Council."

I've never seen her behave this way. Usually, Willow stands confident, living life by her own rules. But she has been reduced to a strictly worded person, pleading for her life as if less than twenty-four hours ago she wasn't kicking ass and taking names.

The boy tilts his head slightly, taking in everything she says, only to stare off into the space between us again. After another pause, he answers her request in his odd tone. "The Cathedral extends sanctuary to the both of you for the next forty-eight hours. In that time, the continuation of your stay will be decided by the Council."

"This is about more than room and board," Willows snaps, showing signs of the girl I've come to know. She blanches a second after the words leave her lips. "We need help. Things have changed dramatically. The Changelings need to strike while

Death is still shaken up."

His feet swing back and forth. The tips of his toes barely touch the floor. "Another request the Council will discuss." Willow shakes her head in frustration. The boy calls out and the doors open once more.

"You will be shown to your rooms now," Mr. White Robe says. We've been dismissed.

Willow opens her mouth several times like a gaping fish. I grab hold of her shoulder. Her lips brace shut as she looks at me, the color draining from her face.

"I thought we were supposed to meet with a council," I whisper as we walk out of the room.

Lines form across her forehead. "We just did."

I choose to keep the other questions to myself instead of facing her condescending tone again.

We are led in two different directions. I try catching Willow's gaze before we were split up, but she doesn't look my way. She walks with the old man, while a Changeling guard accompanies me, his hand never leaving from the hilt of a sheathed dagger.

The room he takes me to is at the top of a spiral staircase. It reminds me of Rapunzel's tower, except there's no window to dangle my red hair out of. Honestly, it's extremely dreary. A toilet and sink are tucked away in the corner and the bed is more of a cot. My muscles tense up just looking at it. My duffle bag is waiting for me at the foot of the bed.

"After you." The Changeling stands outside the door. The corner of his crystal eyes squint as he watches my every move.

One step inside and he slams the door shut. The sound of it being locked echoes throughout the cold room. Did these people really think I'm dangerous? Do I really deserve nothing more than to kept locked away from the rest of the world?

I push the bag on the floor. The springs creak as I sit down. There's absolutely no support to it. I fight back the forming tears.

Had that interaction really gone that quick? And that Council? There's no way we spent that awkward conversation actually talking to the Council. I didn't know what to expect of this place. By no means was I preparing for a grand entrance followed by a guest of honor dinner. But locked away? Really?

I should've stayed at Aggie's. Hell, at this point, I'd probably be better off seeking out Xi or Quill if they hadn't switched over to the dark side. They'd be more welcoming than this place. I just know it.

My back pocket vibrates. I pull out my new phone to a text from Aggie. At least my phone wasn't taken this time around.

Aggie: How is it?

A sardonic laugh bubbles up.

Nora: Five-star quality.

I hope she can sense the sarcasm headed her way as I hit the send button.

4

Light radiates from a small lamp attached to the wall near the door. I've only been in here for a few hours, but I feel like a prisoner now more than I ever did with Kane. He never locked me away. He never forced me into total seclusion.

At least this time around, I had the phone Aggie gave me. At first, I looked up any information I could get my hands on about this Cathedral. There wasn't much. It was founded hundreds of years ago. It's not an active place of worship, but there are several articles relating to outreach programs. Members reached out to those less fortunate and provide them with food and clothes. Other than that, there's no other information from outside sources. Also, none of the websites mention anything about Changelings or their war on Reapers.

From what Kane had told me, the Changelings aren't people I'd want to glorify either. They are pretty much the souls of dead babies modeled into holy warriors, set out of collect blessed souls. That doesn't exactly give off positive PR.

I've only had two run ins with them. Neither left a great impression. The first, Kane had been attacked. We'd been ready to leave after a night at the playground. Royce had called, warning us of a Changeling sighting. The Changeling almost killed him with one of those glowing crystal blades. The stone is the only thing that can be weaponized against Reapers. It prevents them from healing quickly and renders them disabled. The second had been while Kane was healing from that attack. I was walking to the car when a small group of their kind had cornered me. The one female tried strangling me. If I hadn't gotten a second wind and used the Banshee's sonic waves, she would've gotten away with it. Because of that, I over exerted myself and ended up in a twisted sort of coma. After being overwhelmed with visions and pain, I had sunk deep into my subconscious. It's safe to say that I'm not their biggest fan.

Eventually, I switched my curiosities over to Facebook. Even though she's been dead for years, Willow Alder's page is still intact. Every year, less and less people posted on her wall. For the past four, only people that share her last name have made sentimental comments. There weren't many pictures. The ones that had been posted while she was still alive, her smile didn't reach her eyes; her body was tense and obviously uncomfortable. It wasn't the same girl that I've come to know.

Briggs' last name was lost to me, but luckily, it's not the most common first name in the world. I found him on the second search page. A man's man. A respected war veteran. A loving partner. He didn't seem like such a bad guy. From what I know of him, he sticks to the rules. He isn't a fan of Kane or Royce, but he set his judgements aside in an attempt to rescue them.

A knock comes to the door. I sit up as it's unlocked and

swung open. A woman appears in the doorways with the Changeling beside her.

"Eleanor, my name is Margot."

Like the man we met at the entrance, she wears thick white robes. Her greying hair stops just past her chin; the locks are oddly straight. She smiles at me and her eyes soften.

"Hello."

Her gaze roams, looking me up and down, searching for something. It's a reaction I've gotten used to ever since I found out of my Banshee bloodline. They all stare at me as if they're waiting for something to happen. Fangs to grow? Wings to sprout? Neon flashing lights popping out from the top of my head?

"You must understand the hesitation to welcome in a creature such as yourself."

I shake my head and drop my gaze. From my peripherals, I see the way the Changeling's arm shoots out, trying to stop her from walking in the room. The woman ignores him and sits on the edge of the bed. I don't miss the way her face pulls into a grimace when the springs squeak, nor the space she keeps between us. When I was young, I used to think being teased for my ginger hair was the worst thing. That holds no comparison to the ridicule I've faced these past couple of months.

"Here at the Cathedral," she says in a moderate tone, "we house those who dedicate their lives to serving the greater good. We serve one God - the true God. Banshees were created to benefit the creatures of Hell. They come from Lucifer himself. They are unnatural as they are powerful."

"I'm unnatural?" I bite out. My eyes instantly snap to the man in the doorway as he inches forward, hand on the hilt of his blade.

"Yes, especially an awakened Banshee, such as yourself."

A sardonic laugh bubbles up. "I didn't ask for any of this."

"I know you didn't." Her hand wavers as she reaches out to pat my knee.

And yet, what no one is grasping is that I have no clue what the hell I'm doing with the power that runs through my veins. I didn't grow up using my voice for anything other than talking, and later, drunken karaoke. In my twenty-three years, I've never heard of Reapers or Changelings. At least, not in the literal sense. I didn't know that demons and witches actually existed. And now, that's all my world consists of.

The lady, Margot, clears her throat. "You've made a good friend in Willow. She's done nothing but sing your praises. According to her, there's no need to keep you in a holding room. But under the circumstances, we are unsure how much trust we can place in your hands. As far as we know, the princes are using you as their puppet."

"Listen, I'm not going to kill anyone."

"Of course you wouldn't," she says. The sheepish smile contradicts those words. "We've never housed an awaken Banshee in these walls before. We have the means to care for a dormant one with the intentions that they are remain in the state."

I sigh and run a hand through my hair. If I had known this was how I'd be treated, I wouldn't have come. I'm not about to be some mutant lab experiment.

"Willow has also told us that you've been working with the occult in freeing the bindings of your voice. And that it wasn't until last night that your inner demon brought to life."

"I don't even know if that's what happened."

The corner of her mouth pulls. "A Banshee is unleashed at

the moment of great loss."

My brow cinches together. "How-"

A shadow crosses over her face as she says, "We have our ways."

"Then why didn't you come when you first heard about a Banshee being found?"

She flinches at my hardened tone. All this time, they've had the key to my release and acting like I'm the bad guy.

"We were ensured that your powers were hindered. That you'd never take hold of your voice. There was no need to make a scene, especially being on the tight watch they placed you under."

Shaking my head, I mutter, "Unbelievable." Where Death knew jackshit about their own abomination, all they had to do was take a trip to the Cathedral. "What happens now?"

Margot stands, smoothing the wrinkles out of her robes. "We'd like to convince the Council that you're worth protecting. A caged demon is no good to the devils. It's the wild ones they covet the most. And knowing them, they will stop at nothing to get their hands on you."

"Aside from their own deaths," I tell her, digging my nails into the palms of my hand, "I want nothing to with them."

Light shines from her eyes as a satisfied smile stretches across her lips. "That's what I hoped to hear."

"Does that mean I can get out of here now?"

"Soon, my dear." She gestures to the man standing at the doorway. "The Minor Council will be meeting within the hour. Vincent will escort you down. There are a few things we'd like to go over with you."

. . .

I wasn't looking forward to meeting with yet another Council. Hopefully this time it will consist of more than a little boy. Margot didn't say much else before leaving and Vincent is impenetrable. He barely looks at me, let alone answers any of the few questions I asked. Needless to say, the majority of the walk is silent.

The Cathedral is enormous. The stone work is impeccable, holding intricate designs and pillars in its foundation. And there's an endless amount of doors and hallways. I swear it's more of a labyrinth than a church.

I thought he'd take me back to the room we were in before, but that's not the case. Vincent leads me through the main foyer and down another set of stairs before stopping in front of a door. He knocks twice, then steps aside. The thick wooden door swings open moments later.

The taste of bile rises in my throat. Lennox, the Changeling that brutally attacked Kane, stands in the doorway. His face is emotionless, aside from the stone cold look in his eyes as he stares me down. My heart beats faster as the memory in that alley flashes through my head.

"Lennox, let her in." Reluctantly, he steps aside and I walk in.

A table stretches almost the entire length of the room. Men and women in white robes sit around it; all of their eyes on me as I walk closer. I recognize Margot. She gives me a slight nod of recognition. There's also the older man that met us at the entrance. As for the others, I've never seen them before.

A man stands from where he sits near the center of the table and offers me a warm smile. He's seems to be middle-aged, but his hazelnut colored skin holds no wrinkles or laugh lines. "Welcome, Eleanor."

"It's Nora," I interject.

"Nora, yes. I will have to remember that." Unlike Belial, he seems somewhat genuine. The man gestures to the empty chair, which I sit in after instinctively casting hesitant glances around the room. "You, along with a member of the Accursed, pled sanctuary. What is the cause for this urgent matter?"

My head tilts to the side as I stare at him. "You know why I'm here." The mouths of several people pull down into a frown. I glance at Margot, but her head is tilted down, staring at her lap. "Well," I choose my words carefully, "I guess I'm here for protection - protection against Hell."

"Why should we welcome you into these sacred walls?" A woman older than most of my patients at Beacon Lights asks.

"Because I have nowhere else to go that won't draw attention or bring harm to anyone else." My fingers drum on the arm rest. The table of robes stare at me. No one picks up the interrogation, which only makes the drumming pick up. "I'm a Banshee. I've experienced a major loss," the snicker I hear from behind me makes me dig my nails harder into my palm, "which must've awakened the full potential of my powers. If that's true, they'll want me now more than ever."

"Having you here will only place those at the Cathedral in danger. Why are you worth that?" Another ancient looking member muses.

I run a hand through my hair. "I'm not. Honestly." I sigh. "I'm not worth putting anyone's life at stake. I'm no one important. I wasn't before and I sure as fuck aren't now."

"Eleanor, language please."

"Language?" Sarcasm coats the laugh that bursts from

inside me. "Shit. Fuck. Damn. Bitch. Cunt." I run a hand through my hair again and deflate in the chair. "I'm sorry. That was rude." My cheeks heat up. "Agreeing to protect me may be one of the worst decisions you ever make. I'm a hazard. I don't have grasp on my powers. But I hate the princes just as much as you do. I want them to pay. I want revenge."

"Vengeance is ugly." Margot finally speaks.

I lock eyes with the woman. "Yes, it is. But what they did to me, to those that I love-" A rush of emotion washes over me, forming into a lump that settles at the base of my throat. "The things that they did to those that I loved were some of the ugliest and cruelest acts I ever could've imagined."

"Are you willing to accept any and all requirements that would be put in place?" Margot stands, placing her hands on the table.

I glance around the room. More rules. More restrictions. They might be able to help, but their guidelines aren't much better than Death's. I'm a grown woman. And yet, I've spent the last several months grounded like a prepubescent child. But if this means I will be able to hopefully avenge Kane, then so be it. What could it hurt?

"Yes."

Her expression doesn't change, but her eyes widen slightly. An odd sort of smile pulls at her lips.

5

The locked room has a terrible draft. I keep wrapping the poor excuse for a blanket tighter and tighter around me. The bed has a bar that presses into the middle of my back. Needless to say, I have yet another sleepless night. When the time on my phone passes seven in the morning, I get out of bed. I did what I could in readying myself with the small sink. Prison bath.

After meeting with the Minor Council, I was escorted back to the room. About an hour after that, Vincent brought me a plate of food. Breaded chicken with a baked potato and a cup of water. Prison food. Cathedral my ass. This is a prison in hiding. Food. Housing.

Better not drop the soap. The cynical remark makes me groan.

My adrenaline-fueled mind keeps wandering to Willow. I haven't seen her since we were separated. I wonder if she's getting the same treatment. Doubtful.

Before I tried getting some sleep, I texted Aggie to find out how Briggs is fairing. According to her, he's been drifting in and out of sleep since we left. He hasn't stayed awake long enough for her to get him to eat anything, but she's kept him hydrated. I hate that I had to drag her into this mess, but I had no other choice. Well... I did, but Briggs would've died. I couldn't handle yet another death on my conscience, especially not after he helped in trying to rescue Kane and Royce. He deserves to live.

The door of the room swings open. No knock. No announcement. Speaking of the devil, Willow bounds in, completely dressed and ready for the day. Unlike me, shadows don't haunt her eyes and she doesn't move like her muscles are made out of wood.

"*This* is where they stuck you?" She looks around, eyes wide as she takes in the cramped space.

"I take it you didn't get the five-star treatment?" Sarcasm drips from the words. She shakes her head. "You're missing out."

She comes over and holds her hands out. "Come on." I glance over to see the Changeling, Vincent, standing in the doorway. Willow follows my gaze "She's good to go, right?"

Hesitation coats his face, but he gives a subtle nod. My lips separate, gaping at the chance of freedom. "How?"

She smirks triumphantly. "Margot pulled a few strings. Apparently, you made a good impression."

I take Willow's hand and follow her out the door. As we descend down the stone staircase, Vincent stays close behind. Of course. I can leave the confines of my room, but only with a tag along. I bite back the bitterness. At least I'm out of my prison cell. For however long it is, I'm going to take it and run.

More hallways and closed doors. Sun light cascades in through stained-glass windows, making colors dance on the floor. Unlike last night, we pass people on our walk. Men and women in white robes nod their heads. I recognize some of their faces from the meeting with the Minor Council. In the main foyer, there's a herd of children walking in two single file lines. The boys are dressed in black dress pants and firmly pressed white shirts. The girls have their hair neatly pulled back in ribbons that match their white collared dresses. Each of them have heads of blonde hair.

"Who are they?" I lean in, pointing to the children; their perfect behavior creeping me out.

"Little Changelings in training."

I give Vincent a raised look over my shoulder. "Changelings age?"

Willow lets out a chuckle. "They technically have a loose connection to their souls. It's like a dumbed down version of a soul. After a certain age, the Deacons start them in a classroom set up until they actually begin their combat training."

I keep my eyes on the children as the last disappear inside a room and the door shuts behind them. "The Cathedral is a Changeling mill."

"Pretty much."

"No." Vincent's rough voice cuts through.

"Calm down." Willow flashes him a teasing smile. I can't help but notice how cheerful she is today compared to yesterday. "They get a bit testy when it comes to their upbringing," she whispers, bumping my shoulder.

I follow her into a large, open room. Rows and rows of tables and chairs take up most of the space. Aside from a couple of people, the majority of the tables are barren. We take up seats at one of the nearest tables, while our guard stands in the doorway.

Anxiety claws at my chest. "Where are we?"

A moment later, my question is answered. An older woman in white scrubs wheels out a cart with glasses of water and plates of food. My stomach grumbles at the sight of eggs and hash browns.

She pulls a tight smile. "Enjoy." I don't miss the weary glances she casts my way before heading back up the center aisle.

I didn't realize how hungry I am until I started shoveling food in my mouth, savoring the taste. The scrambled eggs have the perfect fluff consistency. But as the food starts to settle in my stomach, an odd tingle plays at the base of my neck. I look up, meeting several stares. Every person in the room, as few as there are, scrutinize every move I make. My appetite goes out the window.

Putting my fork down, I drown the ball forming in my gut with a large gulp of water. "Aggie told me that Briggs is stable."

"Well, that's good."

"Yeah," I draw out the word. Her bright smile doesn't help my apprehension.

Willow goes about eating the rest of her food, paying no mind to the judgmental attention. She's acting like the last two days haven't happened. *Stop it*, I mentally scold myself. Everything's fine. People handle grief differently. This is Willow. This must be how she handles loss, brushing it off as if it doesn't even exist. Judging her process would only be damning my own. She's fine.

I look to Vincent. "Is there a library or something here?"

He nods his head. "Would you mind taking me there? Or is that not allowed?"

"Do you need any help?" Willow asks.

A weak smile pulls at my lips. "I just want to see if there's something to read. Help pass the time, you know?"

The chair screeches against the floor, sounding worse than nails on a chalkboard. If I didn't already have the rooms attention, I sure would now. I follow Vincent out. The moment I step out of the dining hall, my body relaxes. The tension leaves my muscles and my lungs breathe a little easier.

In all my life, I've never felt visual probed. Each minute movement placed under a microscope and studied. For a place housing do-gooders and holier than thous, they sure aren't very welcoming. Like a rabbit in a den of wolves.

The walk to the library is quiet. Vincent doesn't speak to me. He seems as enthused to be on guard duty as I am to be here. As far as I know, he's been stationed outside my door all night. And now he has to dote around the Cathedral with me. Grown woman turned prisoner. Changeling turned babysitter. What a pair we are.

When he holds a door open for me, I expect to see more stares, but the space is empty. In fact, Vincent doesn't even follow me in. The door shuts with an echoing slam, leaving me alone. After the initial set of stairs, study tables and leather couches make themselves at home. Large glass windows stretch to the ceiling. A split level adds another layer to the room, which holds countless rows of book stacks.

"Hello?"

A man steps out from one of the stacks. Unlike most in this place, he waves his hand when he sees me. He doesn't hesitate to walk down one another sets of stairs. As he nears, he gives me a toothy smile, pushing wire frame glasses up the bridge of his nose.

"Hello there."

His polite tone takes me aback. "My name's Nora. I'm here under sa-"

"Sanctuary," he cuts in. "I know all about you."

"Oh." My face heats up. "Yes, well… I was hoping to find a book to check out."

His blue eyes shine brightly. "Excellent." He has the appearance of a Changeling, but, unlike most, his hair is considerably shorter. It's floppy, but doesn't cascade down his shoulders. Oddly enough, it's a breath of fresh air. "You've come to the right place for that. I'm Micah."

"Nora."

He lets out a pleasant chuckle at my awkward reintroduction and gestures for me to follow. "Are you looking for anything particular?"

I run my fingers over the intricately carved railing. Swirls and flowery shapes run along the entire length. It's not a design you see any more in this modern age. "Not really."

"I should warn you, we don't keep up with new releases. You'll have to settle for the classics. Austen. Dickens. Bronte."

"That's fine with me." The shelves of books go on forever. One stack bleeds into another. The occasional aisle breaks up the walls of spines. "Why is there no one in here?" He raises a brow at me. "Except you, of course."

Nowadays, libraries aren't the most popular of places. But even then, I've never stepped in one as empty as this place.

Micah turns down an aisle. "Most avoid it."

"Why? It's so peaceful." And it is. Sunlight streams in through the expansive windows, creating a bright space for reading. The ceiling is painted with murals of clouds and cherubs. In all honesty, it's like I've stepped into another world. The quiet. The peace. Its breath taking.

We stop about midway down a row. I recognize several titles; the gold scribe stands out against the leather bindings. Of Mice and Men. Odyssey. The Picture of Dorian Gray.

"I'm not the most popular person here. And being that I'm the keeper of the books, this place doesn't see many visitors. But you're welcome here. Anytime." He gives me a small smirk. "Books are my friends. They don't bite. The worse they do is make you cry or give you papercuts."

I look at Micah, taking in his thin build. He doesn't scream powerful. With his glasses and the sleeves of his button down rolled up, he's comfiest looking Changeling I've seen yet. Aside from Margot, he's also the nicest person housed in these walls. Even knowing who I am, he's been nothing but friendly. Polite. But then again, Vincent didn't even step inside. He let the door close completely. I find it hard to believe this man is a bad person, deserving of complete isolation.

"Don't fret about it," he whispers. "I don't."

His words pull at my chest. "It must get lonely in here."

"Why would I get lonely?" He reaches up and grabs hold of a book. He holds it out for me; the burgundy cover cool to the touch. "I have plenty of friends and adventures to keep me busy." I trace over the letters on the front cover. Pride and Prejudice. The subtle humor isn't lost to me. "This must all be strange for you."

My eyes travel upwards, locking with his. Sunlight reflects off their sky-blue color, making them glow. "It's not what I expected."

"Most things aren't."

"Do you think I made the right choice coming here?" The question slips from my lips before I even realize I asked. He might know who I am - *what* I am - but that's no reason to assume much else.

A shadow passes behind his eyes, while a turned-up smirk wavers on his lips. "You made the decision to seek out the Cathedral. You did what you thought was right. There's nothing wrong with that."

He keeps his gaze honed in on mine for a moment longer before flashing a wide grin. He pats me on the shoulder and backtracks, leaving me alone with the aisle of books and his haunting words.

6

I don't think I've ever experienced a night as long and cold as this one. The dropping temperatures have seeped through the walls. It didn't matter that I have on two pairs of socks or that the blanket is bundled tightly around me. I can feel the cold all the way down to my bones. My phone reads sometime after six when I give up on sleep. With the lack of outlets, I've been trying to save the last bit of charge my phone has.

I've limited my use to keeping tabs on Briggs. He's still confined to bed. While his stitches seem to be holding, he's not ready to walk or sit up on his own. All is ruled out. It'd be different if we'd taken him to a hospital. He could've gotten the transfusion he desperately needed, as well as the correct medication. Tylenol doesn't exactly suppress a severe infection or the pain radiating from the wound. I just hope he's able to pull through this.

Earlier, after settling on Pride and Prejudice, I had Vincent guide me back to my room. Even though it's probably the dreariest place in the world, it's four walls are better than all the shrewd stares.

Later on today, I'll find out the Council's decision. Not that I'm looking forward to that. With how I've been treated, I don't think I'll be staying here much longer. For people that supposedly know about Banshees, you'd think I was a double-headed gnome. On top of that, Willow isn't herself. I don't know what she ate since we were separated, but she's happy - too happy. My anxiety is at an all-time high being in this twisted Wonderland of angels. All it's missing is a frantic rabbit and an evil red headed queen. Oh, wait! Maybe that's supposed to be me.

Letting out a groan, I sit up. The poor excuse for a bed creaks, sends a haunting echo through the room. *How did my life get to this point?* It's a question I find myself asking again and again. I can't help it. A year ago, I was grabbing as many shifts as I could. I rarely slept. Free days with Hannah and nights off with Aggie are what I looked forward to. Kane's face flashes through my mind. Those coppery eyes sear right through me. They always do.

Did.

A sob wracks through my body. This isn't fair. He should be here. Well, not *here*. He would've known what to do. He wouldn't have sought out the Cathedral. No matter what situation we were in, he always had a plan. Hell, sometimes several different versions of a plan. While it's only been days, it seems like a lifetime since I last laid eyes on him. And yet, I can still remember how his hands felt caressing my cheeks as he kissed my goodbye. The soft touch of his lips linger on mine.

Wiping at the tears that spill down my face, I stand. I

shake my arms and bounce on the balls of my feet. I can't let myself go down that road. The moment I stop and grief catches up, I'll be drowning in nothing but sorrow. Not today. Not while I have so much to do - so much to overcome.

The faucet pours nothing but cold water. There's not a separate nozzle for warm. Just cold. Everything is cold. Thankfully, my skin spikes to life a bit as I splash a handful on my face.

"You can do this." My hands grip the edges of the ceramic sink. "If not for you, then for him."

. . .

The same sets of eyes stare down the table at me. The same white robes are starched to perfection. The only difference? The creepy boy now sits at the head of the table. He's out of place in the sea of adults. While their expressions are severe, his is dripping with boredom. Not even that. Acceptance? Patience? I'm used to Hannah's never-ending movements. This level of calm in a child weirds me out. It's unnatural.

My knee starts bouncing. My nerves tick. Nerves. I'm swimming in them. And the way some narrow in their gazes on me only makes the bouncing pace quicken.

I didn't pay attention the last I was in here, but I can't help my own gaze from wandering. Thick curtains hang down the walls. Every few feet, a mural breaks up the fabric. Each frame is as intricate as the wooden rails in the library. But, despite being midday, the room is encased in darkness. The only light stem from the lantern chandeliers that hang high above.

The door opens from behind me. I twist around in the chair. A man's tall frame blocks out the light streaming in from the hall. My heart lurches as the door shuts. Lennox's gaze scalds mine. My mouth dries instantly.

"Eleanor."

My attention snaps back to the table of robes. The older man, from when we first showed up on the steps of the Cathedral, stands from his seat.

"In your short stay with us, you've witnessed the many people that the Cathedral houses. That being said, you must understand our hesitation about accepting you into our holy grounds. There are lives at stake - children's lives."

My eyes cut over to where the little boy sits.

"I'm not - I'm not asking for you to put the kids on the front lines." Lead has replaced my tongue, weighing it down. The words I want to stay have trouble forming around the lump in my mouth.

The old man clears his throat. "But in a way, you are."

His words are violent, striking me across the face. "I asked for help. I still have no idea what I'm doing."

"Even more dangerous." A woman with frizzy brown hair sneers.

I take in a deep breath, fighting to keep my calm. "Margot told me you know about Banshees." Several turn their deathly glares to the woman. Her lips purse. "All I'm asking for is help."

"How will assisting you benefit us?"

"Death wants me." *Holy fuck.* These people are impossible. "I don't have control over my voice. Until I do, I can't fight off the demons - the demons you all know they'll send to sniff me out."

Despite unintentionally throwing her under the bus, Margot's kind voice breaks through the tension. "But you have in fact awakened your inner beast?"

44

Images of the caving foundation flash through my mind. The hollowing sound of my wail mixed with the rush of power. Something I hadn't felt in any of my previous training.

My voice cracks as I say, "Yes."

"The Playground is in ruins. There's nothing left." Several people at the table look above my head. Lennox's baritone voice sends a chill down my spine.

A mixture of impressed and incredulous expressions turns my way. The little boy offers me an awkward smirk. I can't help but wonder if he even knows what's going on.

"Nora," Margot says, standing from her seat, "what if we told you we have access to another Banshee - a dormant one?"

The palms of my hands burn as my nails dig in deep. A wave of anger spikes, making it hard to keep my temper in check. "You know of another Banshee and you kept it from me."

"Her existence wasn't information for you to know."

"Bullshit!" The chair screeches against the stone floor as I stand. My hands land hard as they slap against the tabletop. "You've all been treating me like a leper, even though you've had a Banshee in your keep?"

"You cannot compare-"

"Try me!" A tingle sparks at the base of my spine, slowly creeping up. "I'm asking for help. For being *righteous* people, you sure aren't very accepting."

The room falls deathly quiet.

I run my hand through my hair. This meeting is getting out of hand. And of course, no one is on my side. Squeezing my eyes shut, I take a deep breath and whisper. "I don't know where else to go. Death has done nothing but threaten the people I love. They killed Kane." My voice cracks. I squeeze my fists tighten, refusing to let them know just how badly I'm broken inside. "I can't sit by and watch as they hurt more people. I won't."

"Will you vow to follow the rules instated to protect the longevity of the Cathedral?" The older man asks.

When I open my eyes, I keep them trained on the table. "Yes."

"And will you dedicate your time to improving your skills?"

Yvette's smartass smirk shadows the back of my mind. "I will."

I raise my gaze. The little boy wears a satisfied smile. Even Margot, who'd maintained a blank expression, gives the slightest nod of her head.

"At this time," a woman older than time itself speaks. Her attention is on a paper laid out in front of her, "the other Banshee is not in a healthy state of mind. Once she is well, she has offered to help you in understanding your voice."

I bite down, clenching my jaw so my anger won't escape. I can't believe there's another Banshee. Who's to know how long she's been here. Hell, there might be an entire colony the Changelings have kept hidden.

"While she heals, we want to ensure that you have the skills needed to handle your own welfare." The woman looks up, but she avoids looking directly at me. Instead, she focuses above my head. "Lennox, you are to help Eleanor in combat training."

All the blood leaves my body. The man that attached Kane and I, almost killing him, is to be my trainer. *Him*. I stood my ground against him. Kane was on the ground, bleeding to death before my eyes. The Banshee took over, sending Lennox several yards. His body flew across the air like he weighed nothing. I could've killed him. Hell knew I wanted to. But I spared his life. Getting to Kane was my first priority. It'd be my luck that one of the people that I despise the most will be in charge of teaching how to stay alive in a fight.

"Excuse me, Council," he steps up, voice filled with disdain, "but I don't think that's a wise choice. It'd only be destined for disaster with our history."

"Your history is exactly the reason we chose you," Margot snaps. Her eyes sear into him. His knuckles cracking as he fists his hands sounds like gunshots ringing in my ears. But he takes a step back, pulling the tension between us tighter.

"Does the Council agree to these terms?"

The attention of everyone at the table instantly turns to the young boy. Any amusement falls from his face. While my nerves skyrocket under all the pointed stares, he just looks...bored.

Several minutes pass. The only noise comes from the drumming of my pulse. "They accept the terms, deeming them appropriate. The length of the Banshee's stay in these walls will be determined on her willingness to cooperate."

Even though the table of robes remains neutral, it's easier to breathe - the energy is no longer high strung. I glance at Margot. She doesn't say anything, but the corners of her mouth pull up for a mere second.

No matter how saintly they all may seem, I can't help but feel like I just signed a deal with the Devil.

7

"Faster."

I push harder, doing my best to ignore the fire scorching my lungs. For being the first day of official training, I thought Lennox would've made it somewhat easy. Run a lap or two. Jumping jacks. Taking into consideration that I don't work out, he set his expectations high. I've been on the treadmill for close to three hours. After stretching, I hopped on. I've been alternating speeds. It all started out with a brisk walk, but quickly escalated to full sprints and even a lopping jog.

"Faster."

I've lost all feeling in my feet and legs. I'm barely breathing. I don't dare tell him any of this though. I'll be damned if I complain. Not only will my pride be wounded, but I doubt he'd care much.

"Faster."

Clenching my jaw harder, I keep pushing. My arms swing wildly at my sides with terrible form. Every inch of my body is sweating, including my hands. When I returned to my room last night, I ran them under cold water. Blood was caked on my palms; crescent moon shaped cuts taunted me. Needless to say, the more I sweat, the worse they sting. I haven't been able to take a break to try and dry them.

"Faster."

The memory of me running for my life just weeks ago keeps imbedding its way into my mind. The last time I ran this much was when his people decided to corner me while I was leaving for the Playground. Even now, I can feel the suffocating hold that girl had on my throat.

Lennox reaches over on the treadmill and hits a button. The moving track stops almost immediately. My body lurches forward and I grab hold of the railing to keep from going over.

"What the fuck?" I whip my head to Lennox. He crosses his arms, staring at me with a smug smirk played out across his face. "Is this funny to you?"

"Yes," he says, taking a step forward, "I do. This is a waste of my time. It's not even worth a fraction of the effort I'm putting in."

I open my mouth to speak, but snap it shut. Saliva fills my mouth and an uneasy quake stirs in my stomach. There isn't time for me to look for a trash can or toilet. Vomit erupts, forcing me to double over, clutching my stomach.

"You've got to be shitting me." Lennox's voice is filled with disgust, breaking through the pounding in my head.

When my stomach finally settles, I take a few deeps breaths and pull myself together. I wipe my mouth on the sleeve of my shirt, avoiding looking at the mess on the floor.

"Is this going to happen every time?"

I clench my jaw and look up. The corner of his nose if curled up in a snarl. "What is your problem?"

Keeping his distance from the puddle on the rubber mat, he moves closer to me. "*You're* my problem." Hateful blue eyes pin me down. "If you didn't make ties with Hell, I wouldn't be in this situation. I wouldn't have to babysit a grown woman, let alone pretend that any training is going to help her. You're weak."

His words cause a mixture of embarrassment and anger to flood through my body. My cheeks burn. "Do you honestly think I want it to be you that helps me? No. I don't. As far as I'm concerned, I'd rather see you burn. But I don't make the rules...unfortunately."

"You're lucky you're under the protection of the Council."

"Watch yourself, Lennox."

He lets out a cynical laugh. "You don't scare me, Banshee. And that Reaper isn't here anymore to save you. I tried stepping in. If you weren't brainwashed, you would be better off. Neither of us would be in this position. As far as I'm concerned, he deserved everything that happened to him."

I falter backward, thrown off by the low blow. A tremble takes over my hands. "How dare you say that. You didn't know him."

"I know more than you think." He keeps his gaze locked in with mine. Pulling away, he gestures to the floor. "Get someone to clean this up. Be here tomorrow morning at five."

Lennox looks me up and down before turning on his heel. As the door to the gym shuts behind him, I let out the breath balled in my chest. No matter how much I want to prove how wrong he is, I'm glad he's gone. I can't feel my legs. My stomach is in knots. And all I want to do is cry.

A hand touching my shoulder scares me shitless. I turn to see a man in white scrubs stands behind me.

"Are you alright?"

A chuckle slips out, coated in the irony of the question. "Not at all. Do you know where I can get a mop or something?" I gesture to the mat. "Me and running aren't friends."

Repulse shadows his face as he looks down, but he smiles at me anyways. "I can get this taken care of."

"No, I can clean it. You shouldn't have to do that."

He gives a slight shake of his head. "I saw you on the treadmill. You worked hard today. Why don't you go rest?"

"Are you sure?" I can see the apprehension in his eyes, but he nods his head. "Thank you. I can stay and help."

"Go lay down. You should rest."

I nod and thank him once more.

After the meeting yesterday, the group of robes agreed on changing my living situation. I wouldn't be kept locked away in a high tower. I'm no longer a prisoner. A three headed dragon, maybe. But, at least for the time being, Rapunzel is free from her tower. They allowed me to share a room with Willow. And no wonder she was shocked when she saw where they put me. Even the walk to her from room was nicer than the spiral stone staircase. Mural tapestries flanked between floor to ceiling stained-glass windows. This particular wing of the Cathedral is set up as a college dorm: girls to one hall and boys to another. It's a lot quieter than anticipated. Every now and then, a door might slam or a muffled conversation would slip under the door. But it's a completely different atmosphere.

I knock before opening the door. Willow sits on her bed and looks up from the magazine in her lap. Both of our beds are shoved into corners; dressers shoved under their lofted frames. Thankfully, we have a connected bathroom instead of a communal one. The room isn't much bigger than the prison tower, but we're able to make it work.

"You don't have to knock." She smiles at me from across the room.

I shrug, shutting the door quietly behind me. "The last room that was mine was kept locked."

"Well," she says, going back to her reading, "what's mine is yours."

I groan the moment my body hits the bed, "Fuck." Unlike the shit excuse of a cot, this one has somewhat of a mattress.

"That bad?"

"I puked."

Willow sits straight up, chucking the magazine on the floor. "You're kidding! What was he having you do?"

"Run. Lots of running." Kicking off my shoes, they land on the ground. "He's such an ass."

"Lennox? Really?" I shoot her a glare from across the room. "I never thought he was that bad."

I throw my arm over my eyes, blocking out the light. It also keeps her from seeing the murdering glower that's taken over my face.

Has she forgotten that he didn't show up when she asked? That his horde of angels countered me in an alley? Or, better yet, that he almost killed Kane?

"It'll get better."

My jaw clenches and teeth grind together.

If this how working with him is going to go, I don't know if I'll be able to make it. He'll kill me in the training room before I even get out in the real world.

Her mattress creaks, and a moment later, the end of my mattress dips as she sits by my feet.

"It's really not that bad, Nora. I wish you could see that."

"Once again, my life is uprooted." I keep my voice low. "I'm surrounded by people I don't know. I have to go through yet another trial. I don't know who I am anymore." A sigh creeps past my lips. "I've lost myself."

"No, you haven't." She pats the top of my foot. I don't even want to know just how soaked with sweat my socks are. "It's just a rough patch."

A rough patch? I pull my arm away and look at her. Willow's eyes are shining bright; a tight smirk pulls at her mouth.

"What is wrong with you?"

Willow's head tilts, making her dark mane of hair fall over her shoulder. Confusion paints her face. "What do you mean?"

Her words strike, freezing me in the moment. Sitting up, I pull my knees close to me.

"The fact that you're sitting here all calm and collected, catching up on the latest celebrity gossip…" I can't believe I just said that about Willow. Shaking my head, I tell her, "You've been acting like nothing happened. You sit there and smile like you didn't just watch Royce get brutally murdered."

The light slowly fades from her eyes, but her expression barely wavers. You would've thought I told her someone hit the neighbor's dog.

"Nora-"

"Don't *Nora* me!" I stand up, no longer able to lay down. My nerves splinter as the base of my neck tingles. "He died, Willow. Royce died. He's dead. Kane's dead. Where's the fiery girl that didn't take no for an answer?"

She lets out a breath, shaking her head back and forth. "It's not worth the fight."

"What do you mean, 'It's not worth the fight'? You were the one that wanted to get a move on with this whole revenge plan."

"There's no reason to get upset over it. It's done and over with."

"Like Hell it is!"

Clucking her tongue, Willow stands and walks over to me. "I knew you wouldn't be able to think clearly."

"Excuse me?" My body jerks backward from the verbal slap in the face.

"You heard me."

My face hardens as I say, "I wish I didn't."

Walking past me, she climbs back into her bed. The magazine is up and shielding her face within a second's time. Reaching out, I rip it from her hands and toss it to the ground.

"You don't care that Royce died?"

The corners of her mouth fall. "That's not what I said."

"That's what you're acting like."

"There's no-"

Holding up my hand, I cut her off before she can say another word. Taking in a deep breath, I say, "You loved him, remember? You loved him so much that you went on a suicide mission just to save him. While we're at it, remember Briggs?" A sheen of tears rims her eyes, but none fall. "He can still die. Just because we stabilize him, doesn't mean he's out of the clear. *This* was your plan. We were to get to the Cathedral. The Changelings would help. *That's* what you kept saying. We're here, Will. I've been stripped of my humanity and locked away like a fucking fugitive. I'm forced to work with a man I hate. But

I trust you. You were so sure about all this. What happened?"

Running my hands down my face, I try to calm my nerves. A tremor threatens to unleash itself, but I hold it down. The last thing I need is to send her through the wall. Then again, it might knock some sense in her.

"The only man I ever loved was taken from me. You're at risk of losing not one, but two men you love. I don't know what's gotten into you, but this? This isn't you. This isn't the Willow I know."

Shaking my head, I turn away. I can't stand to look at her any longer. If we weren't confined to sharing the same room, I'd leave. But I don't exactly have anywhere to go.

I lay back down in my bed and slip under the covers. My body practically melts into the mattress. Rolling over on my side, I turn away from her and close my eyes.

Her mattress squeaks and a moment later, the lights are turned off. The only noise is the sound of our breathing. Well, until she whispers, "Not everyone handles grief the way you do."

"I'd rather feel the pain than act like their deaths don't mean anything. The hurt is the only way to keep their memories alive." My voice cracks, but I choke down the lump that rises in my throat. "They're the reason I'm here. I *will* get revenge for their deaths. And if I have to do it alone, then so be it."

8

I should've kept my comments to myself. Maybe then I wouldn't have to endure this form of torture. Then again, Lennox just shouldn't speak. Period.

When I woke up this morning, I couldn't feel my legs, let alone move them. Despite only running yesterday, every part of my body ached. Arms. Back. Stomach. Sitting on my ass was borderline masochism. Tears trickled down my face as I sat up, lifting one leg over the side of the bed, then the other. Willow laid awake in bed. I was thankful that when she saw I was finally up, she simply rolled over. I didn't know what I'd say to her. To get away from the tension, I readied myself as quick as possible trying my damnedest not to groan in pain with every move I made.

Wishful thinking had gotten the best of me. I hoped Lennox might have taken me standing up to him as a good thing.

Maybe he'd give me a break. I was wrong. So very, very wrong.

Yesterday's running wasn't the worst of it. Today is much worse. All I can do is try and keep my mind preoccupied. I made a list and put it on repeat. Reapers. Demons. Death. A constant reel of faces and names rolled through my mind. Some from the Devil's Playground. Some not. Regardless, the list was filled with people I want dead. It fueled my body to keep going - keep pushing.

Then a new kind of Hell began. Sit ups and jumping jacks. Lunges and squats. I pushed through it all. That didn't seem to satisfy Lennox though. If anything, it only added gasoline to his fiery hatred.

"Burpees," he had said.

He stood over me, glaring as I scrambled to stand from the plank formation. I had to remind myself to thank Aggie later. If it weren't for her gym stories, I wouldn't know what the fuck a burpee was. Taking in a deep breath, I push down the bile threatening to come up. Impatience emanated from Lennox as he crossed his arms, causing the material of his thermal to stretch over the muscles underneath. And then it started.

By this point, my body had become all but numb. I was able to get through the first three without any issues. But as I went to jump up, my leg gave way, sending me down. Pain radiated from my knee. Stars popped in my vision. I cried out as throbbing and burning sensations washed over me.

"What are you doing?" He had growled, trudging forward.

Tears betrayed me, pouring down like a dam. "Please? I need a minute."

"You're wasting time."

"Fuck you." My voice cracked as I gasped for air. The shooting pain in my knee slowly began subsiding, but the throbbing joints and muscles throughout the rest of my body immobilized me. "Have a fucking heart."

"We don't-"

"Why don't you just kill me?" A loathing tone infected my voice. "You've been wanting to kill me since you first heard of me. Just do it already and you can go back to your happy fucking life."

He didn't answer. Aside from the sound of my forced breathing, silence took over the training gym.

Raising my head, I feared he'd take advantage of the situation and put an end to it all. Lennox lowered down to my level. I had never been that close to him before. Eyes that seem ghastly from afar have a million skies twirling around in them up close. A sigh slipped past those full lips as a shadow clouded his face.

His breath was hot against my face. "I don't want to kill you, Nora." The deep drop in his voice sent a tingling jolt down my spine. "You're weak. Nothing good will come of this."

"Well when the time comes, be sure to stand back so my blood doesn't splatter on you."

His sharp jawline clenches down as he grinds his teeth. A string of words leave his mouth in a language I've never heard before. And then… he left.

Which brings me to now as I lay on the training mat. I try not to think of how much sweat and other bodily fluids are probably caked into the material. Fire has scorched my lungs, singeing each breath I take.

Lennox is right. As much as I don't want to admit it, it's true. The motherfucker is actually right. I'm weak. Whoever thought me going through training would be a smart idea is clearly in the wrong. There's no way I'll be able to stand in a fight against a Reaper, let alone Death. But I'll be damned if I don't try.

Pushing myself to my knees, my teeth clench down as I push past the pain. Nothing wants to move. Every part of my body screams for me to stop. Standing, I can practically hear my knees creak. Ankles, feet, knees, shins, thighs - every inch of my lower extremities beg me to give in. The daunting echoes fill my ears, but I push on.

People eye me as I creep back to the dormitory wing. I move at a snail's pace, inching my way through the halls. A few Deacons stop and ask if I need help, but I decline. I need to do this on my own.

Luckily, Willow isn't in the room when I get back. I can't bare another argument, not like this. Stripping down, I turn the water on in the shower. I never thought I'd be thankful for a connected bathroom. A sharp gasp pierces out of my chest as ice cold water cascades down my shoulders, spiking more goosebumps along my flesh. And yet, it soothes my muscles. I stand rooted in place for the longest time, unwilling to move.

By the time I actually get out of the shower, my skin's colder than ice, but it helps tremendously. As much as I just want to sink into the mattress and sleep, that'd be the worst possible thing for me right now. I have to keep moving. Reluctantly, I change into loose clothing and head back out.

Despite being in the training room all day, I'm not even the least bit hungry. Lunch has been over for a while. One of the rare good things about the Cathedral is that they keep select portions of each meal aside for those who aren't on a normal eating schedule. There may only be a few people in the dining hall, but I can't eat. I won't risk the possibility of throwing up again, especially not after how voluntary my upchuck reflexes were yesterday.

I wind my way through the many twists and turns, trying my best to remember the way to the library. It's not the most evident place to seek solitude, but it's the only place that I've had any sense of calm.

Standing outside the doors, my fingers trace of the intricate designs carved in the wood. It oddly feels alive, as if a thousand lives are behind them. Well, in a sense, there are. Millions of people live inside the tales of books, even the non-fiction works.

Opening the door, I step inside. I make sure to be as quiet as possible when shutting the heavy door behind me. Like last time, there isn't anyone here. And yet, the silence is welcoming.

I step further into the room, looking around for someone. Sitting behind the main reception desk is Micah, the Changeling that resides in the library. His head lifts from his work when he sees me near and a smile breaks across his face.

"Nora," he beams, "you came back."

I shrug. "If that's okay."

"More than you know." As I near, a frown pulls down the corners of his mouth as his brow creases together. "You look like shit."

His comment makes me laugh, which I instantly regret. My sides cry out, pleading for the movement to stop.

"I had training again today."

"Is Lennox trying to kill you?"

"You have no idea," I mumble under my breath. Shaking my head, I sigh, "It's just been rough."

Coming around the expansive desk, Micah gestures to a leather couch. "Have a seat. I'll go make us some tea."

He slips past me before I can express what a bad idea that might be. I turn to the sofa and an odd pull tethers me to it. The brown leather is overstuffed, welcoming me to collapse in the cushions. My feet move before I even have a chance to recognize what I'm doing. The moment all the weight is shifted away from my feet, my muscles sigh in relief. I sink deep in the comfort of the couch. It's probably a terrible idea. Hell, I probably won't be able to get up from here. Micah will have to accept that I'll be sleeping here tonight.

By the time he returns, my eyes are heavy. My body perks up as though he comes closer with a tray on his hands. Steam escapes from the spout of the teapot. He pours each of us a healthy amount and drops in two sugar cubes.

"Thank you," I tell him, accepting his generous offer.

He waves off my comment. "Don't thank me. You look like you need it." Sitting down in a chair opposite of me, he crosses his ankle over his knee and blows at the steam. "I just can't believe what a beating he's been giving you."

My brow raises. "Really? He hates me. They all do." A sardonic laugh pushes out. "He probably sits around with his friends and tries to find ways to make my life more of a Hell than it already is."

"They're all assholes. Don't mind them."

Don't mind them. How am I supposed to not mind them when I'm being pushed to the brink of exhaustion? I'm not wanted here. That's clear. But at least we're on the same side, want the same thing: for the hand of Death to be severed.

Shaking away the damning thoughts, I turn my attention back to Micah. He stares off into his cup, pushing his glasses up the bridge of his nose.

"Do you mind if I ask you a question?"

He smiles. "Of course."

"The last time I was here, you said you aren't the most

popular person and that's why everyone avoids the library. Why is that?"

A shadow crosses behind his eyes. It's a subtle movement that I would've missed if I wasn't paying attention. His smile wavers, but eventually pulls into a tight smirk.

Taking a sip of his tea, he explains, "Back in my time, I was the Angel's Child." Confusion blankets my face. Sitting his cup down, he bridges his fingertips together. "You met with the Council?"

Nodding my head, I say, "The Minor Council too."

"The child that was there is the current Angel's Child."

The little boy that sat alone in the dark room flashes through my mind. His quiet disposition had been haunting. He seemed completely out of place in the sea of white robes.

"His name is Meyer," Micah continues. "Every thirteen years, a new Child is brought in. Set aside from the others, he trains to connect with the angels and higher beings. When they're around two, they take over in relaying the messages to the others."

I had found the way the boy would grow silent, only to speak again a moment later, extremely odd. But it makes sense now. He's a communication link. Instead of cellphones, they use children. But at two-years-old? Most toddlers are running around without major verbal skills.

"And you were of those kids?"

He nods his head, sending a few strands of his floppy blonde hair out of order. "Two seating's ago."

"How old does that make you?"

"Twenty-eight."

Numbers and dates flood my mind. "Then how old is Meyer?"

"Five." My mouth gapes up. Words have escaped me. Clearing his throat, Micah's voice drops and each word comes out slowly. "There was another Child between me and Meyer. It all became too much for him. He was seven-years-old when he jumped from one of the highest windows."

Blood drains away from my face. I move to reach out and comfort him, but my body screams out and I recoil. "I am so sorry, Micah. That must've been terrible."

"It was. In the time from his lost life until Meyer took up the seat, things were rough. The lack of communication got to everyone, especially the Deacons. The tension was impenetrable."

"Doesn't this all seem a bit weird to you?"

The framed glasses slip down Micah's nose. "Do you mean the whole Angel's Child thing?" I nod. Sipping from his tea, he pushes his glasses back in place. "Extremely. But the higher beings need someone who is completely innocent. Let's just say that I didn't have a normal upbringing." A subtle laugh springs from him. "Hell, no one in the Cathedral has had any normal childhood memories. But to answer your question, that's why. I didn't have the same upbringing. My opinions are drastically different."

Leaning back into the plush cushions, I let the ease of the moment take over. There's no judgement. Micah doesn't talk to me like I'm a nuisance, but more like a friend. I'm able to find peace and seclusion in the library's walls.

"Do you have any tips on how I can survive Lennox?"

"Ha!" His biting laugh makes me jump. "There's no surviving that man."

Rolling my eyes, I say, "Thanks for the support."

He waves away my comment. "He's not as bad as you

think. He's had his mind toyed with, which messed with his views on life."

"Really?"

Nodding his head, Micah sits down his cup. "Remember the whole high-tension thing and lack of a Child? He gained his ranks during that period."

"Makes sense," I mumble under my breath, taking a large gulp of tea.

"Just stand your ground. He just wants to be sure you're an equal and not a risk. Keep doing what you're doing."

9

Blood pounds in my ears, mixing with the music streaming in through the headphones. I don't know what song it is. I lost track of the lyrics long ago. All I hear is the amplified bass.

Taking Micah's advice, I've been trying to beat Lennox at his own game. Our scheduled training starts every day at six in the morning. I've been showing up an hour early and hopping on the treadmill. Sleep and I are no longer on good terms. All I do is toss and turn through the night, and my alarm goes off far too early each morning. But one thing Lennox can't say is that I'm not dedicated.

I still have yet to talk to Willow. I honestly have no clue what to say to her without sparking another fight. Her behavior has changed. She won't tell me what she was doing or why, but she isn't herself. Especially not in the sense of Royce's death. She's always gone, which doesn't give me a chance to talk to her. In the morning, she's still in bed when I get up. When I stop in after training, she's not in the room. And she creeps in after I've gone to bed. Sometimes I'm still awake, hovering over the pull of actual sleep. Other times, I'm wide awake. I just can't find it in me to roll over and try to fix things. So, I just lay there, pretending I'm asleep.

I've been spending my free time with Micah, talking and learning more about the Changelings. We hole up in the library, drinking tea and eating sandwiches. It's an odd little friendship we've formed, but I've come to treasure it.

Micah isn't like any other Changeling I've met. His face isn't carved from stone, softening only to flash hatred fueled sneers. No. He's kind and caring. He listens to everything I have to say, even the rants about Lennox. Through our talks, I've learned more about not just him, but the community here at the Cathedral.

When Micah was two, he was seated in the Council room. He didn't grow up like the rest of the young Changelings. While they were being cared for in a school environment, Micah's training had a spiritual focus. Working to open his senses to the angels and higher beings, he was marked as a social leper from his rebirth. And once he was seated as the Angel's Child, there was no return. He remained in the room, hearing all the information needed to be passed down to the Deacons and other Changelings. He didn't learn combat or the extraction of souls. He learned to keep an open ear. Except by doing that, Micah heard everything. From politics, to strategies, to secrets that were never meant to surface. They couldn't exactly force him out in the mortal world, nor could they risk placing him in any public forum. So, they stuck him in the library's secluded stacks. And there he's stayed.

Micah wouldn't tell me who the infamous *they* are that he kept referring to, nor the secrets he overheard. I didn't push him. I wouldn't. As much as my curiosity keeps trying to get the best of me, I value his friendship. Especially in this place.

Another positive about befriending Micah, he can charge my cell phone. There are no outlets in the room I share with Willow, but the library holds plenty of them. When I go to visit, I can charge my phone. Aggie's been sending me daily updates about Briggs. His wound is healing nicely, but he's had a fever that keeps fluctuating. No matter what she's tried, Aggie's been having a hell of a time getting it to break. She was able to smuggle a few things from work, but most is heavily inventoried.

I've asked Aggie to try and keep tabs on Hannah in between work and being an at-home nurse. I was relaxed and comforted in knowing Kane had hired the caretaker, Carrie, to help her. With her pay no longer being covered, I don't know how that will unfold. So far everything seems to be going well with her, but it's only a matter of time.

My conscience hasn't stopped clawing at the back on my mind, begging me not to bring Aggie deeper into this mess. She shouldn't have any idea about the Accursed and Reapers. She shouldn't know that her best friend is a Banshee. I should listen to my gut, but I don't. I need her. She's been one of the only things keeping me grounded during this past week. From her texts, to her early morning Facetime calls, I've realized just how much I've missed her. And she doesn't seem to mind. Taking care of Briggs has been giving her something to do. Just her knowing and being able to talk to her has been extremely comforting. Something completely in contradiction to how I've been spending my daylight hours.

I hear the way the training room door slams shut, but I

ignore it. I keep pushing. My lungs don't burn as much as they had the during our initial training session. In the morning my legs are stiff, but I stretch them out and keep moving. My body is slowly getting used to the daily strain.

Lennox steps around the treadmill and in my line of sight. My jaw instinctively clamps down. By this point, there are crescent shaped scars in the palm of my hands from where I've dug my nails. I'm constantly reopening the small wounds. The less comments I make, the less we argue. But biting my tongue has never been easy for me.

Pressing the button, I slow my pace and pull out my ear buds. Lennox crosses his arms over his chest, showing the bare sinewy muscles that are usually hidden under the thermals he wears. He's by no means as bulky as Briggs, but he isn't weak.

"I told you to meet me here at six." His voice deepens as he speaks. His eyes dart to where I turn the machine off, following my every move.

Grabbing the hand towel I slung over the rail earlier, I wipe off the sweat that pours down my face. "Okay? I'm here. I figured I'd get a head start."

"It's not all about running and cardio, Nora."

Sweat burns my palms as I dig into them. "That's the only thing you've had me do."

"Because you have absolutely no training. If you were to go up against even the weakest of Reapers, you'd wind up dead in record breaking time."

"Then show me," I bite out, finding it hard to contain my lack of patience.

Rolling his eyes, he simply states, "You aren't ready."

He doesn't give me another glance. Walking past me, he heads toward a rack of weights.

"I won't ever be ready." The truth of those words weighs heavy on my tongue as I follow him. "But at least you can show me something. Anything."

"You aren't ready."

A growl rips from my throat. "You're supposed to be training me. That's the whole point of this."

"I *am* training you." The muscles along his back become rigid.

"Running and sit ups aren't considered training."

Lennox turns around abruptly and stands just inches from my face. Being this close to him, I can see how long his eyelashes are as they all but dust the tops of his cheeks.

"The longer you run, the more your stamina will grow." His nostrils flare as he takes slow, deep breaths. "Exercises to tone your abdomen will allow you to take a blow and absorb the shock better."

While Lennox has always come off as a dick, I've never seen him this riled up. When he attacked Kane in the alley of the Playground, everything happened too quickly for me to narrow in on any details. But this? I see why he's respected among the Changeling community. He oozes strength - a power that demands to be noticed.

"I know damn well you won't survive a fight against a low life demon, let alone Death. If you find yourself in a fight that you can't win, the only thing to do is run. And if you can't, you're dead. Then this," he gestures between us, fingertips brushing against the skin of my bare collarbone, "would've been a waste of my time. Understand?"

Swallowing hard, I push down the lump drying up my mouth. "I'm not as weak as you think I am."

The way his eyes darken makes me feel as if I'm standing

bare in front of him. Breathless and open. A shiver spreads along my arms and across my chest, hardening my nipples into tight buds, begging to be touched - tasted. *Stop it*, I scold myself. It's the adrenaline. Nothing more. He's despicable. Attractive and powerful, but he's still my enemy.

"Show me." His honey-dipped words are tempting.

Heat fills my cheeks. Shaking my head, I rid my mind of the sinful thoughts; my mind a nasty traitor to my heart. "What?" I ask breathlessly.

The corner of his mouth lifts, spreading a knowing smirk. "Show me you're not weak."

Lennox walks toward the boxing ring in the center of the room. We had yet to step foot inside the ropes. I knew we'd eventually move to the ring, but just the sight of it leaves me hesitant. Grabbing hold of the middle rope, Lennox pulls himself up and over. Like always, every move he makes is filled with a swift grace. I jump up to where I'm sitting and crawl through them. The ropes are harder and more resistant than I thought.

"You want to be cocky, Nora," he presses, placing his hands on his hips, "then show me."

My mouth opens, gaping at what he said. "You want me to, what...? Fight you?"

"Yes."

I wait for the punchline to follow. Hell, I'd be okay with a "Sike!" Neither come.

"Okay then," I mutter.

Raising my arms, hands curled into fists, I take in a deep breath. I've seen several movies with fight scenes. There were a few that had been about an athlete training. I try recalling all those scenes, moments, and knockouts.

I move first, practically running up to him. That's my first mistake. Lennox takes a quick side step and I stumble into the ropes. They give way, but push back almost instantly. I'm not even turned around before he pushes me backward and I fall on my ass.

"Let me stand!"

He bites out a sharp laugh. Grinding the back of my teeth together, I go after him again.

Each punch I throw, he takes hold of my fist, covering it with his entire hand. Punch after punch. He blocks everything. Sucking in a breath, I use all my force to lift my leg up in a kick. He grabs my ankle, suspending it in the air.

"You done?"

"No," I growl, pulling to free my foot.

A Cheshire grin slithers across his face as he forces my leg up and I lose my balance. I land on my back, shoulders digging into the mat.

Scrambling to my feet, I attack again. He pushes me to the side like I weigh nothing.

"Come on, Nora," he goads. "Show me what the Reaper liked so much."

Blood freezes in my veins. The mention of Kane from his mouth causes me to lose grasp of my senses.

"Don't fucking talk about him." The words leave my tongue in a low, warning snarl.

His brows raise. "You mean Kane?"

My lips pull back as I stand. "How dare you say his name. You almost killed him."

He shrugs. "But I didn't." Lennox takes a predatory step. "Too bad." And another. "That would've been such a satisfying kill."

Pushing the balls of my feet into the ground, I take off

toward him. I tuck my head down and hit him with my shoulder. He stumbles backward, but grabs hold of my upper arms, forcing me away. Taking advantage of the space, I send a fist into his side.

"Kane deserved to die."

A sob escapes from my chest, but I push through the forming tears. I throw another round of punches, all of which he blocks.

"I just wish I would've been there to see it."

"Shut up!"

The tingling at the base of my neck forms quickly, shooting up with lightning speed. I cry out, sending a wave in his direction. Lennox flies several feet backwards, his body jamming into a corner of the ring.

As the wail fades, my chest heaves. A leftover quiver of emotion washes over me, forcing out another choking sob. I press the heel of my hand to chest, hoping to ease the gaping hole that's formed.

Lennox lowers his arms from the protective stance he held them in. His eyes narrow, running from the top of my head to my feet. Deep lines etch themselves in his forehead as he assesses what just happened.

"You," I say with hoarse words, "will never speak of him again. Understood?"

Straightening up, he clears his throat. "Today's session is over."

I bite down on the inside of my cheek as he walks by, climbing out of the ring. Swallowing the metallic taste that's formed in my mouth, I wait. The loud bang not only echoes throughout the room, but in my chest as well. A malicious cry pushes its way out, dousing me in unrelenting grief.

10

A knock on the door startles me awake. Grabbing my phone from under my pillow, the screen momentarily blinds me. 3:54. Sitting up, I look over at Willow's bed. She must not have heard the knock, because the lump of blanket she's curled into doesn't move.

Slipping out of bed, I quietly pad over and open the door. Every bit of air in my lungs is pushed out. Rainy images flash through my mind. Weeks ago, I was attacked and nearly choked to death by a brutal angel. Long, silky hair with porcelain features. She was beautiful beyond belief - a face I'd never be able to forget. And in the early hours of the morning, here she stands.

My first instinct is to slam the door, but she snaps her hand out, stopping it. Panic floods through my body.

She rolls her eyes, shaking her head. "Get ahold of yourself."

"What do you want?" My voice is still a bit hoarse from the cry I unleashed yesterday.

"Lennox will not be meeting with you today."

Her comment takes me by surprise. "Why?"

Those pink lips pursed together. "His duties aren't your concern. He just asked me to relay the message so you aren't running yourself into a grave."

"That's hard to believe." Before I can say anything else, she spins on her heel and walks down the hall. I shut the door quietly, enclosing the room in darkness once more.

The sheets are still warm when I climb back in between them. Pulling them around my shoulders, I close my eyes and try to drift off to sleep. Despite the rude interruption, I find myself able to quickly fall back into my dream world.

Rain pours down from the black sky. The stars are all hiding. The moon has runaway too.

"Hello?" I call out, but only the echoing sound of my voice answers me.

I stand in the center of a roofless space filled with mirrors. Hundreds of different versions of my reflection surround me. With every turn I take, they change, adapting to my movements.

Stepping closer to one, I reach my hand out. The moment my fingertips touch the cool glass, it splinters into a million pieces.

As they fall down, they reveal someone standing behind them. It's a girl. With her back to me, all I can make out is her petite frame and blonde hair.

My heart beats faster in time. Swallowing hard, I open my

mouth to speak as the person turns around. The cruel angel stares back at me. Her arm snaps out and encases my throat in her grasp. I try to cry out. Kick. Scream. Claw. A sinister smile turns up her lips as darkness clouds my vision.

Sitting straight up, I inhale a sharp breath. It takes my eyes a minute to adjust to the room. I'm no longer in the mirror filled space. I'm in my bed, tucked away at the Cathedral. Sunlight streams in through the small window. It was just a dream.

I run my shaking hands down my face, trying to calm my nerves. My skin is clammy and cold.

"You okay?" Willow's question makes me gasp. I didn't see her.

Swallowing hard, I nod. "Bad dream."

She pulls a tight smirk and steps back into the bathroom.

Sections of the sheet are now damp with sweat. Jumping out of bed, I quickly pile it together, wanting to rid myself of any memory of the dream. *Fuck*, I can't even call it a dream. It was a nightmare. Moments from that night crawling back to the surface and breaking through.

I try to pay no mind to the way my knees quiver with each step I take. I can't remember the last time a dream affected me like this. My dreams stay locked away in my head. I rarely remember them. They don't follow me out into reality.

Willow emerges from the bathroom with her hair pulled up and in her usual black attire. Her steps falter the closer she gets to me. My mouth opens to say something, anything, but nothing comes. She ducks her head down and rushes out the door.

I have to pull myself together and talk to her; actually sit down and talk, refraining from any type of argument. The longer this goes on, the harder it'll be to reconcile things between us.

Willow is more than a valuable ally - she's a friend. I need her beside me. If we're to stick to our original plan to go back against Death, there can't be a fissure keeping us apart.

Groaning, I stuff the sheet in the small hamper for the cleaning staff. Just when I think I can't fit any more on my plate, shit keeps piling up.

. . .

With there not being any training today, I decide to give my body a break. It might not be the best idea, but pushing myself to the brink of exhaustion every day isn't good either. Today will be dedication to strategizing.

Despite knowing I'll be gawked at, I swing by the dining hall. It's unusually packed for this time of day. Children, Deacons, and Changelings all crowd around tables. Pulling out my phone, I check the day. It's Sunday. That explains why it's packed. Sunday at the Cathedral is dedicated to reflection and worship. I haven't attended a mass here. Honestly, I haven't stepped foot in the church for years. I'm not a religious person. Plus, most of these people probably thought I'd catch fire if I sat in a pew.

Grabbing a small bowl of oatmeal from the buffet line, I eye my choices of tables. Each one has someone sitting at it. And as I walk down the main aisle, people shy away, leaning into their neighbor and whispering. Biting down on the inside of my cheek, I keep walking.

In the back corner, a table is empty save for one chair. A little boy sits and toys with his food. It's not just any boy. It's Meyer, the current Angel's Child. Seeing that he's the only one at a table set for eight pains my heart.

One thing I've always feared is how Hannah would be treated once she started school. Kids are mean. Hell, they're meaner than some adults. While I was able to slip into the background, that's not Hannah. She has too much personality. Her heart is as wild as her spirit. I dread the day someone pushes too hard and she shuts down, dimming her light. I don't want that for him either.

Pulling back my shoulders, I walk up to the seat across from him. It takes him a moment, but he slowly lifts his head. His blue eyes widen when she sees me.

"Do you mind if I sit here?" I cast him a bright smile.

Apprehension takes over his face. He wearily glances around the room. When his eyes meet mine again, he shakes his head, causing his hair to flop back and forth.

I hide my grimace as the chair screeches against the tile. Sitting down, I give him another smile and take a bite of oatmeal. Surprisingly, it's not bland. It's topped with cinnamon and sugar. Small chunks of apple are spread throughout it too.

Meyer eyes me from under thick lashes. He's nervous. From what Micah has told me, he doesn't have friends. He's by himself from sun up to sun down. Well, except for the voices.

"What's your name?" I ask sweetly.

His little mouth opens and closes several times before he clears his throat, saying, "Meyer."

I hold my hand out to him. "My name's Nora."

He stares at my hand as if he's able to see some contagious disease lingering on my fingers. But after a moment, he shakes it.

"You have a strong grip," I comment, causing his cheeks to burn red.

Meyer quickly goes back to his food, crawling to the

safety of his bubble. My heart honestly aches for him. No child should be forced into a seclusion, making them awkward around other people.

Running through the thousands of conversations I've had with Hannah, I try to pick a topic to get him going. She'd talk about anything and everything. We had an hour-long talk to one day about why trees pick a certain place to grow. Apparently, the old pine tree in the back just knew a little girl would live there one day. She would love Christmas so much that the tree wanted her to have her very own Christmas tree every day of the year.

"Hey, Meyer?" He pops his head up again. "Can I ask you a question?" It takes him a few seconds before he nods. "Why do you think the stars twinkle?"

"Umm." His gaze darts past me, lips pressing tightly together. "I guess because they get too hot."

His answer takes me by surprise. I didn't learn much about the solar system until I was nine-years-old. But here he is, knowing that stars actually have their own temperature.

Leaning my elbow on the table, I rest my chin in the palm of my hand. "You think?" His little shoulders shrug. "I always thought they were winking at us."

His brow knits together. Meyer's scrutinizing glare narrows and he says, "Stars don't have eyes."

"How do you know?"

"People study stars." He speaks each slowly.

From the other two times I've faced him, he's been very articulate. Hannah is very smart, but she still talks in her silly way. Not Meyer. If I didn't know better, I'd say he was older than five.

"That doesn't mean there can't be something fun about them," I tease. "Think about it. There are millions of stars out there. But when we take a moment to look at them, I think they're winking and wishing us luck."

"But they're stars."

A chuckle bubbles up, which only makes the corners of his mouth twitch. "Well, yeah, but we wish on stars, hoping our dreams come true. Maybe they wink at us to let us know they're working on them."

This time, he's the one to giggle. "Like they don't want us to lose hope."

"Exactly!" I exclaim. He flashes me a toothy smile. "Do you ever wish upon the stars?"

The amusement that momentarily overtook Meyer's face is clouded. He expression pulls downward and he shakes his head.

I feign shock. "You've *never* made a wish and sent it up to the sky?" His eyes fall to the table. "What about tossing a penny in a wishing well?" He shakes his head again.

Glancing around the room, I notice that the majority of the people have returned to their own conversations. They aren't bending over backwards to get a glance at the two of us. And those that still haven't learned to mind their own business, shy away the second I lock eyes with them.

Leaning across the table, I whisper, "I may have some change in my pocket. And I think I might have saw a fountain when I came in last week. Am I right?" The way his eyes light up is the only answer I need. "Why don't you and I take a walk, and see if we can't make a couple wishes?"

Indecision floods over Meyer's face. His hesitation is blatant, but after offering another smile, he shakes his head.

"We have to be sneaky," I say quietly, holding up a finger for him to be quiet.

Sliding out of his seat, he follows me and we make our

way out of the hall. Meyer's little feet run to keep up, but he stays right in line. His mouth has solidified into a smile. Just the sight of his excitement makes me feel better. Honestly, this is the happiest I've been since I stepped foot in the Cathedral.

With Meyer tailing close behind, we make it to the door in record time. But the guards standing on either side make me stumble to a stop. He runs into the back of my legs.

Crouching down to his level, I whisper, "We may have a problem."

Meyer peeks his head around the wall. I expect him to deflate with disappointment, but he looks back at me with a sly wink, just like those damn stars. Pulling his shoulders back, he motions for me to follow.

"Can we help you, Child?" the one Changeling asks.

"I need you to open the door," he tells them. "Nora wants to see the fountain."

They share a look before the other says, "No."

I open my mouth, ready to accept our failure, but the boy steps forward.

"You will open this door," he instructs, his tone strong and demanding. "You cannot refuse an order from the Angel's Child."

Both of their faces instantly harden. Anger and hesitation flashes behind their eyes. Nevertheless, they turn and hold open each of the doors. Meyer lets out a satisfied giggle, practically skipping outside.

The beginning signs of winter have taken over. The temperature has drastically dropped. A light layer of snow dusts the grass. It's only a matter of time before the blizzards start. The last time I was outside these stone walls, it was just chilly. Snow hadn't even been in the forecast.

Wrapping my arms around myself, I try to keep as much body heat inside my sweater as possible. We walk over to the fountain centered in the turnaround style driveway. The water's been shut off, but there's still a few inches at the bottom.

"What now?" Meyer stares giddily up at me, his eyes wide and bright.

"Well," I lean down once more, "we need to take these pennies and hold them in our fists."

Reaching in my pocket, I pull out a handful of change. We each take a penny and squeeze them tight.

"And now?"

My lips quiver, fighting a smile. "And now we have to close our eyes and make a wish."

"Okay!" Meyer shuts his and mutters, "I wish for a monster truck."

I don't have the heart to tell him that he isn't supposed to make the wish aloud. I don't want to ruin his fun. He repeats his wish two more times before tossing the coin in the fountain.

Eyes snapping open, he looks over to find where it landed. "Did I do it right?"

"Yes, you did."

"What'd you wish for?"

"Oh." Realizing I hadn't tossed my coin, I shut my eyes for a moment then toss it in. "I wished for things to be okay."

Reaching out, Meyer takes me hand and I follow him back inside. "They will be. You wished for it after all."

Oh, Meyer.

If only it were that simple.

11

The clock hanging on the wall ahead ticks by slowly. I've been counting the time that's passed since I sat in this leather chair. Twenty minutes and 13 seconds. Now 14 seconds. That's a total of 1,214 seconds.

Like yesterday, Lennox isn't available for our daily training. But unlike yesterday, I wasn't woken up in the buttfuck hours of the night. I had just changed into some comfy workout clothes and was headed out the door when I ran into a wall of a person. Vincent reached out to steady me, staring down as if he never saw a person stumbling before. He was today's messenger. But unlike yesterday, I didn't get the day to myself. I was being summoned.

1,282 seconds have gone by now.

I followed Vincent through the halls, slipping past the room that I had met with the Minor Council. Two doors down, he knocked and we waited.

Honestly, I'm not sure what I was expecting when he told me I was being *summoned*, but I can guarantee you it wasn't seeing Cranston opening the door. I don't know if it's the permanent scowl on his face, but every time I see him, he reminds me of those old men in the mall that yell at the younger boys to pull up their pants. Apparently, he's doesn't approve of my workout attire of leggings and a tank top, because he sneered at my bare shoulders.

1,587 seconds have passed.

The two of us sit in silence while he mills through paperwork. He occasionally clears his throat or signs off on something. Never once does he look up.

The door of Cranston's office opens, startling me. Twisting around in the chair, I catch Margot shutting the door behind her. She flashes me a warm smile. Her gray hair hangs pin straight along either side of her face - not a strand out of place.

"Good morning, Nora," she says brightly.

Cranston clears his throat behind me.

"Morning."

"I hope I didn't keep you waiting long." Margot walks over to the seat neighboring mine, her white robes flourish with each move she makes. She reaches of and pats my arm. "I haven't seen you for a while. How are things going?"

I shrug. "They're going."

Telling them about the Banshee cry I unleashed on Lennox probably isn't the best thing, so I clamp my lips together and keep that little incident to myself.

A grin spreads across her face. "I'm glad to hear that. Sessions with Lennox are going well?"

"I guess," I tell her. "Where's he been?"

Margot's face falters for a slight moment. She pats my arm again. "We needed him to run few errands. Don't worry. You'll have your trainer back tomorrow."

I bite out, "I'm not worried."

"Of course not."

Cranston clears his throat again and I glance over to him. He set aside the mounds of paperwork and looks at us, both hands folded on the desk. "Your training is what we wanted to speak with you about."

"I'm doing the best I can." Defensive walls bare themselves.

An awkward chuckle leaves Margot. "Yes, we know. We wanted to discuss furthering training for you."

"Oh." Heat floods my cheeks.

"As you remember," she goes on, "we've been protecting another Banshee against the hands of Death."

How could I forget? I spent months fumbling around in the dark, trying to grab hold of even a vague piece of this fucked up world. Banshees have supposedly been extinct to our current world. Yvette, the leader of the La Croix coven, who had personally worked and befriended Banshees in the past, wasn't aware of there being another one running around. But guess who has one up their sleeve?

"There have been more and more sightings of demons and Reapers scouting for you."

"*Scouting?*" Cranston spits. "They've been creating enough chaos that the mortals will soon know every one of our secrets."

The older woman lets out an exasperated sigh. "Word it how you will, but it's dire that you have a full grasp on your powers."

I glance between the two. "Lennox has no clue where to even begin with that sort of training."

Another awkward laugh. "No, we won't be placing this training in his hands. The other Banshee has been going through an upset, which is why she hasn't been available. She's recovered though, thank the Heavens."

"You will be training with her," Cranston cuts in. "The mornings will be dedicated to honing your abilities and the evenings will be spent with Lennox."

"All day trainings? Isn't that overkill?"

As much as I'm ready to dive back in after my free day, I wasn't anticipating working my ass off all day, every day. At least now I have the evenings to myself. Getting to hideout with Micah has been the saving grace for my sanity.

Clearing his throat, the bitter man narrows his gaze. "You agreed to partake in the training and tasks demanded of you. Being granted Sanctuary wasn't a unanimous decision. It's a privilege that can be withdrawn at any moment."

"Cranston," his fellow Deacon hisses.

"Don't you dare scold me, Margot. She understood the rules when she agreed to them."

"I'm sitting right here," I say in a low voice. "I didn't refuse. I simply asked if that was doing too much."

Cranston leans back in his chair, teeth grinding together. I hold his gaze, refusing to shy away from his grumpy ass.

"The other Banshee has agreed to work with you, but it must be in the mornings." Margot tries to direct the conversation back on point. "While her voice is dormant, she can still offer insight that we cannot."

"Why in the mornings?" Right when I've started getting used to waking up at the ass crack of dawn to train, my schedule is going to be thrown off.

Margot's face falls. She keeps her eyes trained on the wall behind me, avoiding my gaze. I can see thought after thought running through her mind.

When she finally speaks, she says each word slowly and with a purpose. "When a Banshee is born, their voice is intended to be used. When one is kept locked inside, instead of unleashed, unfortunate things happen. They become overwhelmed by their inner being, which takes a toll on them."

"What do you mean?"

"Voices. They begin hearing the voices that want to come out, mentally punishing their host for keeping them trapped."

A bitter taste fills my mouth. "If I hadn't found out what I am or hadn't unleashed my Banshee, I would've just gone insane?"

She nods her head.

A twisted laugh suddenly erupts, startling the both of them. If it hadn't been for Kane accidentally discovering me at Etta's, I would have eventually lost my damn mind. And no one would've been able to help me, because even doctors wouldn't know how to diagnose me. So even if I spent the rest of my life unaware that I'm a twisted creation of Hell, I still would've suffered consequences.

I shouldn't be laughing, but I can't help it. No matter how I look at it, I've been fucked ever since I was born. Which, the more I think about it, is hysterical. While I've been busting my ass, it wouldn't have made a difference either way. The Banshee has been destined to take over my life one way or another.

"Nora." Margot's mouth pinches together, eyeing me as if I just spurt dragon wings from my back.

Taking a deep breath, I try to calm myself, forcing the

laughter to stop. "Come on," I mutter, "you have to admit it's pretty funny."

They look at one another. They're weary glances only cause a final chuckle to bubble up.

"So, I'm to start training with this other Banshee," I redirect the conversation. "What's her name?"

Cranston clears his throat. "Her name is Marcie."

It's as if he dropped a fifty-gallon drum of frozen water on my head. All the blood in my body drains away, leaving nothing but dry ice in its place. My mouth gapes open, but nothing comes out. Margot reaches her hand out, but I snatch mine away.

"I think I misheard you."

"Marcie." Cranston says again, "Her name is Marcie."

"Marcie McKinley?" My mouth grows instantly dry as my heart sinks to the pit of my stomach.

"Ramsey," Margot mumbles. "She reverted back to her maiden name after taking refuge in the Cathedral.

No longer able to sit, I stand and begin to pace. Back and forth behind the set of chairs, my body shakes as I keep moving.

"You're telling me you have her here?" I ask, my voice growing frantic. "My mother. She's been here this entire time?"

Margot goes to stand, but I shoot her a glare, daring her to move. She slowly sinks back down "She didn't want us to tell you."

"Ha!" I bite out. "Why would she? It's not like she gave a damn about me to begin with."

"That's not true. She love-"

"No, she doesn't." Anger and rage creep up my spine. "Don't you dare there sit there and try to say that. She left her family. She abandoned her only daughter, not giving a damn that she'd get put into a nut house."

My mother isn't a person I remember much about. A few broken memories, but nothing of importance. She left me and my father to fend for ourselves. Her leaving tore him to pieces, creating a man I no longer recognized. I had to grow up and learn how to care for myself, because he couldn't pick himself up long enough to actually be a father.

"Nora-"

A forceful sensation grounds itself into my spine. "Don't." My voice grows thick. "Don't you dare say another word."

"I don't know who-"

"I said don't!" Snapping in the direction of Cranston, I cut him off. The tremors rush up and out, forcing his chair into the wall. Photo frames crash to the floor, shattering around him.

Margot lunges out of her seat, hands flying to cover her mouth. They both stare wide eyed. Pushing out a deep breath, I trudge toward the door. Neither of them move to stop me.

My mother. My fucking mother. All of this is her fault. And the worst part about it? She fucking knew! She knew that when she gave birth to a girl, the Banshee bloodline would pass down to her - to me. And then she left! She didn't leave any instructions or a note. She packed up and left. She didn't go far either.

Pushing my way through the halls, I don't shy away from the timid looks cast my way. I don't even bother stepping out of the way of others. Barreling past everyone, I keep walking.

Everything about this place is fucked up. While I've been treated like a spawn of Satan, they've kept my mother hidden. They sent out Changelings to kill me, and yet they house a Banshee of their own. But *I'm* the one they're worried about.

Pulling open the training room door, I let it slam shut. The forceful echo fills the space. No one's here. They sectioned off time for my training with Lennox, leaving the place deserted. The fact that we are missing two days' worth of training doesn't change that.

With heavy steps, I make my way to the heavy bag dangling from the ceiling. The first hit is such a euphoric moment. The second? Even better. Clenching down my back teeth, I keep it up - one hit after another.

All this damn time she was here. She knew I would acquire the powers of the Banshee. Instead of guiding me, she left. She abandoned me when I need her most.

Another punch barrels into the bag.

She could've answered all my questions. I wouldn't have felt as alone. I was told I'm the last Banshee, but that's a lie. Not that anyone knew. She fled, cowering behind the walls of the Cathedral.

"Feet apart."

The stern voice scares the shit out of me. Whipping around, Lennox leans against the door jam. His hair is tied back into a knot, showing off those harsh facial features. Dressed in a combat uniform, he looks dangerous, even from a distance.

"What?"

Pushing off from the wall, he walks over. "Keep your feet apart and hips squared."

Coming up behind me, he places his hands around my waist, positioning me. The touch of fingers grazing an exposed sliver of skin causes me to gasp.

Holding my fists up, I hit again. This time, the bag sways a bit. When he steps back, I throw a more forceful punch.

"Breathe."

Not realizing I was holding in my breath; I push the air out my mouth. Inhaling, I pull back. Exhaling, I hit. Inhale. Exhale.

Over and over until all the built-up frustration and rage has been exhumed from my body.

Uncurling my fists, they scream in pain. My skin is red and raw. Each knuckle is cracked and bloodied. But I don't pay any mind.

"You feel better?"

His question lacks the condescending weight it'd usually carry. Turning around, he looks at me with soft eyes.

My voice cracks when I tell him, "Yes."

Those blue eyes flicker to where my hands hang at my sides, then he drags them up ever so slowly, meeting mine again. He simply nods his head and turns to leave.

I don't holler after him. There's nothing to be said. And yet, when the door shuts once more, my chest pulls. An abrasive gasp forces itself from my lungs, leaving me numb.

12

"You're telling me that she's been around this entire time and hasn't tried contacting you?"

"Yup."

Snow finally falls from the sky. Large, soft puffs drift down as I stare out the window. After this morning, I don't want to be around anybody. At least, not anyone here. With my mental and emotional state in turmoil, I found locking myself away in an empty study the best idea for everyone's sake.

But as I curl up in the window seat, thoughts and hypothetical situations keep milling through my head. What if my mother came back into my life? Would she have me keep the Banshee dormant? Become mentally unstable like her? If she did, would I have even met Kane? Willow? Quill?

I found myself calling Aggie, searching for even the

slightest normal thing in my life. She sounded distracted at first, but she wrangled her attention in. And then... I shared the load of shit I've been carrying around. I just dumped it right in her lap.

"Isn't that weird?"

"Yup."

"But no one else thinks that's a little fucked up?"

"Nope."

"And they want you to work with her?"

"Yup."

"Fuck."

"Yup."

Leaning my head against wood frame, I shut my eyes. I want to be far from this place. I probably could leave; it's not like they're locking me up anymore or have a tracking device implanted in my neck. But that would put me right back where I started.

"But if this is really what you want to do, you'll have to get over it," Aggie says, her voice turning sullen. "I'm sorry, Nora. I truly am."

As much as I want to argue, I can't. Aggie's right. If I want Death to get what they deserve, I have to suck it up. I have to train with Lennox and I also have to work with my mother.

Letting out a sigh, I thank her. "How's Briggs doing?"

"He got up and walked today."

Briggs is in the best care possible at the moment. I doubt taking him to a hospital would've help matters any. And leaving him on his own would've secured his fate.

"That's good. Fever broke?"

"Yes, it did. But now he's being impatient and wanting to leave."

Of course. "That's the last thing he needs to be doing."

"You hear that?" she hollers on her end. I yank away the phone, saving my eardrums from rupturing. "Nora said you leaving wouldn't be a good idea."

A faint male voice comes through the phone. I can't make out what he's saying, but by the deep tone, I know it's Briggs.

"Well, I don't care. Sit your happy ass down before I sit it down for you."

A bout of laughter escapes passed my lips - a hearty laugh that makes me toss my head back. I can see her petite frame trying to force him into a chair. He'd probably just end up tossing her over his shoulder with one arm. Calling her was just what I needed.

"I'm glad you're hitting it off," I say. Part of me has been worried how he'd react once lucid.

Aggie groans. "If you can call it that. He's a pain in my ass."

"You'll just have to put him in his place then." I can practically see her rolling her eyes. "Have you had a chance to check in with Hannah?"

The phone call falls silent. My heart rate quickens at a dangerous rate when she says, "Listen."

I can't help my sister in my current situation. Going to her would cause red flags to pop up everywhere. Despite my mother popping up and my father still alive, that little girl is the only true family I have left – blood relation, at least.

"I went over to your house and the nanny was leaving."

"Carrie," I tell her, remembering the first time I saw the two of them together at the park. I never thought I'd be okay with Hannah's care in someone else's hands. My she seemed happy and Carrie was attentive. She'd send Kane report of Hannah's progress too.

Aggie clears her throat. "Yeah. Anyways, I told her I'm a friend and was just stopping to see how things were going."

"And?"

"She's really nice. A huge smile plastered her face when she started talking about how well your sister's doing. I asked her about how long she's planning on working with her. She said a while."

"A while?"

Silences breaks through yet again. I can hear the deep breath she takes on the other end. "Did Kane really not tell you about any of this?"

Finding out that he took the time out to research hiring an at-home caretaker had blown my mind. It was yet another sign of how wrong I had been about Kane from the get go. He could be kind and caring. He protected his people with everything he had. He didn't have to do anything in regards to Hannah, but he did. And that's a big part as to why I fell deeply in love with him.

"No, he didn't."

She clears her throat once more. "He didn't tell you about any future plans?"

"Aggie." What little patience I have left is starting to wear thin.

"Alright, alright," she concedes. "He didn't pay for just a couple months of care. I guess he had her sign a contract, securing her employment until she enters into high school. From there, he already arranged for her to attend that private school over by the lake."

My jaw drops, coming completely unhinged. It's hard to accept what I'm hearing. But then again, so has everything else I've been through lately. Kane had gone above and beyond. He didn't even have to hire a caretaker for her, let alone secure the wellbeing of her future. But he did.

I brush away the tears that slide down either cheek. That man truly was something else. Such a generous person hidden under a stone facade.

"Nora?" Aggie's voice breaks through.

"I can't believe that."

"Neither can I," she agrees, voice softening. "I wish I could've met him."

The wall around my heart splinters and cracks even more. "I wish you could've too. He was an astonishing man."

"It'll get better. I promise."

"Yeah." The lump rising in my throat won't be ignored any longer and it causes my voice to crack in a hideous way. "I have to go. Thank you, Aggie."

"Of course."

Ending the call, I toss the phone on the floor. It hits hard against the cold stone, probably cracking the screen. I can careless. Wrapping my arms around my knees, I bury my face and cry. My shoulders shake violently with each wretched sob. I let the pain and grief out. After forcing them into the corners of my mind, an odd sense of relief comforts my muscles and bones, like welcoming an old friend home with each tear that's shed.

. . .

After the phone call with Aggie, I keep thinking of how uneasy my relationship with Willow is. I honestly don't know what's gotten into her and why she thinks it's okay to make light of what happened. I don't. And if that's how she's going to be, then I don't really care to know what she's been doing to make her this way. What I do care about is the us being on the same page. There's still a long list we need to get through to avenge Kane and Royce.

But, first things first, we need to sit down and talk.

Thankfully, when I get back to our room, she's there. She's curled up reading yet another magazine, oblivious to the world around her.

When I walk in and shut the door, she glances up over the pages. I give her an awkward smirk as I climb on my bed. The tension in the air is stale.

"Willow," I say, startling her. She lowers the magazine and raises her eyebrows, "I talked to Aggie and Briggs is doing better. I thought you'd like to know."

Pink floods her cheeks. "Thank you."

"He had a fever that was a bitch to break, but he's on the mend. Just being ornery and impatient."

"That's him." The corner of her mouth pulls up.

She doesn't hesitate in bringing the magazine back up and blocking me out of her line of sight. I can't exactly blame her. The last time I had a full-length conversation with her was our fight. It's just been short responses ever since.

"Willow," I say again. This time her eyes narrow as she looks at me, "we need to talk."

Willow is a force to be reckoned with. She's strong and capable. Putting up with bullshit isn't something she does. I've seen her in action, moving swiftly and with lethal grace. This version of her is a mockery of the woman I've come to know, but I bite back the comments. Picking a fight won't help. If anything, it might just push her over the brink and I'll be stranded.

"I need to apologize to you."

Pacing myself, I make sure to choose the right words. Just

because I disagree with how she's handling her own grief; doesn't mean I have the right to bash it in.

Unlike Aggie, I know she won't glide around with her head held high in petty retort. That's not Willow. She's the type of person that will look me dead in the eye and not give a damn about what I have to say. She'll know if I'm lying.

"We came here looking for help," I continue on, "and we found it. The Deacons have welcomed the both of us in. As much as I hate it, I think the training with Lennox will eventually pay off. I mean, I won't be as good as you."

A small grin pulls at her lips. "You're stronger than you think."

"Yeah, well, that's still to be determined." Swallowing hard, I run a hand through my hair. "But I overstepped. I shouldn't have said the things I did. You're handling Royce's death the only way you know how."

"You were upset and-"

"Willow," I bite out, instantly regretting it. She flinches. Taking in a deep breath, I bring my temper back down to a simmer. "Willow, I need to get this out."

Sheepishly, nods. "Okay."

"That argument shouldn't have gotten that far. It put us in a tough position. If I would've just reeled in my emotions, we wouldn't be here," I admit. "We have to work together."

Uncertainty blankets her face, lips wavering to speak whatever thoughts are running through her head. "I've been having a hard time with his death. I can't deal with my emotions the way you do - not about this."

"This isn't easy for me either." My voice cracks with the admission. "Waking up every day, knowing he's not here, is the worst thing I've ever experienced."

Climbing out of bed, she limps over and wraps her arms around me. Pulling her close, I bury my face in the crook of her neck.

Her fingertips drum on my back. "We will get through this."

A shaky breath rattles my chest. I let go of the tension and just melt in her embrace, yet another foreign behavior from her.

"I've been working on a plan." Pulling away, I can't help but scrutinize her vapid expression. "I'm trying to schedule a meeting with Xi. We'll get what we want one way or another."

"Do you really think so?"

She nods her head, shaking loose a few strands of wavy hair. A bubble of emotion pushes its way up my chest, escaping with a gasp. A smile stretches from one cheek to another. Pulling her close once more, I hug her as tightly as I can.

"I'm sorry."

"So am I."

13

I've tried yoga a few times. Not my thing. I'm not flexible enough to tuck my foot over my shoulder and twist like a pretzel. The only pretzel I can get down with is covered in salt and dipped in honey mustard. Crystals. Chakras. Feng Shui. While these types of mind-centering things can help a lot of people, they don't work for me.

A couple years ago, Aggie dragged me out on one of my very few days off. It was midsummer. Sweat seeped out of every pore, making it uncomfortable to walk. It was terrible. Plus, I had baskets of laundry to get done, which kept gnawing at the back of my mind. Nevertheless, I followed along. In the middle of a park near the nursing home, a decent size group crowded around. Some carried those foam mats people used when they self-inflicted the tortured art of twisting your body into a pretzel - or practiced yoga. Aggie and I? We didn't have anything.

Everyone found a spot, centering around a middle-aged woman in spandex. Come to find out, it was a meditating circle. There weren't any risky maneuvers involved. Just peace. We spent an hour just taking deep breaths and focusing our mind. It felt odd at first, knowing we were probably getting looks from all the foot traffic. But that day has stuck with me ever since.

I don't think I'd ever be ready for today, but here it is. I didn't sleep at all the night before. Thoughts kept racing around my mind like a carousel. After mumbling, "Fuck it," I climbed out of bed and changed, then made my way to the private training room assigned to us. I sat in the middle of the space and used the tactics I learned years ago.

Pulling in a deep breath, I slowly exhale, pushing away all the weighted thoughts bombarding my mind. I need to focus. I can't be overwhelmed with all these *what ifs*.

"What are you doing?"

The voice breaking through the silent seclusion scares the shit out of me, causing a yelp to pop out. Twisting around, Lennox holds open the door. He stares down at me with a skeptical look and his top lip pulled up in a sneer.

"Meditating," I say, cursing how breathy my voice sounds.

His brow knits together. "Why?"

For shits and giggles, I want to say, but I reel in the sarcasm. "Today's a day I never thought I'd see and it's safe to say that I'm a little stressed."

"It's just another Banshee."

"No," I bite out. "To you she might be another Banshee, but she's my mother. Two different ends of the spectrum."

A faint shade of pink colors his cheeks as his mouth forms a perfect circle. "I didn't know she's your mother."

"Sure."

"I'm not lying to you, Nora."

Walking over, he sits down beside me on the padded floor. Unlike the last time I saw him, he's in his usual workout attire: joggers and a t-shirt.

"Have you met her?"

He shrugs. "Once or twice."

"What's she like?"

Eyes searching mine, he says, "She's nice. We're not friends or anything. I've bumped into her around the Cathedral, but that's it. She spends most of her time in the greenhouse."

The oddity of the conversation isn't beyond me. A man who I loathe is telling me about my mother that walked out on me. Add in a unicorn and the situation might be more believable.

"Why are you worried?"

Looking up, I meet his gaze. Those pale sapphire eyes shine under the fluorescent lights. "She left me when I was a child. And now I have to depend on her to get a full grasp on my powers. What if nothing's changed? What if she doesn't think I'm worthy enough to teach and abandons me again? I don't think I'm ready to handle that. Not again. Not now."

"You *are* worthy, Nora." His comment takes me aback. I can't stop my mouth from gaping opening as I stare at him. Rolling his eyes, Lennox gives me a whisper of a smirk. "Don't let it get to your head."

"Why are you being nice to me?" The words race out before I even know I said them.

His face falls, but his eyes still hold the light. "I may not be a fan of how you were brought into our world, but you aren't weak. You've proved that there's strength in you. As long as we're on the same page-"

"Putting an end to Death," I cut in.

He nods his head. "As long as our end game is the same, I'll help you."

I stare at him, waiting for the punchline of a joke to come at any moment. But it doesn't.

Clearing my throat, I say, "Thank you."

The door of the training room opens and Margot walks in. A few seconds later, a woman follows, jumping as the door slams shut behind her. She's frail. Her eyes are sunken in with heavy shadows. Several shades of grey stains her frizzy red-orange hair. There are fragments, different angles the light catches, in which I can see her - the old her. My mother.

"Good morning, Nora." Margot smiles. Lennox and I stand as she walks toward us. "I hope you slept well." My mouth pulls in a grimace-like grin. Clearing her throat, she continues, "Anyways. This is Marcie."

"We've met."

A wavering smile dances on Marcie's mouth. She steps forward and reaches both arms out. I don't run into her arms though. She's a stranger to me, just like every other person in the Cathedral. Her green eyes, the same shade as mine, rim with tears when I don't uproot myself and go over to her.

"Nora."

Despite the way her voice croaks when she says my name, I don't let on to the effect it has on me; the ache that gnaws deep in my bones. Pulling my shoulders back, I announce, "Let's get this over with."

Marcie becomes flustered and Margot gives me a downcast look, but I stand my ground. The pressure of Lennox's hand on the small of my back pulls me away from the dark, impending thoughts.

"Well," the Deacon clears her throat, "I'll leave you to it.

Lennox will see to any needs you may have."

As she turns to leave, I glance at the Changeling towering over me. As much as I loathe him for attacking Kane and saying those cruel words the other day, I can't ignore the thankful tingle that loosens the pull in my chest.

He gestures to the corner of the room. "I'll be there if you need me." His comment is directed to me as he saunters over and takes a seat on the floor, leaving me and Marcie to it.

Turning my attention back to her, I avoid looking her dead in the eye.

"It's nice to see you, Nora," Marcie tries again. "You've grown into a beautiful-"

Holding my hand up, I stop her. "Don't. We're not doing this." My heart dips at her pained expression. "I'm here for training. That's all."

Her mouth gapes open and shut a few times before she shakes her head. "I guess that's it then." I nod. Sadness blankets her face. "Well, have you tried using any of your abilities?"

"I didn't know I had any supernatural powers until a couple of months ago. But I have a friend - had a friend - that was helping me."

"What all are you able to do?"

I blow out a puff of air. "When I sing, I'm able to see souls. I can toy with them. There have been several times that I've seen what has damned a person, but I'm still not sure how that works."

"Anything else?"

"I can conjure tremors and use them as an invisible force."

Her eyes widen. "That's impressive."

I shrug and hope she can't see the way my cheeks heat up. Her approval is the last thing I need – the last thing I want.

"What do you think you'll be able to teach me?"

"Control," she states.

While Kane had been put up while he healed, Yvette helped me focus on my powers. It didn't go as smoothly as I may have liked, but I was able to learn quite a bit from all those failed attempts. And yet, since the tremors stem from an emotional upset, it's harder for me to reel them in.

"And you've unleashed the Banshee's full potential?"

I mumble, "That's what they say."

"Then let's start with trying to hone in on your voice. You'll need to focus and sing."

"I already told you, I know how to do that."

She takes a small step back. "You know how to do that with just an inkling of power, not with the capacity of an unleash Banshee."

"What's the difference?"

"Before," she says in a low tone, "you were only able to tap into those with a soul. Now, you'll be able to take on the lifeline," she gestures to Lennox, "of a soulless being."

My mouth dries. "You want me to practice on him."

She nods her head. "I'll stop you before you go too far."

I glance over my shoulder at him and he simply nods his head, reassuring me.

Okay then...

Whenever Yvette wanted to try something new in my training, Kane always put up a fight. If he thought I'd be hurt or it'd be too much, he stepped in. But I don't have him here to play referee. And as much as her request has my nerves all riled up, I don't want Lennox to have a change of heart in my training.

Turning full on to face him, I take a deep breath and begin to sing.

"When the days are cold and the cards all fold."

Narrowing my eyes, a blacken haze slowly begins to form along Lennox's frame. Just a hint and nothing more. But, eventually, the haze grows, much like the way souls do around humans. The harder I push, the more it grows.

"No matter what we breed, we still are made of greed."

Underneath its form, Lennox's eyes widen and his mouth opens, gasping for air. A delicious sensation crawls through my veins, chilling every nerve end it touches. The panic settling in Lennox's eyes should be setting off an alarm and pulling me out of my head. But it doesn't. If anything, I want more. I want to feel the wave wash over me and pull me under. The more I push, the deeper I dive.

"When you feel my heat, look into my eyes. It's where my demons hide."

Hands grip my shoulders and shake me. I rip away from the tunneling vision sucking me in. In the corner, Lennox collapses and clutches his chest. Rushing over, I kneel down in front of him. I scan him from head to toe, looking for any sign of injury.

"Are you okay?"

He pulls away, limbs shaking. "What did you do?"

"She almost killed you." Marcie's voice echoes around us. "That's what she did."

I whip my head around. "You almost let me kill him? What the fuck is wrong with you?"

This time, she isn't taken aback by my harsh tone. Her brow creases as she looks at me from a distance.

"You're stronger than I anticipated."

"Maybe you should've figured that out before you had me toy with his lifeline." Turning back to Lennox, I reach my hand out, his skin cool to the touch. "Are you okay?" He nods slowly. "I'm sorry."

The words leave an odd taste on the tip of my tongue. I never thought I'd be apologizing to a Changeling - to *this* Changeling. An image of Kane lying in that alleyway floods my vision. Pulling away, I stand and walk back to the center of the room.

"Again," I croak, fighting back any and all emotion.

Marcie steps in front of me and taps my temples with her fingers. Deep lines are etched in her skin. "This time, try and keep your mind open."

"It was open."

She shakes her head. "No, it wasn't. You would've been able to stop. Lock in with your voice, but it keep your mind *open*."

Fisting my hands, I dig my nails into the skin and try again. This time, the black haze comes on quicker and stronger. I push my voice to reach out more. Just when I think I'm making a decent attempt, Marcie pull me out again.

. . .

By the time we're finished, I'm pretty sure Lennox is more tired than I am. Serves him right though. Karma's finally setting in. After what seemed like a million tries, I'm able to bring out the haze around his body and push it back. It took forever before I didn't need Marcie to reel me back to reality.

Marcie. Just her name irritates the living fuck out of me. She kept making side comments, but I shut them down quickly. Aside from training, I want absolutely nothing from her.

Making plans to meet in the same training room tomorrow,

she slips through the door. She casts a longing look over her shoulder before disappearing.

"How do you think it went?" Lennox asks.

Shrugging my shoulders, I tell him, "Good. I guess. Could've been worse."

"Yeah," a harsh chuckle follows, "you could've killed me."

Following him out the room, I nudge his shoulder. "I still can."

He turns his cheek, hiding the way the corner of him mouth quirks upward. Peeling off the sweatshirt, I toss it on one of the pieces of workout equipment, leaving me in just my spandex leggings and tank top.

"What do you want to start with?" he asks me.

Turning my attention to him, I narrow my gaze. "What do you mean?"

Combing through his hair, he uses the tie around his wrist to pull back him mane of hair. "I figured we'd move onto some combat training. You'll have to keep up with your daily cardio and prep exercises though."

"Really?"

His mouth hardens into a thin line. "I don't see why not."

I do my best to cover up the excitement that starts stirring around, igniting my veins. *Finally*. We're finally getting somewhere.

14

Inhale.

"Jab."

Exhale.

Inhale.

"Jab"

Exhale.

Inhale.

"Knee."

Exhale.

It's been a week since I started split sessions with Marcie and Lennox. In the mornings, we spend time honing in on the different abilities that stem from the Banshee. I've been able to master control over my voice while toying with lifelines. Even though he keeps volunteering, I know Lennox isn't a fan of it. He keeps his mouth shut though. I almost wish there was someone else to practice on. The sensation of pulling on his lifeline is addicting. But as much as I want to take over and pull his lifeline away, give into the delicious chill, I don't. I can't. I've always wondered how addicts can give in as easily as they do. I know now. It's a temptation that's just out of arm's reach, which only makes it that more dangerous.

Similar to how Yvette trained, we've been using dummies to practice aiming and expelling sonic waves. Their power is a Hell of a lot stronger than before, and they don't take as much effort to spark anymore.

Every day, Marcie has tried talking to me about my life. It's as if she's mistaken my training for a bonding session. No. She hasn't mistaken. She knows. She just won't accept that I don't want to talk to her. Nevertheless, she's persistent and sneaky, which only irritates me even more. I don't want her to know anything about me or my life. She walked out on me. She doesn't deserve that luxury. Our relationship is based on training and training alone.

Lennox has moved onto combat based exercises. I still have my daily running and cardio workouts, but rest is more hands on. And as much as I hate to admit it, the basics have helped tremendously. The hits don't hurt as much and my reflexes are quicker. It's taken time, but I'm finally starting to see just how much of a difference the training is making. I've never been a workout buff. I have cellulite and my thighs jiggle. But pushing my body has tightened the muscles in my stomach. Indents run up the sides of my calves. I've always had an ass, but it's become more pronounced in my leggings. Places that I never thought could tone, have taken on a new form.

"Alright," Lennox calls out, lowering his hands covered in thick foam gloves. "Let's call it a day."

My chest moves in time with each heavy breath. Placing my hands on my hips, I lean forward, trying to calm my heart rate.

"You sure?"

Normally, I'd mentally scold myself, but the progress is addicting in its own way. Knowing that I have a better chance against a Reaper or a demon fuels my motivation. It makes me want to keep pushing.

He nods his head.

I walk over and take one of his hands in mine, undoing the Velcro strap. His hands are red from the base of his palms, up to the tips of his long fingers. Undoing the other one, I run my fingers over the irritated skin. Lennox's warm breath cascades down my face as I do. Glancing up, his nose is just mere centimeters from my own. Those blue eyes shine brighter than a summer sky.

"Thank you." His voice is deep and tempting.

Air catches in my chest and I simply nod my head. Swallowing hard, I take a much needed step back and use the towel I draped over the edge of the boxing ring to wipe the sweat from my face.

"You've been doing really well."

"Thank you," I say, slinging the towel across my shoulders.

"I think tomorrow I'll enlist some help. That way you can get better one-on-one experience."

My brow cinches together as confusion swarms my brain. "Why don't you just practice with me?"

The corners of his mouth quiver. "I'd rather pick on someone my own size."

He has a point. While I'm average height for a woman, my

five-foot six-inches is still a foot shorter than him. He constantly towers over me.

"Who are you thinking? Micah?" I ask, knowing that the librarian is only an inch or two taller than me.

Shadows cross over his face. "No," he snips. "And you'd stay far away from him if you know what's good for you."

His words cause my to flinch. "He says the same thing about most of you," I reply quietly. "Why is everyone against him?"

Lennox bites out a sardonic laugh. "Of course he has you thinking that we're the bad guys."

Dunking under the ropes, he climbs down, feet landing with a thud. I walk over and he wraps his hands around the sides of my waist. I force back the gasp that threatens to unleash itself as his fingers slide across a sliver of exposed skin. I don't know if it's the adrenaline or sweat, but every time he touches me lately, my skin ignites - a rivaling feel from the cooling effects from the Banshee's powers.

"When he was the Child, Micah was the star pupil," he explains. "But the older we got, the more closed off he became. While the rest of us started our training, he shied away from any and all form of contact."

"They go through different training than the rest of you."

He shrugs his shoulder. "They can go through and learn combat skills, but most choose not to."

"Interesting," I mutter.

"Near the end of his seating, rumors from the Deacons kept flying around that he was trying to overturn the Cathedral. It was terrible. When the Child after him passed, things started to go off kilter. Fights broke out. Deacons were exiled. Changelings abandoned their posts." Lennox tosses me a bottle of water. The cold liquid tastes like heaven running down my throat. "All Micah kept saying was that he warned us. Everyone thought he went insane. They prescribed him treatments in the infirmary and allowed him to take over the library. To this day, he still believes that this place is corrupt and that the Changelings are serving under a false rule."

"What do you mean they prescribed him treatments?"

For as long as I've known Micah, he hasn't mentioned anything about needing medical attention. I remember him talking about how he uncovered secrets, but he would never elaborate on them. He kept them locked down. But treatments? He left that out completely.

Clearing his throat, Lennox continues, "Holy water."

"Like what people are baptized with?"

The side of his mouth quirks up. "Not exactly. *Real* holy water is blessed by the Archangels. It has curing powers to help the body and soul." The confusion still swarming my mind must be showing on my face, because he explains further. "Has Willow seemed off to you?" I nod. "After she settled into her room, she sought out help from the infirmary. The holy water allows her to block out the memories and emotions that are causing her pain. Once she allows the water to dissipate from her body, she will be back to normal."

You've got to be shitting me. Now everything makes sense. I knew she's been off. It's a mask - a facade. Taking that holy water has turned her into a completely different person. She's been medicating to ignore the pain, instead of facing it. No wonder she don't really react when I bring up Royce. She's forcing herself to stop feeling.

"I never would've thought of that."

"Most don't."

Everything he says makes sense. Unless you're a Changeling or live in the Cathedral, it's a whole new world. Most know nothing about its inner workings. From the people, to the way they're taught, to their duties - it's like a community walled up in solitude.

I follow Lennox out of the training room, letting the door slam shut behind us. It must be nearing sometime after six o'clock. There aren't any children roaming the halls and sky outside has darkened. With each day that passes, the colder it gets. Snow's been a constant force; the grass and trees are coated in white.

"Are you planning on stopping by the dining hall?" Lennox's voice cuts through my thoughts.

My face reddens. I almost forgot he was still walking along side me. Usually we split off and go our separate ways.

I shake my head. "No. I have to stop by the library after I shower. I asked Micah was able to get his hands on something for me."

"Did you now?" His words slow in a cautious pace.

"Yeah. I figured running errands isn't on the list of things I'm allowed to do."

"You could've asked me."

Tilting my head up, I catch the way he looks at me. Eyes soft and lips slightly parted. Shadows from the lights around us contrast his face, making his jawline sharper.

Lennox is far from unattractive. In his own way, he's hot - really hot. Being a Changeling, he has these angelic features: silky, long hair, clear complexion, and bright eyes. All he needs is a glowing white backdrop and he'd be set. I remember first seeing him. He stood outside the building that housed the demonic board room. He and Kane had an argument - light versus dark. The two of them had their own air of power. I remember thinking that he was attractive, even back then. Nothing like Kane. Hell, they were from opposite ends of the spectrum.

Damn. That day seems like it was a million years ago.

"I'll keep that in mind."

He gives me a tight grin and looks forward.

I don't know when he all of a sudden stopped hating me, but I'm not going to complain. Lennox can be extremely harsh. His intensity can be just as overwhelming. It's a relief not having him breathing down my neck, ready to break me in half.

"This is me," I say, gesturing to the hall at the right.

He nods to the left. "Me."

"See you tomorrow."

Those blue eyes roam my face. "Good night, Nora."

I can't help from looking over my shoulder as we go our separate ways. His tall frame walks down the hall, legs moving at a graceful stride. As I turn away, my heart pulls.

Walking into the room I share with Willow, I shut the door and lean against it. I press the heel of my hand into my chest, trying to subside the growing pressure. I shouldn't be feeling this way. I shouldn't feel as comfortable around him as I do. He's the enemy. No. *Was.* He *was* the enemy, but not anymore. Now he's… what? An ally? A friend?

"You okay?" Willow steps out of the connected bathroom, running a towel through her wet hair.

I nod and kick off my shoes. My socks are soaked through with sweat. They'd probably drip if I tried wringing them out. It's disgusting.

"You sure you're okay?"

Running my hands down my face, I let out a sigh. "I don't

know."

"Talk to me. What's up?"

"Lennox is what's up."

Rolling her eyes, she asks, "What'd he do now?"

"He's being nice."

A loud, obnoxious laughs bubbles up from her. I let out a groan, but her laughter overshadows it. "You're upset because he's being nice to you."

"I'm upset because he makes me forget."

Silence deafens the room. The admission terrifies me. Willow tosses the towel on the floor and rushes over to me, wrapping me in a hug. I sigh and melt into her arms.

"Every day he makes me forget how badly I'm hurting. And I feel like I'm betraying him," I admit, my voice low. Tears rim my eyes, daring to fall. "And then I have to stop and remind myself of who he really is. He's the Changeling that almost killed Kane. From day one, he's hated me. If I died, he wouldn't even blink an eye. But it's not like that anymore."

"You're not betraying anyone. It's okay to feel."

My fingers instinctively curl, clawing back the comment that fights to come out. The fact that she can stand there and say that, knowing damn well she's been taking something to make her forget, is beyond hypocritical. She's the last person that should be saying that to me.

"Kane would want you to be happy."

Yanking away from her, I seethe, "I'm not going to fuck the guy. I don't even know if Changelings can do that. It's probably against some code." A sigh drags out from my lungs. "I'm just saying he makes me forget."

"And that's okay."

"No," I rebut, shaking my head. "No. I just have to be

careful. I have to keep my guard up."

She gives me a small smile. "You're human, Nora. It's okay to feel. It really is."

"I'm not human. If I were, we wouldn't be here." She lets out an exasperated sigh. "I'm a Banshee. And until Death gets what they deserve, I can't let things like emotions cloud my head."

"Whatever you say, Nora."

Patting my shoulder, she steps away and continues to get ready for bed. And yet, an uneasy feeling rocks my stomach. But I don't say anything else. I can't. We just squashed the tension. No need to add more.

15

The walk to the library will forever be imbedded in the back of my mind. I make two right turns and a left. The Cathedral had once been like an unsolvable labyrinth. While it's expansive size is still intimidating, I've been able to locate a few places on my own. As long as the walls don't twist and turn, creating new pathways, I'll be okay.

When I step into the library, the lights are dim. There have been several times that Micah and I stayed up and talked long into the night. The darkness that covers the room never bothered me. Not when I had him with me. But as I walk up the staircase and farther into depths of the library, the shaded lights are creepy. Disturbing.

Clearing my throat, I call out for him. No answer. "Micah!" I call out once more. A chill runs up my spine. As goosebumps form along my arms, I promise myself only a few more minutes.

I'm used to working nights; roaming the halls of the

nursing home with the lights on their lowest settings. Groans from the patients. Odd noises or doors being shut would always echo in the deserted halls. But it's not as unsettling as walking through this abandoned room.

"Micah!"

Only the sound of a low, groaning creak answers me.

I'm out of here, I say to myself. Turning on the balls of my feet, I head back for the stairs.

A door slams, followed by footsteps. I stop dead in my tracks. Holding my breath, I try to be as quiet as possible, despite my heart thumping away in my chest.

"Nora," Micah finally answers, "is that you?"

Relief unties the built-up tension. He looks down from the upper level, smiling at me. Those big frames take over most of his face.

"I thought maybe you forgot," I admit, climbing my way up to him. I flash him a cheap smile, hoping he can't smell my cowardice. Afraid of the dark. Hell, that's a fear only children have.

He shakes his head, sending a few strands of his floppy hair flying. "I wouldn't miss a date with you for the world."

"I don't know if you'd call this a date."

"Super-secret spy mission. Tomato. Tom*a*to." He shrugs. "Looks like you got a good work out in."

I glance down. A few sweat spots remain on my shirt. I crinkle my nose and he laughs.

"Were you able to get it?"

He winks from behind those large frames. "Even better."

My brow instantly knits together and lips purse. I didn't think anyone could get much better than what I asked for. But then again, this is Micah.

Wrapping his hand around my wrist, he motions for me to follow. I staying close as he walks through the stacks. We travel deeper into the fortress of books than I have ever been. The farther we go, the more it seems like I'm heading down a rabbit hole. Instead of a white rabbit though, I'm tailing behind a mad hatter. Micah opens a door and we go in. The space is set up like a studio apartment. A small fridge sits on a counter, while a bed is pushed up against the corner.

"Micah, where-"

"Shh!" he snaps, raising his finger to his lips.

Eyes wide, I nod my head.

I stand back as he grabs hold of the metal footboard and scoots it across the floor. The screeching pierces my ears and I plug them with my fingers until it's over. Crouching down, he grunts as he lifts up a piece of the stone floor.

"Do you need help?" I ask quietly, peering over the mattress.

"Almost done," he says as he pulls up another piece. I take it from him and set it on the ground. When he turns to me, his face has fallen. His usually full lips have thinned and his eyes are steady. "You need to promise me that what I'm about to show you will never leave this room. Understood?"

I nod, feeling anxious from his suddenly serious tone. It's a good kind of anxious though. Like a child ready to hear how to win a board game. Or learning the password of parental controls.

"You also can't speak until we're in the clear. We need to make as little noise as possible."

"Okay!" Eagerness takes hold of me, raising my voice. His eyes narrow and I hold up both hands. Whispering, "Okay."

Micah lowers himself through the hole he's created. It's not big. I'm honestly shocked that he's able to fit down there.

But then again, he's probably the only person that knows about this - whatever it is. Following suit, I climb in after. Images of lowering myself down from the roof of the abandoned warehouse hatch flashes through my head. A night that seems like it was forever ago, even though it's only been a couple of weeks. I follow close behind him. Unlike the tunnel that connected the conveyor belt to the basement of the Playground, there aren't any lights leading the way. But Micah holds tight to my wrist and leads me.

Even though he said to keep quiet, I find it hard. The slightest noise is amplified as it echoes around us. I keep my breathing shallow and step lightly. But even then, I fear that I'm being too loud. I just take Micah not whipping around and shushing me as a good sign. It's not long before we reach the end of our secret adventure. My inner child is living her best life at the moment. The whole growing up quick thin really put a damper on exploring and imagining new things when I was younger. I know for a fact Hannah would love this though. Her imagination would be running wild.

An aged iron gate covers the exit. Disappointment sinks into my chest. But with a nudge of his shoulder, Micah pops it loose and sets it aside as we climb out. The backside of the Cathedral towers high above. Only a hedge line separates us from the holy Wonderland.

I go to speak, but he shakes his head just as I open my mouth. *I guess we're still keeping quiet.* The temperature has drastically dropped since we left the warmth of the library. Our breaths cloud in front of our faces. While the cold is nice for my worn muscles, it quickly fades and my jaw starts to chatter. I wrap my arms across my stomach, burying my hands to keep them warm.

Up a hill and through a section of trees, we walk out of sight of the mountainous building. The farther we move away from the Cathedral, the clearer a figure standing in the tree line becomes – pacing back and forth. I fumble to grab hold of Micah's shirt, but he simply smiles and slips away. He moves at a running pace, closing the distance. My heart catches in my throat as I prepare for the figure to attack him. Instead, the two embrace. Arms wrap tightly around one another. With hesitant steps, I keep moving. And as I near, I swear the two of them are close enough that they could be kissing. *Nope.* They *are* kissing.

"Micah?"

Pulling away, he lets out a little laugh – a childish giggle. My friend takes a step back. The once shadowed figure comes into the moonlight. Embroidered jacket and a cashmere scarf. Flawless complexion. Lined eyes.

A wrecking ball of emotions barrels into my chest. "Xi!" I lunge forward, wrapping my arms around his neck. He laughs, returning the hug. "Is it really you?"

"I sure hope so," Micah chuckles.

Loosening my death grip, I look back and forth between them. "But how?"

They both share a coveted glance. Even in the dark, I swear I can see the way Micah's cheek tinge pink.

"Let's just say we've known each other for some time," Micah says.

Xi rolls his eyes. "My dear, we've been stuck in a lovers tryst for years. But enough about us," he reached out and touches my cheek, "I want to know what's been going on with you."

I let out a sigh. "A lot. Things aren't the same since the last time I saw you."

"I know. One night I had a wildly profitable bar. The next?

A pile of rubble and ash."

"I can't tell you how sorry I am about that." A wave of guilt washes over me. "We went there to save Royce and Kane, but-"

"Nora," Xi levels his tone, "you don't need to apologize. You couldn't control what was happening. No one could. You went to save the man you loved." His eyes dip low for a brief moment. "And now all we can do is move on from it."

"I'm trying."

"I know. Darling here has been telling me all about it - all the work you've been doing." He gives me a small smile. "That's why I asked him to bring you tonight."

His *darling* clears his throat. "He's my outside source if you haven't figured that out."

A large cloud bursts in front of my face as I laugh. Despite the bitter cold of the weather, it warms my heart just seeing these two.

"You are not alone in your fight," Xi says, bringing the conversation back on subject. "There are many of us that don't agree with how things have been. Not all of us are big, bad soul eaters. Some of us just want back the peace that this world once held."

My mouth gapes open, finding it hard to form words. "But isn't-... aren't you-," I sigh. "It's your job to follow Death's orders, isn't it?"

"And you've seen just how hands on I was with that."

Back before I tore his business to the ground, Xi would alternate the decor and atmosphere of the Playground. With a tight guest list and an ever changing interior, it was a bar - no, an experience - that everyone wanted to be a part of. It fueled their envy. Xi found a way to manipulate humans without ever laying a hand on them. All by the appearance of a bar, he was able to get mortals to do anything and everything to get in - to just get a glimpse inside.

"Don't lose hope." His words cause a lump to form in my throat, emotions trapped. "You have allies all around. Ones you never knew you had."

"Is that what Willow has been meeting with you about?" A deep line cinches between his brow. Why does he seem confused? That's who she said she's been trying to meet with. Sighing, pushing aside my comment, I run a hand through my hair and give him a sheepish smile. "Now you have me wanting to watch my back from now on. You never know who's watching."

Xi gives me a playful wink and pulls me into another tight hug. This is the most emotion I've ever seen come from this man - this demon. While he may be the most eccentric person I've ever met, he's not one to socialize. I don't blame him. People suck. But in the time we've spent together, he grew on me. And I got to see a rare, more spirited side to him.

"Time is of the essence," Micah points out.

Kissing me on the cheek, he keeps his voice low when he whispers, "Keep an eye on him."

I give him a knowing smirk when I pull away. Thanking Xi once more, I turn and started heading back the way I came. As thankful as I am that Micah brought me tonight, I know it cut into their alone time.

But as much as I love knowing that two people that I've come to cherish share a forbidden love, I can't push aside the envy that's sprouted in the pit of my stomach. Jealousy. Yearning. Not that Micah, nor Xi, did it on purpose. They found love. I found love. They get a few fleeting moments here and there. I lost the man of my life, and I will forever be longing for one more moment. One more touch. One more kiss. I've dreamt over and over again what I would do if I had one more day with Kane. Not that we'd leave the bed. But the in-between. The things I would want him to hear - to know before-... I would tell him how much I loved him. He would know. He would've died knowing that he stole a significant piece of my heart.

"Told you I did good." Micah had crept up behind me, nearly scaring me shitless.

"How did-"

"Did you really think I was locked away in the library?" He lets out a quiet laugh. "Curiosity got the best of me. Snuck out a few times. Ran into him. You know what they say about love at first sight and all that jazz."

"I honestly had no idea."

"That's the point."

Micah hands me a decent size box that I hadn't seen him carrying until now. Lifting the lid, a smile sparks across my face at the sight.

"I can't tell you how much this means to me."

He rolls his eyes. "You already owe me your life and first born child. I'll just keep adding to your tab."

16

I've been alternating between using the sonic waves to knock out wooden dummies and luring out Lennox's lifeline. And let me tell you, it's fucking exhausting.

Marcie had the Deacons make a contraption that allows the dummies to pop up in different locations on a track. It's supposed to help me get a better grasp on the sound waves. Summoning and focusing on one target is simple. But when they pop up in a different location, forcing me to stop and reload quickly? That's a bitch. I'd rather spend a whole day just running. And I can say that because I've done it before - many times before. In the midst of tunneling sound waves, once a buzzer sounds, I have to stop and locate Lennox. While I knock out targets, he keeps moving. I have to pull at his lifeline, only to let go before I go too far. And then it's back to aiming for targets.

When the session is called, I collapse onto my back. I no longer have a headache. That's been taken over by a pounding migraine. Plus the desire to never move again.

"Are you okay?" Marcie asks.

Opening an eye, I squint up, trying to make her out from the fluorescent lights overhead. The shadows haunting her eyes are darker than they have been. She looks tired. Exhausted. From what I remember, she was always well kept. The woman standing above me has a frizzy red nest piled on top of her head. Her cheeks and eyes are sunken in, giving her this haunted stare. While she has my mother's name, I wouldn't have recognized her if I passed her on the street. Honestly, I'd probably clutch my purse tighter and pick up the pace.

"I'm fine," I mumbled.

She sits down beside me. Looking over, Lennox is working to put everything away. He must've sensed me watching, because he glances up and we lock eyes. The comforting sense that warms my blood brings on waves of defeat. *No.* I can't. Pulling away, I sit up.

"I want you to know that you are doing an amazing job."

"Just stop it," I spit. She flinches, just like she always does. "Why are you not getting it? I don't want to talk."

Her thin lips gape open as moisture collects in the corners of her eyes. "I just need you to know how sorry I am. I didn't want to-"

"Then why did you?"

Her eyes glances over to where Lennox is stacking up wooden targets. As much as I don't want to admit that I'm anything like this woman, we look too similar to deny it. With her being this close, I can look past the haunting features. Same eyes. Same nose. I got my father's full lips, but other than that, we could be twins in another life.

"There was a lot happening and they got whiff of a Banshee. I had to run. You hadn't shown any signs yet, so I thought the bloodline had thinned out enough, leaving you free from the curse. If I would've known your voice would surface, I would've stayed."

"But you didn't," I bite, raising my voice. "You left. You abandoned me. Did you know you sent Dad into an alcoholic state?" Eyes wide, she shakes her head. "And that I had to work before and after school just so I could eat? And that I'm stuck raising my little sister because I don't want her to end up like me? Oh, wait," I hold up my hand, letting out a cynical laugh, "I'm not raising her. Instead, I was forced to leave my job, my family, my friends, all because people found out that I'm a Banshee. And that was news for me, let me tell you. For all I know, my sister could be starving in that house. But you're sorry. That's supposed to make up for everything, huh?"

Tears pour down her face. Guilt tries butting its way into my stomach, but I block it out. *No.* She doesn't deserve to be pitied - to be forgiven. She did this. She knew there was a chance that I could become a Banshee and she still left.

"I wish I could take it back - take it all back."

"But you can't."

I don't wait to hear what else she has to say. Storming out of the room, I step out into the main training area. There are a few Changelings using the equipment. They cast weary glances my way as the door slams shut behind me, echoing around the room.

"What?" I snap, fuming where I stand.

Their attentions are quickly redirected back to their workouts. Taking in deep breaths, I try and rein in the anger.

When I was little, I used to stay up late into the night. I kept wondering what I must've done that was terrible enough that my mother no longer wanted to be around me. Those thoughts lingered, returning night after night. It took years for me to get over the abandonment. I didn't have the luxury to float around and let all the different scenarios fill my head - give me hope.

Growing up, especially in high school, I didn't have friends. I didn't have time. Between school, work, and trying to keep food on the table, friendships were too exhausting. But then Aggie weaseled her way into my life. I was thrown off when she first asked about my mother. But I told her. She'd been pissed and just as confused as I had been those many years ago. I have to give her a call later and tell her why my mother walked out. She'll get a kick out of it. It's just an excuse. She had a lot going on. *Ha!* It's bullshit - all of it.

"Nora."

My elbow lodges itself in Lennox's chest as his voice breaks through my mental rant, scaring the shit out of me.

"What?"

His eyes narrow as he rubs the spot I hit. "What's with you?"

"Nothing." His gaze doesn't leave mine. "It's nothing, Lennox."

"Liar."

"Excuse me?" Taking a step closer, I have to tilt my head up to look at him. A faint layer of stubble coats his jawline.

"I called you a liar."

"Whatever," I mumble. Shaking my head, I go to turn away, but he grabs hold of my upper arm.

"Tell me what it is or we're not training today."

Rolling my eyes, I let out a breathy chuckle. "Fine by me."

His mouth thins. That piercing gaze holds me in place. "Again, you're lying."

"What do you want from me?"

"I want you to tell me what's turned you into such a bitch."

The air in my lungs forces its way out in a gasp; my feet stumble backwards from the verbal blow. My hand brazenly strikes his cheek, but he doesn't move an inch. He takes the blow. The only sign that I hit him is the stinging of my palm and the red splotch forming on his porcelain skin.

"You're a fucking bastard!" Tears rim my eyes. Anger and rage force its way up, filling my words.

"And you're an ungrateful little bitch."

I feel like I've been punched in the stomach. My instant reaction falls in line next, fueling the way my hand slaps across his face.

Ungrateful. Ungrateful? Why the fuck would I be grateful about any of this? If he were to take me home so I could forget about all this, I would be grateful about that.

Those coppery eyes harden, daring me to say another word. A sinking feeling fills my stomach. Kane towers over me, casting a shadow. He's never looked this big before. Has he always been this tall? This menacing? Swallowing hard, I try to ground myself.

Kane reaches out, taking hold of my chin. He grips it hard enough that I fear he'll leave bruises as he raises it up to meet his eyes level.

"I'd think twice before trying that again." His voice is painted with rage and laced with anger. "Little Banshees don't

need   fingers   and   hands   to   sing."

"Nora?"

Blinking away the forming tears, I glance up at Lennox - those inquisitive eyes now concerned. Stepping back, I shake my head. My heart feels heavy in my chest as if all my emotions and tension dangle from it, weighing it down. Sorrow and grief. Anger and rage. Frustration and confusion.

"Let's just- let's just train," I say, hating the way my voice cracks. "Okay?"

He stares me down a moment longer, waging a battle in his mind. Push me into telling him? Take a step back and let it go?

Please, please, please... just drop it, I silently plea.

Clearing his throat, he gives and curt nod and relief washes over me.

"We better get a move on then." He holds out a hand, pointing to the door. While his tune might've changed, his eyes haven't softened.

"We're leaving?"

He shakes his head. "Not really. I planned a little crash course. Is that alright?"

I shrug, glancing around the room. "I guess."

. . .

When Lennox said that we weren't really leaving, he wasn't lying. Slipping out a side door, I follow him out into a courtyard. Walls of the Cathedral close in the space. The weather outside is cold, but not too bad. There's no wind, which helps. A couple inches of white snow dusts the ground. It's untouched, other than a few footsteps.

I cross my arms over my chest, thankful that I didn't change out of the long sleeve shirt. The spandex material stretches, but helps keep in the warmth already radiating from my sweating skin. Aggie hadn't been sure what to pack. But, thankfully, she made sure to stuff several cold weather clothes in the duffle bag.

"Lennox," I call out as he walks toward the middle of the courtyard, "what are we doing?"

He wipes off a stone bench and sits down, uncaring that his balls might freeze to it. In the white snow, he looks majestic. With his long hair layered around his shoulders and those piercing eyes, he's like a dream come alive.

"He hasn't told you?"

Whipping my head around, I catch a girl stepping out to join us. Her hair's pulled up, exposing her perfect face - one that haunts my dreams.

"What is she doing here?" I ask, letting every ounce of disdain drip from my voice.

"Training," Lennox simply says.

"I agreed to train with you. Not her." I gesture over to where the Changeling stands, the heavenly bitch that almost killed me. This is the second time I've seen her since I've been here. I was hoping our last encounter was going to be, well... our last. Apparently not.

"Nora, this is Celeste," he continues on, ignoring anything I just said. "I assume you two haven't been formally introduced."

"Yup. Nope."

Spinning on my heel, I trudge back in the direction we came. This is bullshit. I didn't agree to this. I agreed to training. I agreed to training with Lennox. I agree to training with my mother. But this bitch? No.

"If you walk through that door," Lennox's yells out, "then forget our deal."

My feet falter in their step, freezing in time. Heat floods my face from the blood now boiling in my veins. Turning around, I lock eyes with him - emerald green meet pale blue. His brows quirk up, testing me, daring me to take another step.

"Fuck this place," I spit, "and fuck you."

All of this is fucked up. Ever since I walked through those doors, nothing has been as it seems. I get told one thing, but then it turns out to be just a crock of shit.

I'm struggling to keep my head above water. With bigger and more powerful waves crashing down on me every day, I should've just given in weeks ago and let them drag me to the sandy floor. I should've just let Death kill me when they had the chance. Or the girl. I know damn well the princely demons would've been beyond pissed if Changelings were the ones that stepped in and ended me.

It would be different if Kane was here. He knows me. He'd keep me safe, yet allow me to learn. If I said I didn't want her around, she wouldn't be. But then again, if he was here, I wouldn't need the help from the Changelings and the Cathedral. I'd be back in his apartment, tucked away in his bed

Kane is dead though.

As my hand hovers over the metal handle, my fingers

shake. Tears prick my eyes, fighting to take over, but I blink them away. He's the reason that I'm here. His death is why I'm here.

"Fuck," I mutter under my breath.

Turning around once more, I head back down the little walk. Lennox and the girl, Celeste, haven't move. They both stare at me as if they were expecting me to backtrack - expecting me to give in. That only pisses me off more. Lifting my head and pulling back my shoulders, I glance between them. With their almost white hair, paler than pale skin, and blue eyes, they could be twins. They aren't, but they could be.

"What do you want me to do?"

The corner of Lennox's mouth pulls up ever so slightly as he explains, "I want you to fight."

"With pleasure."

"Her?"

Celeste and I speak at the same time. A cocky grin slithers across her face as I cross my arms over my chest.

"It's more sensible for you to start off one-on-one training with someone who has similar characteristics." He leans forward on his elbows. "When you can over power her, we'll move forward."

"That'll never happen," she mumbles under her breath.

Rolling my eyes, I strike at her ego. "Says the girl whose body left a permanent hole in the side of a brick wall."

It's a low blow, but the way her face falls and cheeks burn red makes it worth it. It doesn't last long though. Before I even have time to react, the she-bitch lunges forward and grabs my shoulders, kneeing me in the stomach.

Groaning in pain, I try and push past the stars exploding

in my eyes.

Fuck. This is going to be a long day.

17

"Hold still."

Lennox dips the corner of a towel in peroxide, then dabs my lip. The fizzing sensation burns. I try and do what he says, but it's hard. Between my now split lip and the gash on my cheek, it's clear how bad of a beating I took. That doesn't even include the bruises that now cover the rest of my body.

After Celeste pulled the dick move of kneeing me in the stomach, we spent the next few hours fighting. And when I say hours, I mean *hours*. I was able to sneak in a few good shots, stunning her. That's about it though. She'd react with faster and harder blows, knocking me on my ass. While I'm not a fan of hers in general, I do have to admit that she's a good fighter. No. Celeste is lethal. She knows how to handle herself.

Scooping up a small amount of salve from a tin can, Lennox smears a bit on my lip and under my eye, covering up the area where the skin broke open. The smell of it makes both of my eyes water, but the cooling sensation is worth it.

"What's the verdict?" I ask, grimacing as I stand.

There's no one left in the training room. I can't even explain how happy I am about that. After snapping earlier, there's no doubt in my mind that they'd find me getting my ass beat more than amusing.

Closing the lid on the tin can, he looks me over. "You'll live. At least for another day."

"Gee," I mumble, "thanks."

"I know you're still not happy about me springing her on you."

A sardonic chuckle slips out. "What gave you that idea?"

"Pretty sure if your looks were as deadly as your voice," he smirks, "I'd be six feet under by now."

I shrug my shoulder.

Each and every time I got knocked to the ground, I'd sneak a look over to him. Leaning on his elbows, he kept a close eye on every move either of us made. He didn't leave his perch on that stone bench the entire time. After a while, I couldn't help but wonder if his ass was actually frozen to it. It wasn't though. He stood up with ease and walked over when it was all said and done, holding out a hand to help me up.

Sitting down on the edge of the boxing ring, he crosses his arms over his chest. "You need to be able to work your way up. If you were to take on anyone with any added height or weight to them, you'd go down in a second," he explains.

"But did it have to be her?" I ask, still brooding over his choice of opponent.

"Celeste is one of the best."

I walk over and sit down beside him, our shoulders barely

touching. "What's going on between you two?"

His head snaps in my direction, brow drawn tightly together. "There's nothing going on between us."

"You sure about that?"

"Changelings don't have relationships. Not with the Accursed, not with humans, and especially not with one another."

Sounds a lot like how Reapers interact. Nothing more than physical relations allowed. That's what got Royce and Willow in trouble in the first place. They were ratted out and forced to end things between them. Not that they actually did, but it has been a scandal at the time.

"Are you going to tell me what happened earlier?"

Sighing, I rub my eyes. "My mother left when I was a child. No reason. No good-bye. She just left. After that, my father wasn't much of a parent. He slept, worked, and drank. I had to pick up little side jobs just to have money to eat. Later on, after I was able to get a real job, he stopped paying bills."

Even now, I can't remember how many times he'd forget to pay some type of bill. Water would get cut off in the middle of a shower. The house would be pitch black for days until I was able to scrounge enough money to turn the electricity back on. I was a child caring for a grown man. He changed for a couple of years, when he met his new wife, but that didn't last long.

"He met my step-mom, Dina, and they had my younger sister," I tell him. "That's great and all, but she'd not a better parent than he is. I've stepped up to take care of her. That's also why I didn't try running away from Death. They used her against me. They threatened to sick every demon on her and condemn her soul to Hell."

"Nora," Lennox's voice drops, taking on a gravelly sound,

"children are not to be touched. Not by the light, especially not by the dark. Her soul is untouchable until the day she can make her own decisions."

Blood drains from my face, leaving me cold and empty. I curl my fingers in to stop them from shaking.

"What do you mean?"

"A child's soul is off limits. Once they've reached the point that the Archangels can't exchange their souls, a child cannot be sent to Heaven, nor Hell. At least until they're able to make their own choices. That's when we can make a play for their soul. But not a minute sooner."

"Hannah's been safe this entire time?"

He nods his head, eyes squinting in the corners He doesn't even try to hide the sympathy radiating off of him.

Standing up, I tangle both hands into the mess of hair tied up on the top of my head. Hannah was safe. I didn't have to fall in line with Death. They used the love and devotion I had for my sister to twist my allegiance. A dawning thought rushed in my head, causing my muscles to stiffen.

"Did Kane know about this?" After a moment, he nods his head. "Fuck!" I bellow out.

He knew. He fucking knew and didn't tell me. Even after everything we had gone through. I get why he didn't tell me at first, but after? He couldn't steal a single moment to tell me that. He knew how important she is to me. Was he afraid I'd leave? I wouldn't - couldn't. He had me - *all* of me. I gave him everything. I just handed it over.

I don't even hear Lennox stand. Hands rest on my shoulders; thumbs circle at the base of my neck. "Don't go hating him. I can't believe I just said that. But they probably had something over him. Changelings and Reapers, we don't have anything to live for. That was stolen from us long ago. But that doesn't mean Death didn't have something dangling over his head."

"You mean like a *do as I say or this will happen* deal?"

He nods.

Pushing out all the air in my lungs, I squeeze my eyes shut. Lennox is right. The princes are master schemers. For all I know, they had his world tied together in a bow.

When I open my eyes again, Lennox still stands right in front of me with his thumbs hooked in the pockets of his pants.

"Have you ever been in a position like that?"

If I hadn't been looking directly at him, I would've missed the way his mouth pulls down a fraction. "Reapers and Changelings live in two different worlds."

"That doesn't mean you haven't been coerced into doing something. Even the brightest lights can dim."

"I've only done what is best. Others may not agree with what I do and how I get it done, but I don't let them affect my decisions."

"You wanted nothing to do with me, but you agreed to train me," I counter.

A shadow passes behind his eyes, darkening the pale blue for just a second. "That's something completely different. I cannot go against what the Council wants. It's my duty to follow through with their demands."

"That doesn't mean you agree with everything they want you to do. Same as the Reapers." I remember the way Royce and Kane behaved. They'd do as they were told, even if it took a toll on them. At least until they had enough. "Have you ever went against what they wanted?"

His gaze dips, glancing down at my lips for a moment.

"I've never had a reason to." Clearing his throat, he admits, "If they had given me a choice to train you then, I would've said no."

I tilt my head and gaze back at this man, taking in every inch of his statue face. "And now?"

Lennox's lips part as he draws in a breath. "Now I want nothing more than to see you succeed."

"And you'll help me do that?"

His Adam's apple bobs as he swallows. "Even if it kills me."

I wonder if he can hear the way my heart pounds in my chest. A man who I loathed has been doing nothing but helping me. He wants Death dead just as much as I do. He could've given up on me long ago, tossed me into the pits of Hell to lure the princes out, but he hasn't. An electrifying tension tethers between us. I want to reach out and touch it - to run my fingers through the current and grab hold. *Kane*, guilt whispers, gripping at my chest.

"Nora-"

A loud bang echoes through the room as the training room door flies open. Startled, I jump away from Lennox. And yet, I can still feel the weight of his eyes on my skin.

Meyer's little frame comes bounding across the room. Blonde hair flies everywhere as he holds tight to a box in his hand.

"Nora!"

Glancing at Lennox one more time, I bend down to the little boy's level. My muscles and joints groan in protest.

"What is it?"

He all but tosses the box in my hands. "The pennies came true."

My brow knits together. With his small finger, he taps the lid of the box. Lifting it up and off, I'm met with the sight of a toy. The wheels of the truck raise it up a couple of inches. Light reflects off the bright red paint and silver accents. Just what he wished for.

"Wow! Where'd you get this?"

Lennox leans over and looks in the box. Confusion paints his face as he glances between me and the little boy.

A wide smile stretches across Meyer's face. "I went to my room after sitting today and it was there! The penny wish came true!"

"That's amazing," I tell him. A grin matching his own pulls at my lips.

"You were right! We should bring more pennies next time."

His eagerness makes me laugh. I can't believe how happy a simple toy has made him. I hand the box back to Meyer and pat the top of his head.

"Next time," I tell him, "we'll bring a whole bag full of pennies. Maybe even nickels."

Those bright eyes widen. "I bet you those work even better!"

"We'll have to find out."

He smiles once more and then skips back to the door. A Deacon dressed in white robes holds it open, waiting for him to pass. Despite how happy Meyer is, they still give me an incredulous look before leaving.

"You did that, didn't you?"

"Maybe," I say, standing back up.

The once calm and poised Lennox is gone. A much more stern and rigid copy stands in his place. The thin line of his mouth stretched across his face, darkening his eyes.

"You shouldn't get his hopes up like that?"

"Why?" My brow cinches together, insulted by his comment.

He lets out a sigh. "Meyer isn't like the other kids."

"No," I cut in, letting my temper simmer, "he's not. But he's still a child. He still deserves to be happy. Not treated like a leper."

Running a hand down his face, Lennox groan. "You don't know what you're talking about."

"Pretty sure I do."

"No," he bites out, snapping his full attention in my direction, "you don't. Meyer is the Child. That's what he is. His sole purpose is to relay messages from the Archangels. That's it. Once his time is up, he will be placed in a lack-luster job. Nothing more."

"He didn't choose to be this Child," I rebut, pointing at the door. "He didn't choose any of this. He got picked out of a group and is now forced into seclusion, stuck listening to voices in his head."

Lennox steps away, pacing in time. "Nora, all that's going to do is get his hopes up. His fate is already laid out. You aren't getting that. That's his destiny. There's no changing it."

"Ha!" The bitter laugh sneaks out. "I understand more than you think. Just weeks ago, I was in his footsteps, forced to do something against my will. I didn't know what a Banshee was, let alone that I was one."

"Just stop," he says, holding a hand up. "You and him are completely different people in completely different circumstances. He *needs* to stay in line and do as he's told."

"Why?"

"Because there's too much at stake!"

The way Lennox whips around and bellows causes me to stumble backwards. His ferocity snaps loose and hurdles in my direction. His chest heaves as the veins in his neck bulge out.

Taking in a deep breath, he tries leveling his tone. "Meyer has another couple of years. That's it. Once he's done, he can live a somewhat normal life. But until then, he needs to do as he's told."

Swallowing hard, I bite back the string of arguments filling my mind. Filtering through my choice of words, I say, "He's miserable. He needs a friend. Maybe if someone would've reached out to the one before him, he wouldn't have taken his own life. Being kind and being a friend are two qualities that I will not hide. And I can tell you right now, Meyer needs a friend. I will not apologize for that, nor will I stop being nice to him."

I don't wait for what he has to say. Shouldering past, I leave the training room.

People who are supposed to pride themselves on doing the right thing sure as Hell don't give a damn about their own people. It was a little truck - a fucking toy! I wasn't slipping him a list of swear words or ways to sneak out at night. I gave him a present. Children deserve toys and things to play with, especially in a place like this. They call this place the Cathedral. It's supposed to be a haven. A sanctuary. Ha! It's more like a prison.

"Nora!"

I keep walking, ignoring Lennox as he calls after me. I have nothing left to say to him - nothing at all.

18

After storming out of the training room, I head straight for my room. Lennox is on my last nerve. When I think we might be getting some headway, his dick pops up. Not his literal dick. His dick of a personality. Asshole. Self-righteous. Egotistical. Simple minded. He's all of those things. And yet, he can be caring. It's the moments that he actually listens and treats me like an equal that sends my mind reeling.

Maybe he's right. I have no clue where any lines are drawn to stop myself from crossing them. While I find it appalling that Meyer doesn't have any toys and is treated more as an adult than a child, me getting him a monster truck is jaw dropping to those here. The world of the Reapers is a tangled mess of sin and twisted persuasions. It had taken me a while to grasp what was up and what was down. But unlike life at the Cathedral, the Hellish side of life seems to be much more simple. Demons and Reapers know their place and their jobs. They are given direct assignments from Death and that's that.

In the Cathedral, there are countless statutes of life. You have a child that hears the voices of angels and humans that follow through with their orders. They have a school set up for young Changelings, while the older ones go out to collect souls destined for Heaven. Similar, yes. But the amount of rules and strict ways overpowers them, landing the Changelings world at the complete opposite end of the spectrum.

Needless to say, sleep isn't my friend. I toss and turn, unable to slow my racing mind. It doesn't help that my body screams bloody murder with every move I make. The session with Celeste beat me numb. Then the argument with Lennox finished any sense I had left.

Even as the sun streams in through a small sliver in the blinds, I don't move.

When Willow wakes, she gives me a concerned look. "You good?"

Nodding, I roll over and close my eyes. I can tell by the soft steps she takes that she's trying to be as quiet as possible. After a little while, I hear the door open and shut as she leaves. Sighing, I roll onto my back and run my hands over my face. I need to get out of bed. I'm already late for training. Any more time and Lennox will have my head.

I shake my head and lay on my side once more. "Fuck him," I mutter, pulling the blankets over my head.

Life wasn't always this difficult. Well… it was, but only in the whole *adulting sucks* kind of way. I used to get up every day, make Hannah breakfast and then lunch for later on in the day. I'd take a quick shower and change before heading down to the bus stop. From there, I'd head over to Beacon Light. Before all of this, I was there for a couple of years. It's not the greatest place in the world, but I love the residents. And I'm good at what I do.

At least I thought that. The last day that I worked, my supervisor, Casey, pulled me aside about an incident that happened. Protocol trumps patient happiness, even over a simple package of cookies. I can't exactly blame it all on that. When she confronted me, I may have had a case of word vomit. And by may have, I mean I did. That secured my suspension. Not that it mattered much. Death had ordered Kane to essentially kidnap me and bring me to them. That day tops the shittiest of shitty days.

But months later, I'd still rather be donning my scrubs than getting my ass handed to me in training. Finding out that I'm a Banshee literally turned my world upside down. I haven't been able to right it since. More and more shit keeps piling up. And, honestly, I'm over it.

A knock comes to the door, but I ignore it. Closing my eyes, I curl up under the warm blankets. Eventually, sleep finds me, stealing me away from reality.

. . .

By the time I wake up, the room is encased in darkness. I'm still curled up in a ball, covered and warm. Sneaking a hand under my pillow, I pat around until I find my phone.

7:32.

"Fuck my life," I sigh, sitting up. I don't even have to squint at the screen to know that I've slept through the entire day. If I did though, I know I'd find two tiny letters at the end: PM.

By the time I ready myself, it takes everything I have to talk myself out of crawling back in bed. First, I stop by the training room. All the lights are off, deserted by the masses. Just the sight of the empty room makes my stomach churn.

Tomorrow's session isn't going to go well.

I contemplate heading to the dining hall, but if Meyer is there, that will only cause more issues. Finally, I decide to head to the library.

The doors are slightly ajar, which is unusual for the library. No one visits. Micah uses service doors around back, some I'm sure the Deacons don't even know exist. Doing my best to keep quiet, I pull open the door and step inside. Before I can call out for my friend, the sound of voices echo around me. Tiptoeing, I climb the small set of steps and follow the yelling.

"She has no idea what she's dealing with," Micah snaps, his usual gentle tone sharp and dangerous.

The sound of something being slammed makes me jump. Pressing a hand over my mouth, trapping in the yelp that squeaked out, I lean against a stack of books. With my back flush against the spines, I do my best to stay hidden in the shadows.

"It's not your place to encourage her." Lennox's voice mixes in the conversation making my eyes grow wide.

What is he doing here?

Micah laughs. "She's a grown ass woman - not a child. Hiding things from her isn't going to help your case. She's smart."

"She's rash. The slightest thing upsets her and she shoots off like a damn rocket."

"She does, doesn't she?" I can practically see Micah's smile.

Legs of a chair screech against the floor. A moment passes before Lennox says, "Keep your mouth shut. She could ruin us all."

"Is that what you're afraid of?"

An eerie silence follows. A slow spread of goosebumps travel up my arms. "I'm not afraid."

"You're terrified," my friend bites back. "You're scared that she will bring this place down, just like the Playground. But instead of stone and rubble, it will be all the secrets and lies that break the foundation. And better yet," Micah's tone drops, "you're afraid that at the end of the day, none of your hard work will matter. Not if she can't stand to look at you."

"You have no clue what you're talking about."

"You're infatuated with her. And if given the chance, I bet you'd turn away from it all just to save her. But would she do the same if she knew the truth about what you've done?"

The sound of grappling forces me away from my hiding place. Stepping out, a throaty gasp juts up my chest. Lennox, his tall agile form, has Micah pinned to the wall - hand grasped tight around his throat.

"Stop it!" I yell out, startling the both of them.

Lennox quickly lets go, dropping his hand and stepping away. Despite having been shoved against a wall, a knowing smile creeps across Micah's lips.

I rush over, looking my friend up and down. Aside from his now rumpled shirt and skewed glasses, he seems fine. Well, besides red, irritated mark wrapping around his throat.

Glancing over my shoulder, I glare at Lennox. "What is wrong with you?"

"This has nothing to do with you."

"Actually," Micah cuts in, "it has-"

Lennox's predatory step forward shuts him up. Placing myself in between them, I hold up a halting hand. "What has gotten into you?"

Those daunting eyes glance between me and his fellow

Changeling. His body is strung tight - shoulders rigid with tension. It takes a few seconds before he takes a deep breath, releasing some of the strain.

Shaking his head, he grumbles, "Nothing."

"Sure doesn't look like nothing."

His jaw clenched as he towers over me. "Where have you been?"

The change of direction takes me aback. Digging my nails into the skin of my palms, I tell him, "Sleeping."

"All day?" A pointed brow raises.

"Yes," I huff. "I slept all day because I couldn't sleep last night."

A shadow quickly passes over his face, expression falling. "Is everything okay?"

The way Micah chuckles behind me allows for anger to wash over Lennox's once more. Shoving his hands in his pockets, his mouth forms in a thin line.

"Yes."

He gives a curt nod.

"But what why were you two arguing?"

"Difference of opinions," Micah answers, straightening his shirt.

"About what?"

"Nothing."

"You."

Both Changelings speak at the same time. Lennox turns his eyes to the ground.

"What about me?"

"Your dear trainer just wanted to make sure I wasn't filling your head with silly thoughts. Isn't that right?"

Lennox's long hair cascades down past his shoulders.

While he doesn't look at me, the locks ripple as he nods his head. A brooding little boy.

"You good then?" I ask.

They both nod, cutting the tension in the room down by a fraction. Letting out a breath of air, I allow my guard back to drop.

"You missed practice." Lennox meets my gaze. Gone is the softness around his eyes. A scowl etches his face with shadows.

Running a hand through my mess of red waves, I say, "Again, sleeping."

"I came by your room." That must've been him that knocked at the door before I drifted off to sleep. "I didn't know if you weren't faring well after yesterday's session."

"With Blondie?" He nods. "I'm fine. Sore, but fine."

"We'll have to get back into it tomorrow. We'll lose any progress we've made and it'll only hurt worse."

"I understand."

Eyes waver once more between me and Micah; an expression that I can't read masks his face. He turns to leave, those hands still shoved in his pockets.

Once he's out of the room, I turn to Micah. Not only does he wear a shit eat grin, but he crosses his arms over his chest, seemingly unfazed.

"You going to tell me what that was about?" I ask.

He shrugs. "You pretty much heard it all." My lips pursed together in question. "I know this library like the back of my hand. Do you honestly think I don't know when someone walks through those doors? Or hides behind a stack?"

My face warms. There's no doubt in my mind that my cheeks are blazing red.

"Things didn't go over so well with Meyer's present. I guess he felt it necessary to play bad cop."

Just the mention of that toy truck deflates my heart. "All I wanted was to make him smile. He needed to know that he isn't alone."

"I agree with you."

"Who knew a monster truck could throttle the world into chaos?"

Micah laughs, reaching out to pat my shoulder. "Don't stress. I know he-"

"Nora." Lennox appears in the doorway once more. Tension has eased its way back into his muscles. "You need to come with me."

"Why?"

He stands a bit straighter, pulling back his shoulders. "There are two people here to see you. They said they have information about the Reapers."

My chest swells as my heart rate quickens. Nodding, I follow after him. I have to practically jog to keep up with his wide stride though. He all but flies down the small staircase.

A million different scenarios swarm my mind. I know it's not Xi. He'd go through Micah if he needed to get information to me. Willow is here. I try to comb through the list of people that'd possibly know where I am. There aren't many, unless someone let information slip.

As we near the front foyer, my blood pressure threatens to explode. Reaching out, I grab hold of Lennox's arm. The sinewy muscles ripple under my touch, but he stops in his tracks.

Confusion blankets his face. "What is it?"

"What if something's gone wrong? What if something happened to my sister?" My voice cracks.

Acknowledgement flashes in his eyes. Reaching out, he brushes a strand of hair behind my ears, his fingers warm to the touch. Keeping his eyes locked on mine, he says, "Everything will be fine."

I swallow the lump rising in my throat. "What if it's not?"

"Then I'll do everything to make sure it is, alright?"

Fighting back the tears threatening to form, I nod, leaning into his hand as it cups my cheek. Taking in a deep breath, I ground myself and nod. A moment later, we head down the hall. This time though, he slows to my pace.

I see a wall of white robes before anything else. Nearing closer, I catch sight of a few Changelings standing at attention, not just the two on guard all the time. One of them sees us and clears his throat, causing the mass to separate like the Red Sea. In the center stands a broad shouldered man. He's thinner than when I last saw him, but he's still intimidating, even just looking at him. Next to him, over a foot shorter, is a girl with bright eyes and a perfect smile.

"Aggie?"

Jogging over, she almost tackles me to the ground. Wrapping my arms around her, I squeeze tight. I don't fight the tears. I let them fall freely.

"I've missed you," she says.

Whether it's what she said or the way she said it, it's like a bucket of ice washes down over me. Holding her at arm's length, I look her over. Nothing out of place. She's impeccable as ever.

"Aggie," I whisper, "what are you doing here?"

Her face darkens as she takes in a deep breath.

19

"Nora," Margot calls. My attention immediately snaps to her, "let's all go to the Minor Council room." Both of her neatly trimmed brows raise. "I think we'll all be more *comfortable* there."

Nodding, I take hold of Aggie's hand. Even though she's bundled in a winter jacket, her fingers are cold from the weather.

Everyone that had been standing around the foyer herds behind Margot. Lennox stays close to me, as well as Briggs. As we follow, Aggie's eyes dart around. Her wide-eyed expression mirrors mine not too long ago. Curiosity at its fullest. I want to tell her not to think too much. It's not what it seems. Not even close.

It's odd having her here. While I've missed her dearly, I'm still uneasy about Aggie being involved in any of this. Briggs would've been a goner without her, but she should never have found out about this world - this hidden layer of life. Well... life after death.

Margot holds open the door, allowing us inside. Nothing has changed. There are still tapestries and the ancient looking table. Unlike last time, there aren't as many white robed Deacons. Those that are here though, sit at the opposite end from us.

After the door shuts, Cranston clears his throat. "To what do we owe this meeting?"

"Death has Reapers and demons scouring to find Nora," Briggs says, clasping his hands together and resting them on the table.

"We are well aware."

"Are you aware of how rash they're getting?" Briggs asks. He glances around the room. The silence and sullen expressions is the only answer he needs. "They're desperate."

Aggie leans over and whispers, "Who are they?"

"Deacons."

"And him?" She points to Lennox, who stands at attention by the door.

"Changeling."

"Good guy?"

Cranston clears his throat once more and casts us a stern look, mentally scolding us. Forget that we're both in our mid-twenties. We're just like the school aged Changelings to him.

Turning back to Briggs, he asks, "In what sense?"

Margot leans forward slightly, along with one of the other Deacons. I can't help but notice how more relaxed Briggs is in the spotlight. I was a nervous wreck. Then again, there's only a fraction of the people here and he's not an enemy of the state. But Briggs is muscle and brawn. I never took him as a negotiating type.

"They've been hunting any and everywhere. It's like they're searching in the most unlikeliest places, thinking Nora went into hiding," Briggs explains. His voice is deep, commanding the room. "They've gone to her house on several occasions, staking out in case she goes there."

A weight crashes into my chest. They went to my house? They went to my fucking house where Hannah is? Granted, they aren't supposed to touch her, but this is Death talking about. They don't give a damn about mortal souls or social rules.

Aggie pats my thigh under the table. She gives me a tight smirk, but that doesn't ease the spike in adrenaline now coursing through my veins.

"They've been to her place of employment multiple times."

Keeping my voice low, I ask my friend, "You saw them?"

She nods. "A couple times."

An impatient sigh comes from Cranston, causing Aggie's cheeks to redden.

"Is that all?" Margot asks, keeping focus on the conversation at hand.

Briggs casts me a weary look before continuing. "It's to the point now that they're confronting any one she may have had contact with. They've stopped her father and mother-"

"Step-mother," I bite out. The words are out of my mouth before I even realize I'm correcting him. I can't help but blanch, taken back by my own comment.

"Step-mother." Briggs gives me a curt nod. "They went to her work and spoke to her supervisor."

"They tried talking to me," Aggie throws out. Someone who is always confident in herself, now shies away under the huddled gaze of the Deacons. "It was kind of scary, actually. They followed me after work, but I detoured. I didn't want them to find out where I live, because, well... I didn't want them attacking Briggs."

Briggs must not have clued her in. If they really wanted to follow her, they could've and she wouldn't be none the wiser. Reapers and Changelings can cast an incantation to render themselves invisible to the mortal eye.

"I would've been fine," he counters.

Rolling her eyes, she then explains, "I stopped at a gas station. They came up to me and kept asking where the Banshee is. I told them I didn't know. Another car pulled up to the pump next to mine and they left."

"I'm so sorry, Aggie," I tell her. She simply shrugs her shoulder, giving me another small smile.

I've been fearing that something would happen to Hannah. But now that my best friend is thrown into the mess, it's really hitting me that her life is at stake too. She's lucky they simply asked questions. They could've really done some damage. No. They could've killed her. And that would mean more blood on my hands.

"Do we know what they're planning?" the other Deacon asks.

Briggs shakes his head. "No. But I wouldn't be surprised if they start acting with violence. It's only a matter of time."

A low hum begins as everyone continues talking. I tune them out, unwilling to keep listening.

While I've been at the Cathedral, time outside hasn't stood still. It's been moving along. Days have turn into weeks. Training has made me stronger - more resilient - but I'm still weak. The fight with Celeste proved that. As long as I keep hiding, time is going to keep passing. Eventually, it's going to run out and Death will do everything to turn this world into a mortal Hell.

"Take me to them."

No one hears me. Their voices have all mingled into one, arguing back and forth.

"Take me to them."

This time, Aggie turns to me, confusion written all over her pristine face. Her lips purse together.

Slamming my hands on the table, the echoing sound forces their conversations to come to an end.

"Take me to them," I say one final time, raising my voice.

Out of the corner of my eyes, Lennox drumming his thumb on the table catches my attention. His face is set, anger etched in stone. "Not going to happen."

"I'm what they want," I state, airing out the elephant in the room. "If they want me so badly, then just hand me over to them."

"No."

"There has to be another way, Nora." Briggs hops on the bandwagon.

I let out an exasperated sigh. "You just sat there and told me they've been searching for me. They could've attacked my best friend. They already held my little sister above my head once." Memories of the first time I met them flash through my head. "They won't hesitate to do it again."

"We're not sacrificing you like a pig in a slaughterhouse," Lennox rebuttals.

"I can't let them attack-"

"I said, no!"

Aggie squeals as he bellows out. His nostrils flare. A

menacing scowl takes over Lennox's face. It's a look I've only seen once before. While he pale complexion and bright eyes make him seem like a haunted soul, he's more than that. He's strong. He's powerful.

Swallowing down the lump rising my throat, I bite back my temper. This isn't the time or place for another one of our battles to take place.

"We need to do something," I say.

"And we will," he agrees, "but not that. We'll figure something else out."

"Don't worry, Nora," Margot says. "Let us meet and figure out the best game plan."

I nod and dig my nails into my palms to stop me from saying anything. The crescent moon shaped cuts barely get a chance to heal before I reopen them. And yet, it's better than biting down in my tongue. If I did, I'd be lucky if I didn't sever it.

Standing, Margot addresses Briggs. "In the meantime, will you be willing to remain as protection for Miss Agitha?"

He glances over to where my blonde friend sits beside me. She lowers her gaze, seeming suddenly interested in the lines in the table.

"I'd be willing." His voice dips, coming out thicker than before.

"Thank you," I say quietly.

Margot smiles and clasps her hands together. "Then let it be done. The Minor Council will meet and we will go from there."

I barely catch sight of Lennox's back as he flings the door open and trudges out. Cranston mutters something under his breath and the door slams shut against the doorframe.

Taking the dismissal for what it is, the three of us - me, Aggie, and Briggs - stand and file out the door, leaving the Deacons in peace. Neither of us say a word until we reach the foyer.

"Am I the only one that thought they were creepy?" Aggie breaks the silence, causing me to heartedly laugh. Even Briggs cracks a minute smirk.

I shake my head. "Not even close. You haven't seen the children. Some of them remind me of some horror movie shit."

"There's kids here?" Her wide eyes only make me laugh more.

After calming myself, I look to Briggs. "I'm glad you're doing better. You don't even look like you were hurt."

He shrugs. "When you have a little princess pestering you every two seconds with medicine, you can't help but heal"

"And you're welcome for it." Aggie cocks her hip, giving off her usual attitude. Rolling her eyes, she reaches out and runs her fingers through bits of my hair. "You look different."

"I shouldn't."

"But you do," she retorts. "Your hair's grown. And I don't know what they're feeding you, but you've lost weight." Her comment causes me to blanch. "Not that you're fat - were fat," she catches herself. "You look good. Stronger."

"You can thank Lennox for that," I mumble. Briggs catches my eyes, giving me a knowing look.

Most of the Accursed pick a side: light or dark. While Willow fell in love with Royce and had a tendency to lean toward the dark, Briggs and Lennox have worked together many times. Being light sided, he favored the Changelings and their ways, which means he knows how Lennox can get.

"Thank you again," I tell him. "I honestly can't tell you

how much I appreciate you watching out for her."

Those dark eyes waver, glancing to Aggie. "Don't thank me."

"But I-"

"Briggs?"

The three of us turn as Willow bounds down a staircase. Her thick black hair picking up wind as she jogs over. She practically throws herself at her partner, wrapping her arms tightly around his neck. Beside me, Aggie keeps her eyes trained on the ground.

"How are you?"

Reaching out, she lifts up the hem of his shirt, revealing the pink scar of where he'd been stabbed. The scar honestly looks better than I thought it'd turn out. With how many times we had to restitch, I was waiting for it to mirror that of the Frankenstein monster.

"Better," he tells her, lowering his shirt. "And you?"

"I'm good. I've missed you."

Her smile instantly hardens his face. He meets my gaze and I simply shrug. I don't even need to say a word. He knows. Holy water. It's been obscuring her mental state and the way she perceives reality.

"I'll be in the car," Aggie says. She gives me a quick hug and promises that she'll text me. She's out the door before any of us can really react.

Willow looks at me. "What was that about?"

I shrug. "She's probably tired. Did she work last night?"

Briggs nods.

As much as I want that to be the reason for her sudden departure, I know Aggie. She could've worked a triple and be ready for anything. There's something there - something I'll have to get out of her later.

"I should go," he says, gesturing to the door.

"Keep her safe," I say, leveling with him.

He nods and gives Willow a forced smile before retreating for the door. Apparently everyone's making awkward exits today.

Willow gives me a questioning look. "Did I miss something?"

Sighing, I nod. "Let's go to our room and I'll fill you in."

20

Celeste jabs, sending her fist into my abdomen. The blow instantly makes me recoil, only creating access for her to land another hit. Groaning, I duck and try to add even a small amount of space between us. Holding up both of my gloved fists, I take a shot. And miss. She moves quick enough that my arm is just suspended in air. Grabbing hold of my shoulder, she knees my side, sending me to the ground.

"Nora!" Lennox's voice pulls me out of the painful fog of my mind. "What are you doing?"

"Writing a book," I snap. "What does it look like I'm doing?"

Pulling myself up off the ground, I get back into a fighting stance. The two of us circle around, daring one another to make the first move. Celeste goes low, landing her fist into my ribcage. Crying out, I back away.

I can hear the way he sighs, even from across the mat. "It

looks like you're getting your ass kicked."

"That's because she is."

Celeste's snide comment bring my blood up to a boil. Grinding my back teeth together, I run at her. My shoulder collides with her ribcage and I force her into a corner. She doesn't react in the way I anticipated. Instead of cowering and fighting to break free, she wraps both arms around me and lodges her knee into my ribs again. Over. And Over.

"I'm calling it," Lennox says.

Through the tears welling up in my eyes, the disappointment blanketing his face is clear as day. I don't blame him. Even though I didn't have a winning hand yesterday, I was able to put more of a fight. I was able to block some of her hits. Not today. I can't seem to get it together.

The Velcro rips as Celeste pulls off her gloves. When I was first told that we'd be using boxing gloves, I was expecting those bulbous red monstrosities we used before. But these are barely more than winter gloves; your knuckles are covered, but they're a lot more flexible. Plus, Lennox said it's better to experience real pain. It's the only way to handle the shock of getting hit.

Sinking to the floor, I try pretending that the pulsing aches throughout my whole body aren't there. But the second I sprawl out on my back, that's the only thing I feel. Pain. Dulls aches alternating with a sharp jab in my muscles. Fortunately, I don't feel any other parts of my skin searing. The split in my lips and the gash along my cheek are the only things burning when sweat gets inside. And when I'd get hit in those areas, it felt as if she was peeling parts of my skin away.

With the blood pulsing in my ears and the heaving of my lungs, I can't hear what the two of them are saying. There's no a doubt in my mind that Celeste is spewing out hateful shady comments. But Lennox? After the other day with Aggie and Briggs, I have no clue where we stand.

It seems like we can't keep a steady understanding with one another. One day we're fine. Two days later, we're all but clawing each other's eyes out. Poor Micah. He'd been attacked for helping me. Lennox took out his anger out on a fellow Changeling, not giving a damn about any moral code. But the second I even brought up the option of just giving Death what they want, he lost his mind - protesting against the idea. He's been nothing but curt and demanding since. I swear sometimes he's worse than a fucking girl on her period the week of Valentine's Day.

"You good?"

Speak of the Devil. Rolling my head to the side, I look at him. The sun shines in through the window behind him. With his arms resting on the ropes above his head, he almost looks like an angel cascaded in a heavenly light.

Lines crease along his forehead. "Why are you smiling at me?"

I didn't realize a smirk had pulled up the corners of my mouth. They fall though, no longer picturing white feathered wings sprouting out from behind him.

Rolling my eyes, I stare back up at the ceiling. "Too many shots to the head."

"Yeah," he mumbles. "I could've told you that."

"It's a good thing I didn't ask you."

"What's with you today?"

Sighing, I shake my head. "Why are you always concerned about what's wrong with me?"

"That way I can tell the Deacons why you died during

practice." A breathy, sardonic laugh squeezes out, causing my sides to clench. "That's what going to happen if you don't get your head out of your ass."

"And we don't want that, do we?"

"No," he bites out, fast and without a moment of hesitation.

"It would solve everything," I tease.

It would. It really would. With me gone, I wouldn't have to deal with these daily training sessions. Hannah and Aggie would no longer be at risk of being harmed. Death wouldn't get their beloved harbinger.

The sound of the training room door slamming shut startles me. Sitting straight up, the pain that shoots up my body forces a shocking cry past my lips. Celeste is gone. But Lennox isn't here either.

Running both hands down my face, I rub my eyes. I guess they didn't want to join in on my pity party. Slowly, I pull myself up and climb down from the mat. The tank top I'm wearing sticks to my lower back from sweat that's pooled there. I probably smell like twenty different kinds of ripe. A shower is needed - *much* needed.

By the time I make it back to the room, I plan on changing into the loosest clothes after I shower. I don't want anything touching me. Thankfully, Aggie packed only comfy clothes. But she made sure I was covered. Not being able to go home restricted wardrobe options.

Ha. *Home*. The McKinley house was never a home Never will be either. It was a place to sleep.

While in the shower, the steam from the hot water fogged up the mirror of the small bathroom Willow and I share. Using the same towel I used to dry off with, I wipe away the condensation.

My hair's grown a couple inches, stopping at my breasts. The cuts and bruises only make me look scary and possessed, but my cheeks aren't as round. I know I've lost weight in my stomach and thighs as they've toned down from all the workouts, but I wasn't expecting my face to change much. Aside from that, I'm still me. And yet, I don't look like the same person.

That's because I'm not the same Nora that I was months ago. I'm stronger. I have more willpower. I'm not the overstressed mortal I once thought I was. I'm a Banshee. I'm a harbinger. I'm powerful enough to toy with the life of a person; bringing it to an end with just my voice.

Even though I can't help but feel this weighted guilt, nothing that's happened has been by choice. I've taken what's been thrown at me and dealt with it. And even the rare moments that I've actually had a choice in the matter, I did what was best. Maybe handing me over to Death isn't the best thing. It was a rash thought that spewed out in a case of word vomit. At least being here, I can try and better myself. That way when the time comes, I'll have a better handle on myself and will hopefully be able to make a difference. Doubting myself won't help. Even though Lennox and I don't always see eye to eye, he's at least had my best interest at heart.

Sighing, I turn the light off and walk out of the bathroom. Willow stands beside her bed, changing into her sleeping clothes. I barely see her anymore. Even after we reconciled our differences, we've only had passing conversations. I'm happy Briggs didn't ask, because I honestly have no idea what she's been doing with her time. When I've asked before, she's just told me that she's planning something. As much as I want to believe that, I know she hasn't stepped foot in the library. And I know damned well she lied to me about trying to meet with Xi. But with the holy water, I haven't wanted to push.

She glances up as I walk out and smile. "How was today?"

"Shitty," I answer. "I need to go talk to Lennox. Do you know what room number is his?"

She looks up at the ceiling with those dark eyes, milling through the thoughts in her head. "Not off hand. But I know it's the last one on the left when you head down that way."

I grin. "Thank you.

Willow simply nods and continues getting ready for bed. Grabbing hold of the door handle, I look over my shoulder before I open it.

"Do you want to have dinner together tomorrow?" I ask. "It'd be after training, but I can meet you down there."

A smile lights up her face. "I'd like that."

"Me too."

. . .

As dated as the concept may be, the Cathedral split up dorms by sex. Females down one hall and males down another. Being in a religious setting, while also being the home of children, I can't say I didn't expect that type of separation.

Walking down the hall to where all the boys stay, I try and be as quiet as possible. The stone flooring is freezing with each bare foot step I take. Every door is closed. Unlike college dorms, there's not much fraternization that goes down. That only makes the fear of making noise that much worse.

At the very end of the hall, there are two doors across from one another. While one is numbered, the one on the left has no markings or decals. With my heart pounding in my chest, I knock on the door, then hold my breath and wait.

The moment the door opens, my lungs deflate. Lennox stands in the doorway. His sweat pants are low, showing off every dip and plane of his bare chest. With his hair knotted into a man bun, he looks at home. Comfortable.

Brows raised, he asks, "Nora?" Swallowing hard, I offer an awkward smirk. "Is everything okay?"

I nod. "Can we come in?"

His eyes widen.

My cheeks heat up when I realize what I said. Clearing my throat, I try again. "Can I come in? Can we talk?"

Lennox doesn't say a word. He stares at me - blue eyes narrowing. After the hesitation wears off, he steps aside and opens the door a bit wider.

The room that I share with Willow is every bit what you'd expect a dorm room to look like. A small space that's taken up by two lofted beds. His room is much larger. A bed is shoved in the corner that's twice the size of the one I've been sleeping in. A couch is lined up along another wall with a coffee table in front. It's more like a studio apartment, minus the kitchen.

"Have a seat," he says, gesturing to the leather couch.

Shaking my head, I admit, "I'd rather stand.

He shrugs. "Suit yourself."

After shutting the door, he sits down on the edge of his bed. I can't help but taking in the way how at ease he seems. It makes sense though. He's able to drop every guard in these four walls.

"I need to apologize." The words come out before I even know I'm saying them. They're rushed and not how I've mentally practiced them on the walk down. But once they're out, they're out. There's no going back. I take a deep breath and try again. "I've been a bit of a bitch lately." The corners of his lips pull down at my comment. "The whole thing with my mother has had my nerves fried. Then learning that I'd have to train with Celeste - it's been a lot."

"It's better that you train-"

"I know," I say, a bit too loud as I cut him off. His lips thin as he clamps them together. "I know. That doesn't fix the fact that she almost killed me. As much as I hate admitting it, I'm terrified that she will if given the chance again."

"I'd never let that happen, Nora."

A wave of emotion washes over me. Taking in a few more deep breaths, I try calming my nerves. Those eyes of his pool with concern with each inhale I take.

"I'm going to sit down," I mutter.

He moves over so I can sit next to him on the bed. The mattress dips slightly under my weight, closing in the small space between us. The edge of his pinky rubs against mine, sending a shiver down my spine.

"There is too much going on." I cringe at how choppy my voice sounds. "I'm being forced to resolve the pent up abandonment issues I've had toward my mother. I have to train with a woman that tried killing me. I can't do anything without overstepping some sort of line. I've put my sister and best friend in harm's way. You're forced to work with me, even though you hate me-"

"I'm going to stop you right there."

Looking up, my gaze locks with his. The way his eyes hold me causes a whirling sensation in my stomach; my heart tugs in my chest.

"You need to get it out of your head that I hate you," he says. Each word that leaves his mouth is low and with purpose.

"If I didn't want to train you, I wouldn't. You're strong. I want to see you succeed. You deserve to achieve your goals. And, as much as I don't want to admit it, you intrigue me. Working with you has made me want to get to know you."

"Then why do you get pissed off with me? Why are we constantly at each other's necks?"

Lennox rips his gaze away. Laying back on the bed, my muscles sigh with relief as I relax into the mattress. I don't think I'll ever have the strength to sit up.

"Nora," he says quietly, "you're a Banshee. I've been trained to see you as the enemy. The only good harbinger is a dormant one, if not a dead one."

Closing my eyes, I listen to how soothing his voice is.

"You were safeguarded by our enemy. I should want nothing more than to end you, but I don't feel that way."

"Why?" My voice barely reaches above a whisper.

I feel the way he lays next to me. The mattress gives under his weight.

He sighs. "I've come to know you. And I find myself wondering things that I shouldn't. I find myself wanting to know you - inside and out. But because of that, I have to keep you at a distance. You're not something-"

I barely hear what else he says. When sleeps comes for me, it comes fast and strong, taking me into its world of dreams.

21

The smell of smoke fills my nostrils as it clouds deep in my lungs. The only light comes from dancing flames. I cough uncontrollably with each breath I take. The back of my throat is raw. Tears sting my eyes.

Crawling forward, I place one hand in front of another. The ground is warm to the touch, and the further I crawl, the hotter the air gets. Before I know it, my hand slips and doesn't land on the ground. Reaching out, there's nothing in front of me. I have to squint to make out the dark abyss. I'm trapped. If I move forward, I'll tumble down. But I need to get away from this smoke.

An echoing laughter fills the space around me. It's not a woman. It's not a man. It's deeper and more demonic.

From across the way, a light begins glowing larger and larger until several shadows black out the light. One. Two. There are five and two smaller shadows on either side. The light shifts and a troubled cry pries itself from my chest. Meyer. Willow.

Micah. Aggie. Lennox. Briggs. Hannah. All of them lined up and tied to large wooden stakes.

Another light catches my eyes, bringing out a final figure. Once the light shifts, I feel as if my heart is ripped from my chest. Kane.

"Choose."

Tears swell and fall down my cheeks. "I can't," I croak. "I can't."

"Choose."

My bottom lip quivers, giving over to a wrenching sob. I shake my head as I cry.

"Choose."

"Nora."

"Choose."

"Nora."

My body is shaking. I pry open my eyelids to find Lennox hovering over me, his own eyes wide with worry. I all but crawl away from him, placing my feet on the ground. Shaking my head back and forth, tears fall like rivers down my cheeks. Flashes of the dream run through my mind.

"Nora," he says, grabbing hold of my shoulders. Lowering down, he locks eyes with me.

I don't feel the tingle. I don't even aid the wail that comes out. The moment my mouth opens, the Banshee's cry forces itself out and Lennox flies across the room. He lands against the couch. The room around me shakes. The few things he has decorating the room are knocked to the floor. Once the last of the waves taper off, I take a deep breath.

"I can't." The words are but a whisper on my lips before darkness takes over.

. . .

A pounding sensation overwhelms my senses, rounding from the back of my skull to behind my eyes. Even thinking hurts. It takes every ounce of strength I have to open my eyelids. Light from all around blinds me, making me groan. It takes blinking several times for my sight to adjust. A row of beds are pushed along the walls, while stained glass windows allow light from outside to cascade in.

I move to sit up, ignoring the blinding pain that shoots forward. My right arm pinches. Taped to the crook of my arm is an IV tube, running up to a bag of clear liquid.

"Hello?" I croak.

Not even a minute later, a woman comes through a door. She's dressed in a long white robe. Her mousy hair is pulled back with a white nurses hat atop her head.

"You're finally awake." Smiling, she comes up to my bed. She checks the level of the bag and places a hand on my forehead. As she runs her fingers down to my wrist, she looks up at the wall above my bed.

"Where am I?"

A few seconds of silence pass before she looks back down at me. "You're in the infirmary. Don't you remember?"

I shake my head, wincing at the pain.

"Is your head hurting?"

I carefully nod. She holds up a finger and retreats back to where she came from. When she returns, she has a small vial and needle in her hand.

"You had a little incident," she explains as she holds the vile upside down and uses the needle to measure out a dose. She then wipes off an area of the IV line with an alcohol swab. "You've been here for several hours. We did the best we could to make you comfortable." A bitter taste fills my mouth as she pokes the needle into a small port off the line. Within seconds, the mind numbing pain is gone. "How's that?" she asks.

Giving her a small smile, I thank her. "What exactly happened?"

Lines etch along her forehead. "You woke up from a nightmare. You must've been overwhelmed from it, because you passed out immediately after. Hit your head pretty badly."

Reaching up, I find a small patch near my hairline. A dull ache radiates from it, but only for a moment. I don't remember falling. I don't remember the dream either.

"Why don't you rest a little more?"

Nodding, she slips away. I settle back down into the mattress and rest my head on the pillow. It's strange being the only person in this hall of hospital cots. But it's the Cathedral. I shouldn't be worried. The nurse has taken care of everything. I'm safe. Closing my eyes, I allow myself to drift off into sleep once more.

. . .

Sometime later, the slight pressure of someone holding my hand stirs me awake. It doesn't hurt this time to open my eyes, but it takes me a few moments to adjust to the light again.

In a chair beside the my bed, Lennox leans forward and holds my hand in his. Dark shadows coat the patches of skin under his eyes. When he sees that I'm awake, a smile plays on his lips.

"You're up."

I nod. Whatever the nurse gave me for my head is still working its magic. My voice is thick from sleep when I ask, "What are you doing here?"

"I wanted to make sure you're okay."

"I guess," I say. "I don't know what happened. The nurse said that I passed out, but I don't remember why."

A shadow crossed over his face. "I think everything from the last few days has taken a toll on you."

I let out a quiet sigh and squeeze his hand. "Thank you."

"For what?"

"Coming here to check on me. That's really nice of you."

"Don't let anyone know that. It'll ruin my reputation."

A breathy laugh bubbles up my chest. "You're not as big and bad as you think you are."

"Oh, no?" I shake my head. "Keep that in mind the next time we're in training."

The sheepish look that overtakes his face makes him look young. Innocent. His hair isn't pulled back today. It flows over his shoulders. Reaching out, I grab hold of a lock and let it slip through my fingers. Soft as silk.

"There she is." The woman from earlier comes up behind Lennox. She gives me a warm smile as she stands at the foot of the bed. "You're looking better."

"That really helped," I tell her. The memory of how bitter my mouth turned flashes through my mind, but I push it aside. Being a nurse, I've come to accept that sometimes a minute of discomfort can make a world of a difference later on.

The woman places a hand on Lennox's shoulder and he looks up at her as she says, "If she's feeling up to it, I don't see why Miss McKinley can't head back to her room." Turning to me, she asks, "Would you like that?"

"Yes," I answer, smiling at her.

"Would you mind walking her back to her room?"

Lennox shakes his head. "Not at all."

It doesn't take long for her to remove the IV and bandage my arm. Sometime in me passing out and waking up the first time, I had been changed into a set of white clothes. The cotton pants hang loose, as well as the short sleeve shirt. They're soft and warm – a lot better than hospital gowns.

After thanking the nurse for all her help, Lennox loops his arm through mine and guides me out. He walks slow, keeping a steady pace. I have yet to visit the infirmary. Well... until now. It's tucked away into the farthest corner of the Cathedral, in the opposite direction of the dining hall and dormitories. It's going to take a little ways to get back to my room.

"Lennox?" I ask. He raises his brow and looks down at me. "How did I get to the infirmary?"

"I carried you," he nonchalantly says.

"All this way?"

"I could've dragged you, but I didn't think you'd like that very much."

Laughing, I shake my head. "No, not at all. I'm just surprised you were able to carry me that long."

"I could carry your tiny ass all day."

A playful giggle slips past my lips. "No you couldn't. There's no need to try and be a showoff."

"If I had to, I'd carry you for however long you needed."

Heat warms my cheeks. A gentle wave of emotion floods through my veins, causing the corners up my mouth to pull up. I've never seen this side of Lennox. I like it. I like it a lot.

Two Changelings round the corner. They give Lennox a curt nod, but they narrow in to where my arm rests in the crook of his. Something that would normally leave me feeling uneasy, has no effect.

"What time is it?" I ask, taking notice of the sunlight streaming in through the windows.

"A little after three," he says.

"Really?"

I don't remember much from the night before. I know I went to Lennox's room to apologize. After that? Nothing. I can't even remember anything about his room. Were the walls the same color as mine? Did he share it like I did with Willow?

"I'm having a hard time remembering last night," I admit, my voice low.

"We talked. You apologized."

I grimace. "I have been a bit of a bitch."

"No," he says pointedly. "Your feelings are justifiable."

"What else?"

The muscles in Lennox's back and arm tense. If I wasn't this close to him, I wouldn't have even noticed. "You were convinced that I hate you."

"And you don't?"

He shakes his head, sending the long tendrils of his hair dancing along his shoulders. "Far from it."

Turning down the hall to the girls wing of the dorms, we pass another Changeling. She's young. She couldn't be more than thirteen. When she sees the two of us, her eyes dart to the ground and she scuttles by us.

Lennox stops outside my door, letting his arm drop. He turns to me and stands mere inches away. He reaches out, running his thumb along the bandage on my forehead. I anticipate a stinging sensation, but it doesn't come. I find myself scouring his face, taking in every inch. From his rigid jaw line to his straight nose. He's perfect. An angel standing in my presence. As his eyes lower, locking with mine, and air catches in my lungs. This man is so beautiful that it hurts. It's not fair.

"Why does it have to be you?" he asks, voice barely above a whisper.

I narrow the corners of my eyes, confused by his question. He lets out a silent breath of air, leaning his forehead down to rest on my own. I place my hand on his chest and push up on my tip toes, running my lips along his. They're softer and warmer than I expected. Sliding my hand up to his neck, I bring his mouth down to mine. Intoxicating. The pressure of his kiss sends my mind reeling.

As he pulls away, a gasp rips from my chest. He shakes his head, but doesn't move. He stays close; our bodies all but melding into one.

"No." His voice is rough.

"Why?"

"This isn't you. It's the medicine," he says. "They gave you a concentrated dose of holy water. You aren't feeling pain, which means you aren't thinking clearly."

"You don't want me?"

A strained groan rumbles in his chest. Reaching out, he cups my cheek. "Once the water wears off, you know where to find me. It will take a few hours. If this is really what you want, come to me then."

My mouth gapes open, lost for words. Was he rejecting me? Was the beautiful really rejecting me? I'm sure I didn't misread the signals.

Lennox leans up and kisses the top of my head before stepping aside, retreating back down the hall. I watch as he walks gracefully in the opposite direction from where I want him.

I should be feeling a weight in my chest. I should be upset. But I'm not. I'm perfectly fine. Just a few hours. That's what he said. Just a few hours and I can feel his warming touch once more.

22

Willow isn't in the room when I go inside. Next time I see her, I'll have to ask what exactly she's been up to and find out what progress she's made.

Even though I spent the last several hours sleeping in the infirmary, I climb into bed. The sheets are cool, but it's soothing. Comforting. Sliding down, I pull the covers over me and rest my eyes. Every inch of my body is relaxed. My toes. My back. My shoulders. Strain that's been eating away at my muscles and bones has slipped away. Hibernating - if only for a time.

I didn't expect to fall asleep again, but the room is dark when I open my eyes again. A faint throbbing radiates from the bandage on my head. The peace I felt just hours ago has dissipated into a slow ache, tormenting my awaken state.

Reaching under my pillow, I pull out my phone. 8:36. I have a missed call and a text from Aggie. I open my messages and I find hers.

> Aggie: I wish you were here.
>
> Nora: Everything okay?

It takes a moment for her to reply.

> Aggie: Briggs. I think I have feelings for him.

I read over her message multiple times. After the seventh pass, it finally sinks in. My best friend has feelings for the man, the Accursed, I left in her care. That would explain why she left in such a hurry when Willow came up to us in the foyer. Images of how he looked at Willow in that abandoned warehouse flash through my mind. The way he almost died, forcing her to go after another man - one he knew she loves. *Loved.*

> Aggie: Tell me that I shouldn't. Tell me that I need to get over it.
>
> Nora: That'd make me a hypocrite.

My stomach tightens, churning inside me as I stare at the admission. It was a truth I wanted to keep a secret and bury deep in the ground.

Images from the night before flash in my mind, rekindling each and every moment.

I went to his room. He'd been in there alone. I sat next to him on the bed and told him how overwhelmed I was. I admitted how much facing my mother's abandonment has been bothering me. I fell asleep while he was telling me about, well... me. It was an odd bonding moment swept under the rug by an onslaught of sleep.

And then there was the dream. The one where all the people I care about were tied to stakes, even Kane. *Choose.* Remembering the way that voice sounded makes me recoil and shudder. It wanted me to choose. Everyone in my life: Hannah, Willow, Aggie, Meyer. Everyone. Or... Kane. The man who I fell terribly in love with. The man that captured me, body and soul. They wanted me to choose between them. I couldn't. I couldn't choose between the man I love and everyone else that I care about. I couldn't. And that was terrifying in itself.

A mixture of nausea and fear churns in my stomach as guilt tugs at my chest. I couldn't choose between the man that I love - loved - who is dead, and everyone else in my life, who are alive. It wasn't fair. They shouldn't have demanded me to pick. If I had to lose all of them to bring him back, I couldn't. I wouldn't be able to live with myself for ending all their lives. My little sister. My best friend. My trainer. But even being given the option to have Kane back, I would do anything. *Fuck.* Anything, but that. But the fact that I even hesitated scares me shitless.

A sobering cry wracks through my body, making my shoulders tremble.

I have to stop. I have to let him go. I *have* to. I can't keep hanging onto him. All that's doing is driving me insane, obscuring my judgement. I haven't had the time to properly mourn him. I don't know when I'll ever be able to. But I have to let him go. While his death is the reason behind my motivation. I need to refocus my goals and move forward.

If not, I might as well damn every person in my life right along with me.

Taking in a deep breath, I slide out of the covers. My phone begins ringing. I ignore it. The stone floor is cold on my bare feet, just like it was last night. With each step, I take in slow, calming breaths as I leave my room and head down the hall. My nerves crack and splinter more and more. The closer I get down the hallway, the more bile sours in the back of my throat.

I knock on the unmarked door. After a few moments, Lennox pulls open the door. His eyes widen and lips part when he sees me.

"Nora." The way my name rolls off his tongue solidifies every thought in my mind, despite the betrayal settling in my gut.

Stepping into his room, I shut the door behind me. He crosses his arms over his chest, stretching out his shirt.

Swallowing hard, I state, "I'm conflicted."

"Then why are you here?"

A breathy, sarcastic laugh bursts from my chest. "Because it's the only answer I can come up with." Running my hands through the waves of my red hair, I try and calm the turmoil blustering around in my chest. "I used to hate you. Just the sound of your name would sicken me. But you and everyone else here are only doing what you're told. Changelings collect souls for Heaven. Reapers chase those damned to Hell."

Lennox takes a step closer. His eyes are dark, face taunt. "Nora, you don't have to do this."

"Yes," I snap, "I do. You are everything I thought you were, Lennox." His mouth thins. "But you're also this contradiction. Even though I'm getting my ass handed to me most of the time, it's distracting being around you. You terrify me. And yet, you calm nerves, even when we're fighting."

Moving closer to him, my heart beats heavily in my chest. I fear he might hear how deafening it is to me. His arms uncross, dropping his defenses.

My chest swells and my voice shakes. "I don't know what this is - this feeling. All I know is that you have a way of putting all the chaos on hold. You make it easier. You make it okay."

"It doesn't have to be more than that."

"And what if I want it to be? What if I'm curious as to why I feel this way around you - about you?"

His eyes dip, locking in to where I bite my lower lip. When they flicker back to meet mine, they're darker. Primal. "You're nothing like what I've been taught. I shouldn't find myself intrigued by you - curious to know more."

"Show me." Lust laces itself in my words.

Stepping forward, I run both hands up his chest, entwining my fingers behind his neck. Leaning down, Lennox captures my mouth with his. This kiss is unlike the one just hours ago. Need oozes from my pores, mixing with the heat of his skin. His tongue runs along my bottom lip, coaxing my mouth to open. Dipping inside, he claims every inch as his own. It's territorial in every sense of the word.

His hand slips down my waist, cupping the back of my thighs and raising me up. Carrying me to the bed, he lowers me down, never breaking the kiss. Fingers toy at the hem of my shirt. Each brush of his skin against mine is electrifying. His lips move down, kissing my cheek, then my neck. Lennox is attentive. I'll give him that. He nips at the sensitive skin below my ear, making me gasp. Pulling off my shirt, he lifts it over my head and tosses it aside.

"Nora," he groans, voice strained as he puts space between us, eyes graze over my bare chest. My nipples tighten under his gaze, making it unbearable.

I pull his mouth down on mine. Need. Traveling lower, his lips graze over the ridges of my collar bones. Lower. He cups a breast, kneading the flesh. His tongue peaks out, circling the harden bud. My head thrusts back into the pillow as he takes the nipple in his mouth. Sucking. Teasing. Heat pools between my legs. A moan slithers out as he twirls the unattended bud between his fingers.

"I can't," I breathe. "I can't take it."

Unabashedly, my hand skates down. I'm already slick from his attention. Pulling back, his watches as I swirl my fingers around the tight bundle of nerves. Groaning, he sucks the nipple back in his mouth. Circling. Pulling. My hips buck; his mouth sends a sinful vibration straight to my core.

"Lennox!" I cry out as my orgasm hits. He continues with his devious ways as waves of pleasure roll through.

When they finally die out, I'm breathless. I'm worn, but my body sings for more.

Lennox moves vigilantly, placing kisses along my skin. He slips his fingers under the band of my pants, sliding them down, leaving me fully exposed. Traveling upwards, his kiss consumes me. His lips meld with mine.

"You," he whispers in between breaths, "are dangerous."

Tugging at the hem of his shirt, I pull it up over his head.

Stop talking, I mentally will to him. Capturing his mouth with my own, I push his pants down and his hard length springs free.

"Nor- ohhh."

I take hold of him, running my hand down his shaft, cutting him off.

Please, just shut up.

Straddling his hips, I stare down at him. There's no denying just how attractive the man lying underneath me his. The size of his hardened girth nestled between my ass cheeks doesn't hurt either.

Lifting up, I slowly ease myself down to the hilt. I dig my nails into his chest, taken aback by how full I feel. His own fingertips clench either side my hips, holding me still.

Lennox looks up at me with shaded eyes. When I go to move my hips, his head buries into the pillow. Snaking my hands into his, I start with a slow tempo. Heat. Tension builds, hitting just the right spots.

Opening his eyes, a deep, predatory gaze stares back at me. His bottom lip is captured between his teeth, pulling. I move a little faster. Friction builds. Clamping my eyes shut, I roll my hips. The tempo increases and I can feel the pressure of another orgasm building. His hand leaves my hip and travels slightly lower. His thumb runs along that bundle of nerves.

A gasping moan punctures through the surface the moment it hits. Pleasure cascades through me. My body falters. But Lennox? He doesn't. He uses me - uses my body - and allows me to ride out the wave. Just as I start coming down from my sexual high, Lennox stills. I can feel the way he pulses inside of me, releasing.

His muscles relax little by little. The tip of his tongue sticks out, wetting his lips. The very same tongue that helped me come the first time. Taking a deep breath, he opens his eyes and looks at me. The predator is gone. Lax. Ease. Reaching his hand out, I nuzzle against it as he cups my cheek.

"Amazing," he whispers, voice thick with lust.

Heat that radiated at the center of my core now tinges my cheeks. Lifting up, I roll to lay beside him.

"Was it good for you?"

The way he asks breaks my chest wide open. But I cover it with a smile.

You shouldn't have to ask. "Yes." *There shouldn't be any second guessing.* "It was really good, Lennox."

He places a chaste kiss on my lips, then pulls the blankets over us. They're thicker than my own. Rolling to the side, I let him spoon close behind me. His now limp member nestles up against the swell of my ass.

I bite down on my lip, doing my best to keep my emotions locked away. But memories flourish back in my mind. The insatiable kisses. Hands seeking to touch me - all of me. The undeniable sense of satisfaction. I swallow hard to hide the choking cry that threatens to escape. This should feel right. It *should*. But that doesn't stop the tears as they slide from the corners of my eyes, collecting in the fabric of the covers.

Lennox's breathing levels as sleep finds him. It doesn't come for me though. The gaping hole in my chest won't close and all the guilt ridden thoughts haunt my mind. And as his thumb brushes against the underside of my breast, I can't help but wish it wasn't him.

23

I duck to avoid the fist aiming straight for my face. Taking advantage of the open field, I set my target. My gloved knuckles collide with her side. Her compact, yet impenetrable, frame recoils. I swing my leg and knock her to the ground. Taking advantage of her shocked state, I scramble and plant my knees on either side of her. One hit. Two hit. Three hit. Blood.

Satisfaction shouldn't be what I'm feeling. I'm trained to save lives - to keep the blood inside, not make it come out. And yet, seeing the way her skin cracks open from each blow I deliver, excitement overwhelms my senses.

"The fuck?" Celeste cries out between hits.

Out of the corner of my eye, I can see Lennox place two fingers in his mouth and whistle. They're the same two fingers that had been elsewhere just hours earlier, getting a different kind of wet. He must've been thinking the same thing, because his lower lip skates in between his teeth. It's a tell of his. A sexy tell at that.

Climbing off of the battered blonde, I jump and shake my climbs. Adrenaline courses through my veins like a drug. The more her and I spar, the more I learn how she fights. Celeste tends to leave her right side open. Her legs may be strong, but they also have weak spots. They can't handle being hit low with a lot of force. The more I learn, the easier it is to take her down.

Much like Reapers, Changelings have the ability to heal at a rapid rate. Fucking bastards. While my split lip is still healing, along with the crack I took to my head, her face will look like she scratched herself in her sleep in an hour's time.

"Let's call it," Lennox says.

With a nod of his head, he gestures for me to come closer. Plopping down on the edge of the ring, he takes a hand in his. Long fingers stretch across mine and peel at the Velcro. Blood had soaked into the fabric, standing stark against my skin.

He examines my reddened knuckles, running a thumb over the irritated skin. "You okay?"

"Oh, angel's above," Celeste groans from somewhere behind me. The sound of her pulling off her own gloves is much more forceful than mine. "You two make me sick."

"Celeste." Lennox's tone drops. Warning.

"No," she bites back. "You two are fucking disgusting. She's a Banshee, Len. Not one of us. It's against code."

His hands tense over mine. "There's no code. Not about this."

She snips out a sardonic chuckle. "Yeah. Just a code of standards."

Standing up, I march back over to her. One hand still gloved and the other bare. "What the fuck is your problem?"

"You." Head held high, she steps forward.

"Yeah, I got that."

"You come in here, acting like you are owed a favor. You're not. The Cathedral is a safe house away from creatures like you - scum of Hell that found its way up to the surface."

For someone so elegant, so graceful, Celeste's insides are nothing but rotten to the core. A decayed personality oozes through her porcelain pores.

I pull in a deep, calming breath as the base of my neck lights up with electrifying tingles. The last thing I need is for the Banshee to lash out and make another imprint of her body in the wall.

"Celeste, you are the last person that I care about in this world," I admit with a steady tone. "If it came down to it, I'd choose saving Cranston over you and that guys *hates* me. I'm not here to win your favor. If you dislike me as much as you say you do, then leave. Walk out. Don't help me. I couldn't give two shits. But I'm done with your bitchy remarks. This isn't about us. This is about life and death. Heaven and Hell. But for some insane reason, you can't see that we're on the same side."

Her nostrils flare like a dragon whose flames are ready to spark. She holds my gaze for a few seconds longer before turning away and climbing down from the ring. The door doesn't echo when she slams it. Just a loud bang. And then she's gone.

"Nora, I-"

I hold up a hand, not ready to deal with him. My emotions are beyond frazzled. Squeezing my eyes shut, I take in deep breaths. I clear my head and just breathe.

When I no longer fear sending someone through a window, I turn to Lennox. He rests his arms over his head, leaning against the rope.

"You don't need to apologize for her."

"I wasn't going to," he says, eyes narrowed. "What I was going to say was that you need to forgive her."

"Ha!"

His face pulls taunt. "When are you going to get it through your head that things are different here? I don't know what all you learned when you were with *them*, but Reapers and Changelings are two different species. Cats and dogs."

I pull off the second glove and toss it in his direction. "Not everything is black and white."

"No?"

"No. There are countless combinations of people in the world. Race. Gender. Sexuality. Skin color. Someone already tried the whole *let's pick a dominant race* thing. And guess what? It didn't work out too well for him, did it?"

"Nope, but guess where he landed? Mortals go one of two places: Heaven or Hell."

This time, an actual laugh comes out. It's coated with disbelief, but it's there. "That's the biggest crock of shit I've ever heard. Look at you. Look at those Reapers. And what about Willow? And Briggs? That's a bunch of fucked up grey area."

"That not how we're-"

"I get it!" I holler as irritation begins clawing its way back up my spine. "The Deacons are just mini Hitler's running around and teaching baby Changelings there's good and bad. Nothing else. No in-between."

"Nora." That daring tone creeps back into his voice.

Taking in a final deep breath, I surrender. This entire conversation is getting out of hand. In this day and age, I thought people had a pretty good grasp on diversity and acceptance. Oh, no! When you walk through the doors of the Cathedral, that all goes out the window.

Shaking my head, I climb down. Lennox hands me a clean towel and I wipe the sweat off my face. Strands of hair too short to be pulled up stick to my skin. They're plastered like a gross mosaic.

"You did good today," he says, blatantly trying to reroute the conversation.

"Thanks."

Morning training with Marcie hasn't been going well. Ever since my little outburst, me and her haven't been seeing eye to eye. I mean… not that we did before. But it's like she's curled into a hermit shell, hiding away from the other ginger in the room, one more menacing than her. She's timid. There's an obvious strain of hesitation when she talks, as if she's trying to plan exactly what she's going to say. I should probably feel guilty. Hell, part of me wants to be. But as curious as I am about the harbinger history that runs through my veins, I can't apologize. I can't make small talk. I know it's messed up, but I keep getting this thought in my head that if I give her even an inch, she'll take a mile. That she'll twist what she did to make herself the victim.

Just as Lennox as I turn out of the training room, a little form bounds down the hall. The closer it gets, I'm able to make out that toothy smile.

"Nora!"

"What's up, bud?" I ask, crouching down to his level. Lennox eyes the two of us, but I pay him no mind.

Meyer takes in a deep breath, preparing himself, and then says, "There's more than one way to wish."

"Oh?"

He fervently nods his head up and down. "There's stars

and pennies. And they do the candle thing on birthdays. At least, that's what I've read in books."

It's moments like this that not only amaze me, but sadden me. Meyer is barely older than Hannah. While she is wicked smart, he surpasses her with such a magnitude. And yet, her imagination and creativity is her stronghold. I can see her going anywhere and doing whatever it is she sets her mind to. But Meyer... I worry. Will he make it out of this sitting? Will he survive in the world afterwards?

Glancing up at Lennox's figure shadowing over us, I give both boys a smile. "You're exactly right, Meyer."

"But!" His ecstatic outburst squeaks a giggle out of me. "But what about dandelions? You know, the ones that turned white?"

"That's a good one. Did you think about eyelashes?" Those bright eyes widen and he shakes his head. "I guess I'll have to show you that one too."

Those tiny hands clasp together. "We have so many wishes to make!"

A stern voice cuts me off before I have a chance to speak. "Meyer, that will have to wait for another day," the Deacon states, all but glaring at the little boy.

My heart aches as his face falls. A fraction of a second ago, his face was lit and full of happiness. Now, a quieted, sullen boy stands in his place as he nods his head in dismissal.

Reaching out, I take his hand in mine. "Give me a few days and I'll come find you. I think are a few other wishes you may have missed."

The hesitation to smile coats his face, but I don't miss the way his eyes light up. Then, after giving my trainer a weary look, he turns and walks away.

I wait until Meyer is long out of earshot before I stand back up and smack the stone hard muscle of Lennox's chest. And the bastard has the nerve to look confused. Shock.

"Why do you have to be such a jerk?"

The corner of his mouth quivers. "I wasn't being- I wasn't being a jerk."

"He's a little boy," I snarl, pointing down the hall Meyer had long since turned down. "Let him dream and fun. That's what kids are supposed to do."

"Mortal kids. Humans. He's a Changeling."

"A child, nevertheless," I seethe. "Just like you might be a Changeling, but you're still an ass."

I turn on my heel, not bothering to stay and hear what he has to say. Yet another day ending with yet another argument.

I don't stop. I don't make a detour. I venture straight to my room and shut the door behind me. Clothes go flying next as I head into the shower. I don't test the water. I simply flip the lever and climb inside. Scalding hot water meets my skin. I can almost feel my pores opening up, freeing themselves from the sweat that's built up. I scrub, needing to feel clean. Ever since that first night with Lennox, my instant reaction is to get into the shower once I'm back in the room.

Am I shamelessly using him to cover up just how fucked up I am?

Yes.

Does the guilt wear me down, threatening to drown me?

Yes.

Is it making my situation better?

No.

Am I going to keep doing it so I don't have to deal with my own emotions?

Yes.

A million times yes.

I need to leave the cavernous hole I dug myself. Grief. Longing. Everything that I should be dealing with right now. But they're the same things stopping me from doing what I need to. Their weight hinders me to move forward. One day, I'll be able to take the time a mourn the heart I once had. One day, I'll be able to truly accept his death. But until then, distractions are a must.

Scrubbing harder at my chest, I mentally wash away the pain wanting to escape; its hands reaching out to pull me back in.

24

The sound of high pitched alarms wake me from a dead sleep. I grab my phone and let out a groan when I see the time.

"What is it?" I mumble, feeling the bed shift.

Lennox moves swiftly, climbing out of bed and turning on the light. The brightness momentarily blinds me. By the time my eyes adjust, Lennox has already changed into his usual combat gear. Sitting up, I hug the sheets tightly to me as he ties up boots and then slides a glowing stone blade in a sheath at his thigh.

"Lennox!" I holler.

He finally looks up, but shakes his head and points to his ears. The wailing of the sirens is too loud. Even when he speaks, I can't hear. But those lips are easy enough to read. "Trouble."

Climbing out of bed, I grab for the sweats and t-shirt I discarded on the floor hours ago. I get dressed and he's pulling me out the door before I even have a chance to find shoes.

Barefoot it is.

Holding on tightly to my wrist, he keeps me close behind. Nearly every door in the dorm hallways is open and Changelings file out. They part as soon as they see Lennox - red sea and all. Lennox is a force to be reckoned with any day of the week. But when he's in the zone, it's safer to just move out of the way.

My heart pounds in my chest as we race through halls and down staircases. The sirens are inescapable. They follow no matter how far we go but their piercing sound only eggs us on. I do my best to keep up with Lennox; his fast paced walk mirrors my jog.

When we reach the foyer, there are so many pale blondes huddled around. It's an overwhelming sight. Combat suits. Boots. A mob of angelic appearances.

"Move!" Lennox calls. His grip tightens on my arm as we push through them.

Tugging at him, he slows midstep. "What's going on?"

"An intrusion," he hollers out. He's barely audible, even in our close distance.

Blue eyes bounce around wildly as they stare into mine. I nod, handing the reins to him once more. Duty calls.

He pulls me through a door and down another set of stairs. By the time we come to a complete stop, I'm winded and I can hardly feel my toes from how cold the floor is. Changelings crowd around the room. Many of which I've never seen before. The handful that I do recognize, avoid eye contact - all except Celeste.

"What is *she* doing here?" She sneers, eyes locked at where I hold tight to Lennox's arm.

Down in this cavernous basement, the sirens are a mere echo. Her question was heard loud and clear. Lennox ignores it though, stepping past. He nudges his way closer to the center of the room.

An amazon of a woman looks down at me. She has long limbs and elegant features. Gorgeous. As shadows flicker, a jagged scar is revealed, running from temple to cheek. Her eyes darken as my gaze flickers to her only imperfection. But it only lasts for a brief moment.

A door is thrown open, grabbing everyone's attention. The thick wood bangs against the wall as Margot, Cranston, and another Deacon step out. A muffled cry sneaks through before the hinges swing shut once more.

"Hector."

The man standing closest to Cranston steps out. His stout frame is unlike any other Changeling I've seen. They're all length and grace, but he's bulk and brute. A pale imitation of Briggs.

"Inform the others that the threat has been obtained," Cranston orders him. "All are to return to their dorms. Compliance is imperative."

With muttered acceptance, Hector turns to leave and is quickly swallowed by the mass of angels.

Once the sound of the stairwell door shutting is heard, Margot clears her throat. "A demon was found on our grounds." Hushed whispers fill the room. "Luckily, we were able to capture and detain it. We have yet to find out who sent him or what business he had here."

"We can only assume the worst," the third Deacon states.

My hand instinctively curls into Lennox's. A gentle squeeze from him creates an odd sense of security.

"We are in the midst of an interrogation," Cranston explains, eyes darting around the room. "Until then, we advise you all to remain on high guard. For all we know, he's just a distraction for an even bigger scheme."

"You are all dismissed."

The tension in the room eases as the third Deacon sends the Changelings off. Not a single refuse is spoken. Despite being woken up in the middle of the night to gather in a grungy den, no one seems upset. No questions are asked. They all begin to file out like obedient soldiers, despite the anti-climactic events.

Lennox glances down at me and shakes his head. He must see the questions fluttering around in my mind. But I obey his silent request and I clamp my lips tight together, keeping them locked inside. At least until we're alone again.

"Nora," Margot calls out. "Please stay."

My mouth dries. A rush of anxious nerves wash over me. Lennox squeezes my hand again and those ghastly eyes meet mine. I nod ever so slightly and the two of us turn back.

Dark circles haunt Margot's face as she stares at where our hands are joined. "Just Nora."

My lips part, gaping for words - any words. Nothing comes. When word vomit would actually be welcomed, it fails me. Of course. Why wouldn't it?

"As you request." Lennox slips his hand out of mine and backs away slowly. I turn and watch as he makes his way to the stairwell. I wait for him to turn around. One glance. One small over the shoulder gaze. Nothing.

As the herd of footsteps fade, the echoing silence pulls at my chest. I'm alone. Three Deacons stare back at me, each with their own variance of a weary expression.

"Yes?" I ask. My tongue sticks to the roof of my mouth and I have to peel it away to speak.

"We have a feeling you can be of assistance to us,"

Cranston states. His beady eyes narrow as my hands fist at my sides.

Hesitation fills my bones. I want nothing more than to shake my head and run up the stairs. Well, walk. There's no way I could run with how numb my feet are. But I'd do anything to avoid what they want me to do. And yet, like a good little Banshee, I follow them through the door they once came. With the other Deacon and Margot leading the pack, I feel like I'm being led to my persecution. For all I know, there's a hangman's noose waiting at the bottom and Cranston is just tailing behind to keep me in line.

With each step we take, the colder the air grows. Further and further down we go. The Cathedral truly has no end. While it's walls may only run so long, the depth of its roots are never ending.

As the spiraling comes to an end, a low groan bounces along the walls.

"What is that?" I ask, glancing over my shoulder.

I'm not given a response though. Silence. More and more silence. After rounding the stone corridor, the silence becomes deafening. Blood rushes through my veins like a heavy current as it drains from my body.

A man is strapped to one of the stone walls; his arms and legs locked in shackles. Blood pools around his bare feet, growing larger as blood drips from open wounds throughout his body. Countless of deep cuts mar the flesh, oozing with each breath he takes.

My knees threaten to give in as I take a step closer. "What are you doing to him?" I ask. My voice catches in my throat, making the words come out shaky and raw. Silence, yet again. Spinning around, I meet the Deacons' gaze. "I asked you a question."

Cranston's shoulders pull back as his face grows taunt. It's the third that speaks though. "We are doing what needs to be done."

"Ebony," Margot bites out, giving her counterpart a slashing glare. Turning to me, she gives a weak smile. "Nora, we thought you'd be able to assist us in this matter. This... demon," she sneers, "was caught on our grounds. We haven't been able to get anything out of him."

"Because there's nothing for him to tell you."

Her kind mask slips, eyes hardening as she pins me with her stare. "Demons and Reapers alike have been scouring to discover your location. Housing you is putting every single person here at risk. But as a humane gesture, we extended you protection under this roof. It is time that you return that favor."

The shaking in my hands travels up to my neck and head. I can't even form words. My tongue lays limp in my dry mouth.

With just the raising of her brow, a Changeling steps out. Vincent. He places some sort of device on the chained prisoner's ribs. Just like Dr. Frankenstein, an electric shock fills the poor man's body and a bloody cry fills the room.

"Stop it!" I bellow. The weight of my heart lurching in my chest practically pulls me to the ground.

Margot clears her throat and the electrocution stops.

My feet are moving before I even realize. His skin is clammy and cold as I pat at his cheeks.

"Wake up, Xi," I urge, brushing away thick strands of dark hair that fall along his forehead. Xi is a beautiful man. Seeing him like this, its... wrong. "Please, wake up."

His eyelids flutter, meeting mine for just a moment - a solitary second. That's all.

Whipping my head in the twisted trios direction, I taste the bile that forms in the back of my throat. "This is torture."

"*This* is interrogation," Cranston rebuts, stepping ahead of the group. "He was trespassing. We need answers and he needs punishment."

"The punishment isn't yours to give. Was he hurting anyone? Did he signal an attack?" I question, anger weaving in with the hair raising tingles. No one answers. Shocker. "He means no harm. He did nothing wrong. And none of you are God. You have no right to do this."

Vincent is fast, but I am much faster. As he lunges, I expel a mass of waves in his direction, sending his body flying. Ebony, the once unnamed Deacon, squeals, covering her mouth with both hands. Cranston stares with wide eyes. And Margot? She simply looks at me, narrowing her gaze.

Nails breaks through the skin of my palms as I try and rein in any control. Baring my teeth, I demand, "Cut him down."

"You are not in the position to give orders, Nora."

"Then who is, *Margot*?"

The woman I once thought to be level headed is losing the respect I had for her. Quickly. As if reading my mind, a defiant smirk pulls at her lips. Bitch.

Taking in a deep breath, I turn to Cranston. "Bring in Meyer. The Council can decide."

"The Coun-"

"Summon the fucking Council or I will bring this place to the ground, burying you all with it," I snap. Three sets of eyes judge my threat. Turning back to my friend, I run a hand through his sweat soaked hair. "Are you testing me? Last I knew, I don't really have much to live for. Can you all say the same?"

As I wipe at a smear of blood across his cheek, a wave of

ease washes over me as the sound of running feet echoes throughout the room. He opens his eyes. Tilting his head up, I give him a tearful smile.

Nodding, I whisper, "You'll be okay. I'll make sure of it."

It's not long until two sets of feet climb down the stairwell, one quieter than the other. Meyer follows Ebony. He rubs at his eyes, causing the skin around them to redden. I feel bad that she had to wake him up. But this is an urgent matter. When he sees me, he lights up, even in his blue and white striped pajamas.

"Nora." He says my name with a mixture of confusion and glee. Those blue eyes of his dart from me to Xi. I would never allow Hannah to witness something as atrocious as this. It'd scar her and fill her nightmares with more than bees and spiders. And yet, it doesn't seem to faze him. How much has this boy seen? Blood shed? Death?

"Sorry to wake you, Meyer," I say, forcing a smile. "I need your help though. Can you do that?"

"He does not-"

Behind him, Margot stops speaking midsentence, jaw hanging open as I send a forceful glare in her direction. I've never seen her hesitate. Not until today. I enjoy every second of it.

Focusing back on Meyer, I crouch down like I always do and hold out my hand.

"What can I do for you?" he asks, slipping a small hand in mine.

"This is my friend Xi," I say. "There has been a terrible misunderstanding. He's being wrongly accused and I need your help. Well... the Council's help."

He looks up at Xi, curious eyes narrowing. "But he's not one of us."

"No. You're right. But that doesn't make him any less of a friend."

"What did he do?"

"Micah." Xi's strained voice cracks from behind me.

Standing up, I wipe at the blood coated saliva that slides down the corner of his mouth. Tears burn as they form in my eyes.

I gesture for Meyer to come closer. "You were with Micah?" I ask. Xi nods, grimacing from the minute movement. "Micah and Xi are friends," I tell Meyer. "More than friends, actually. And every few days, they find a way to see each other."

A deep line creases between the little boy's brow. "A demon and Changeling?"

Nodding, I can't help the way the corner of my lips curl downwards. I can't blame him. Once upon a time, it was unheard of for blacks and whites to love. But in this fucked up place, demons and Changelings are be the equivalent.

"That doesn't make him any less of a friend," I remind him. "But that's not the point. Xi, who just so happens to be a demon *and* one of my good friends, came to see Micah. That's all. But they-"

"Fraternizing with creatures from Hell is not right," Margot seethes, "and it's forbidden on these grounds."

Biting down, I try to ignore her comment. "They weren't doing anything wrong. Xi had no ulterior motive. He didn't harm anyone, nor was he planning on sneaking into the Cathedral. And yet, he's being punished - *tortured.*"

Meyer takes a curious step forward and looks up, tilting his head. A scene I never thought I'd witness - something that only happens in nightmares - unfolds in front of me. The innocent child stares up at the corrupting demon. Contradictions whirl around in time.

"Do you make wishes?" Meyer's voice is quiet. If I wasn't standing right next to him, I wouldn't have been able to hear him.

A pained smile quivers on Xi's face. "Yes."

Forever seems to pass as the two look at one another. Meyer's expression grows slightly distant, talking to the Archangels. Micah once had the gift. No longer. I wonder what stories he's told his lover - if he recognizes the look on this young boys face.

"He can go."

"What?!" Cranston spits from across the room.

He stalks over. Meyer turns to face him and I anticipate him to cower behind me. He doesn't. He looks up at the pissed off old man with a serious, yet unperturbed expression.

Grabbing hold of the boy's shoulders, he shakes him. "You're lying. You've twisted their judgement."

A shooting sensation travels up my spine as lunge forward, ripping Meyer out of Cranston's hands. Pushing him behind me, electricity crackles in the air. Not from that damn device of Vincent's, but from me.

"You will not touch him," I growl. Panic flashes across the man's face. "You got your answer. You will not lay another finger on him. Now free him from those chains."

25

The walk back to Lennox's dorm is long. Walking anywhere is this damn place takes forever. Going to the bathroom feels like a mile long trek. Maybe I'm just tired. Overdramatic thought tend to happen when I haven't had enough sleep. Or, apparently, when I get woken up in the middle of the night. The obnoxiously loud alarm didn't help, nor did walking down and finding my friend chained and abused. What kind of people do that? And in a Cathedral of all places. With children. The longer I stay here, the more things I find fucked up with it.

Longer.

More.

I let out a groan and rub my eyes. Everything is just too much. This is not how I thought I would live my life. Fleeting thoughts would cross my mind about saving up money and possibly moving out. Aggie's asked me several times about that. Begged is more like it. I kept turning the offer down, time and time again. I couldn't leave Hannah. I wouldn't be any better than my mother that abandoned me. But two more years and I'll be twenty-five. I'll be a quarter of a century and years of time ahead of me. At least months ago, I knew what each day held. Now? I don't even know if I'll wake up tomorrow. People that I've come to know and trust can be tortured and killed. Something's got to give.

I don't knock on Lennox's door; I walk right in. He's wide awake, laying on his bed and reading a book as if nothing was out of the norm.

"You good?" he asks, eyeing me from head to toe as I shut the door behind me.

An inhale - a single inhale - and I'm falling. Emotions, that I didn't even realize I've been suppressing, dig their way up to the surface. My lips tremble as I fight back tears.

Lennox is off his feet in an instant. "What's wrong?"

I can't speak. I simply shake my head. He wraps his arms around me, pulling me close. I bury my face in his chest as a painful sob breaks through. Even as he holds me, my body shakes. Tremors wrack through me as I cry and a dam of tears spill over.

"I can't take this," I gasp between breaths.

Pulling back, Lennox looks at me. He runs his thumbs over my cheeks, wiping away the tears, even as more fall. "What do you mean?"

"They had Xi."

Lines etch themselves in his forehead, blanketing his face in confusion. "From the Playground?"

I nod. Images of the cracked foundation invade my mind.

"They had him. He was chained and they were torturing him. He did nothing wrong."

"He was invad-"

"No, he wasn't!" I push against his chest, forcing space between us. "He was meeting with Micah. That's it."

He runs a hand down his face. "I told him it was going to get him in trouble sooner or later."

"You knew?" I don't even wait for him to answer. I bite out a bitter laugh. "*Of course* you knew. How could you let them do that?"

"They won't hurt Micah."

"They almost killed Xi!"

"Better one of them than one of us."

I whip my head in his direction. A bitter taste overtakes my mouth. "How can you say that?"

"How can you be shocked that I did?" Distaste laces its way in his voice. "Out there, it's us or them. There's no gray area. We're light; they're dark. He may seem like a nice guy, but he's still a demon."

"He's my friend, Lennox," I say. "He befriended me and showed me kindness when I was thrown into this twisted world."

In the early days of me performing at the Devil's Playground, Xi had gone above and beyond. He not only remodeled his whole bar to accompany the singing act Kane pieced together, but he made sure I had everything I could ever need. Granted, they were mostly materialistic things, but he was still a friend. He listened. Hell, if it wasn't for him, I would've never known about the secret entrance. That was the most terrible night - one I will never be able to outlive. But because of it, I unleashed my own demon. The Banshee and I became one. Without his friendship, I would be dead.

Lennox takes a step forward, reaching for me. I simply brush him away and go for my phone that's still sitting on the nightstand.

"Nora," he says my name so sweetly, "don't turn me into the bad guy. This is just how we live. It's all black and white."

"How can you say that? We were just in bed together a little over an hour ago."

He draws in a deep breath. "That's not the-"

"Don't you dare tell me it's not the same. I'm not a Changeling. I'm not a Deacon." Stepping forward, I pointedly poke him in the chest with each word. "I am a creature of Hell. The blood that runs in my mother's veins - in my veins - is tainted. It's not pure like yours. But it's okay for us?"

Those blue eyes stay locked into mine as thoughts mill around his mind. I can practically see the way he's processing them, piecing apart what he should say from what he shouldn't.

When he finally releases his jaw from its clenched hold, he says, "Whatever I say is just going to piss you off. It could be exactly what you want to hear, but it won't matter."

"You're right," I admit, slightly taken aback by my own admission.

"Then just go."

Reaching out, Lennox holds open the door. The stubborn side of me wants to march out, head held high and shoulders pulled back, to take the dismissal for what it is. And yet, as I stare at the way his hand holds onto the doorknob, my chest pulls. An uneven weight attempts to balance on my heart.

Forcing in a deep breath of air, I leave. I don't turn back around, but the way the door immediately shuts behind me, it echoes through my chest. More tears prick my eyes and I force out a gasp.

This shouldn't be bothering me. Lennox is a distraction. That's it. While I used to tell myself that Kane was going to be a distraction, he was much more than that. But Lennox is just that. Nothing more.

So then why does it feel like bits and pieces are crumbling off what's left of my heart?

Like usual, Willow isn't in the room. Earlier today, I feared that she may have up and left me in this twisted haven. I rummaged through her things. Clothes were left in the drawers tucked under the lofted bed frame. Eyeliner and mascara littered the bathroom sink. But, like usual, she was nowhere to be found.

I make quick work of showering, scrubbing away at Xi's blood that had dried on my hands. I can't believe they had him tied up. How many people know about the underground torture chamber? I have to assume that those crowded in the small room know. Deacons. Of course Meyer knows. He didn't flinch or cower at the sight of the captured demon. That only means that Micah knows.

Micah. He must be a wreck.

I don't bother drying my hair. The wet curls hang limp as I throw clothes on. Before I head out, I make sure to put socks and shoes on. I learned my lesson. My toes are still numb, even after they soaked in the hot water.

Kane told me before how Changelings are made. They're essentially souls of born infants or children that couldn't support their hosts. These *back to life* miracles that they make hundreds of Lifetime movies about are just the work of Archangels. They take souls of fetuses that aren't strong enough to survive birth and exchange them for the other souls, which get warped into Changelings. The pale, almost white haired renegades are nothing more than sculpted souls of dead children. It's as fucked up as it sounds.

Knowing this, why am I this distraught? Deacons aid the Changelings and Archangels. They are probably several other torture chambers in this place.

"- we can do."

The sound of hushed talking makes me stop in my tracks. I flatten myself against the wall and inch closer to the door that stands slightly ajar.

"She's corrupted him."

I know that voice. Margot. I once thought she was kind and on my side, despite the stares and harsh judgements. Tonight proved that I was very wrong in believing that. I'm just another pawn to her.

A man clears his throat. "I'm aware. I was in the room. But drastic measures don't need to be taken - not again."

Margot scoffs at the man, who I can only presume is Cranston. "It's the only way this will work. This progress we've made-"

"Will continue," he cuts her off.

I know I shouldn't eavesdrop. Nothing good comes from it. But I can't help myself. I all but melt into the wall and continue to listen.

"Not if he's off spewing all types of faulty commands. They won't listen to us."

Are they talking about Lennox?

Chair legs drag along the ground. "One instance it's going to change all the work we've done. We've come too far."

"Exactly!" Her voice is strained and exasperated. "The second they catch word, things will surely backfire. We have to take care of it. Now."

A pregnant pause keeps the tension strung tight. But

finally, Cranston sighs and says, "It can't be done the same way. It's too suspicious."

"People fall all the time."

"No."

Footsteps pace. "We can see about mixing something into his serums. Hardly anyone knows about them, let alone if they have any side effects. This time around could just be a lethal batch."

My hand flies to face, clamping over my mouth. Micah. They *must* be talking about him. But why wait all this time? They could have gotten rid of him years ago.

"You want to poison the boy?" Cranston questions.

A knot tightens in my stomach, weighing down at my heart. No. They're not talking about Micah.

Margot confirms my assumption. She quiets her voice as she says, "He's gentle. It's only right to give Meyer the same kind of death."

Wrapping an arm around my stomach, I try and keep my body from reacting. Not now.

None of this is right. From the torturous interrogation of Xi, this night has been filled with nothing but treacherous revelations. The last Child didn't kill himself. He was murdered - pushed to his untimely death. And they plan on doing the same thing with Meyer.

Guilt laces itself in the pit of my stomach. If I had listened to Micah and Lennox, none of this would be happening. None of it. They told me to stay away. I should have kept my nose out of it. But I didn't. I kept pushing lines that had been drawn years ago.

I don't wait to hear what else they have to say. There's not enough time. I need to get Meyer and Xi as far away from here as possible.

And there's only one person I could possibly trust to help me with this.

26

By the time I push my way through the thick wooden doors, I'm out of breath. All the training in the world wouldn't have been able to prepare me for this. Every minute that passes, the less time I have. And I will not fail. There will not be any more blood on my hands.

My shoes pad against the stairs as I rush up. I can feel the way my pulse drums. My hands instinctively keep clenching and unclenching - nerves taking over.

"Micah!" I holler out, wincing at how harsh my voice sounds. Nails on a chalkboard. Rough and raw. "Micah!"

The lights are dim, making the stacks look overpowering. Their shadows drape down, tempting to lure one in their pages and drown in the ink.

I head to the back of the library, moving as quickly as possible. A light cascades from the small room tucked in the far corner. I don't knock as I near. Part of me wishes I did.

Curled up in a ball is Micah. The bed is no longer there. A mattress is tossed floor in the corner, in which he's huddled on. The secret door that he had shared with me is open. A dark abyss fills the space.

I rush over and wrap my arms around him. "Micah," I whisper, "please tell me they didn't harm you."

"They should have just killed me too."

I feel for him. The way he says those words causes tears to prick my eyes, threatening to fall.

"Don't say that."

I reach over and try to wipe away the wetness that coats his cheeks. The framed glasses that he wears are on the floor, just a handful of feet away. The one lens is crack, splintering in countless directions.

Brushing back his mop of hair, I tell him, "I need your help. I know that sound-"

"Get. Out." The gravelly way he interrupts me is startling.

"I'm not leaving you."

Sitting up, he doesn't look at me. He stares blankly at the gaping hole in the floor. "I told you to get out." I open my mouth to speak, but he holds up a hand. "None of this would've happened if it wasn't for you. You've done nothing but cause issues since you stepped through that gate. You curse everyone in your life."

Blanching, I rebut, "That's not fair. I didn't tell anyone about the two of you."

"You didn't have to. Everything you touch, you kill."

I choke down the instant retort. Arguing isn't going to help. "Micah, I would never put you or Xi in harm's way."

"And yet he's dead because of you."

"Micah," I say slowly, trying to catch his gaze, "Xi isn't

dead." His jaw clenches down. "He's here. He's in some underground torture room, but he's not dead. He's alive."

Slowly, ever so slowly, he turns his head. Empty ocean eyes look at me as they well up with tears. His lower lips trembles. "He's alive?"

I nod.

He takes in a sharp breath as emotion takes over him. An uncontrollably sob comes out of him as he cries, wrapping his arms around me. The sudden change in behavior throws me through a rift, but I push it aside and hold onto my friend. His body shakes in my arms for what seems like hours.

"Micah," I say his name once the tremors calm. "Micah, Xi's alive, but he's still in trouble. So is Meyer." His brow furrows and lips separate, narrowing in on what I said. "I overheard Margot and Cranston talking. Meyer is in trouble. We need to get him and Xi out of here."

"You know?"

"That they killed the other Child? Yes. The why part of the scenario is what I'm blanking on."

He uses the ends of his sleeves to wipe his tear coated face. I try and hold in the gag reflex when he blows his nose with the same sleeve.

Once he straightens up, he looks at me. "I told you to leave it be."

"I know."

"No, Nora. You don't know. You don't know the half of it."

"Then tell me. Quickly," I urge.

Micah runs a hand through his lackluster hair. "It started with me. The Deacons. They want a bigger slice of the pie. They don't want to just be these lowly workers. They want a say in what happens. They want to control the Changelings."

"That doesn't mean that had to kill anyone."

A breathy chuckle slips past his lips. "No. That's not what they wanted kept from the world."

Moving to stand, Micah unfurls himself up off the floor. The button down shirt he wears is crumpled. Wrinkles have creased their way into the fabric.

"The Deacons want power. They want to be the ones to wield the leashes and not be collared like the rest of us. But that's where they run into an issue. The Changelings don't serve the Deacons. They don't serve the Cathedral. They serve the Archangels and all the higher beings."

What seems like ages ago, Micah once told me just how this holy hierarchy works. Archangels, lower class angels, are able to pass on judgments and orders through the Child. Micah, Meyer, and all the others before them, were trained to heed the words of the holy spirits and pass them on. Hence the creepy child sitting in a room by himself.

"Why not just say they want more authority?"

Micah rolls his eyes and shakes his head. "Because that would be all too easy, wouldn't it? Some Deacons, such as Margot and Cranston, want to have control more than anything. To do so, they would have to weed out the middleman. Or in the Child's case, twist them into relaying messages a certain wait."

"Basically censoring everything?"

He nods.

Standing up, I straighten my top. Dust and dirt found its way onto my pants as I sat on the floor. I dust those off too.

"Some didn't like the way they wanted to play their game. Those people are no longer around," he explains. Pulling out a pair of loafers and slips them on. "But that still left the issue of the Changelings and their duties. They had souls to collect. But with more and more Reapers gaining ground, it became a struggle. They were doing their job and not taking orders from the Deacons.

"The bastards found a way to put an end to that: no more Reapers. If they were taken out of the equations, all they'd have to do is collect the souls of those destined for Heaven."

"But Reapers are created by Belial and them."

He snaps his head in my direction. Those eyes shine brightly as a demented grin plays on his lips. "That's where you're wrong. Only Lucifer can create Reapers."

All the information he bombards me with sends my head spinning. "Kane told me that him and his bride are entombed. How does that work if he's locked away? Reapers are still being transformed."

"Not for several years. Hell doesn't want to come off as weak. They let everyone think that they still have some major power, but they don't."

"How do you know all of this?"

Micah grabs an extra pair of glasses from his dresser drawer and slides them up the bridge of his nose. When he turns to me, his brows are raised.

"You're forgetting that I was a Child once. I heard everything the Archangels had to say. The Deacons teamed up with witches, Changelings, and even Death themselves. After the entombed the Lord and Lady of the Underworld, they had free reign. It's limited, but they've been able to deal with it."

"Your successor found out about all this, didn't he?" He nods. "I bet you he threatened to share their secrets and they killed him."

"Bingo."

A wave of upset washes over me. "I can't believe this. And because Meyer has swayed from their grasp, he's now an enemy?"

"Yes."

"We have to get him out of here," I say, running both hands through my now damp hair. "I can't let anything happen to either of them."

"What's your plan?"

"She doesn't have one. Neither of you do." The voice startles the both of us. In the doorway, Lennox stands with both arms crossed over his chest. He glances between me and Micah. "I can't believe this," he mumbles.

Stepping in front of Micah, I pull my shoulders back. "You don't know what you're doing."

"I'm stopping the two of you from making a foolish mistake."

The patronizing tone that oozes from his words instantly pisses me off. "Just go, Lennox. I'm not going to sit by and let two people I care about die. Not again."

His eyes narrow. The side of his jaw ticks as he glances behind me. "You told her."

"You knew?" I snap.

Lennox doesn't answer me. His lips waver, but remain silently.

"She needed to know," Micah says from behind me. "And she can do what she will with that information."

"What *I* plan on doing is getting them out of here - away from this fucked up Holy Wonderland."

He shakes his head. "Not going to happen."

Clenching my fists together, I pull back on the tingling sensation rising up my spine. "Can you give us a moment,

Micah?"

Lennox keeps his gaze locked in on mine, neither one of us willing to back down. Micah slips out the door, being careful not to bump into his fellow Changeling.

"Margot and Cranston want to kill Meyer."

"I heard that."

My head bucks backward in shock. "You knew about that?" He nods. "When?"

He shrugs. "I had a feeling you'd come here. We need to talk."

I throw out my arm, gesturing to the other side of the wall. "Then why did you ask him if he told me or not? You knew he did."

"I wanted his admission."

Scoffing, I take a step back. "You're too much." I want nothing more than to punch him in the face and bruise that pretty porcelain skin of his – if only for a brief time. "You can't stop me. I refuse to lose anyone else that I care about. I won't let another death sour my conscience."

"You're being irrational."

"I don't fucking care what I'm being, Lennox!" I bark, rubbing my temples with my fingertips. "Xi is innocent. Meyer is innocent. There's no reason that their lives should end. What if it was Celeste? Or Vincent?"

A darkness shadows his eyes. His usually full lips thin. "That's a completely different scenario."

I let loose a sardonic laugh. Taking a daring step closer, I tilt my head up to look him in the eye. "What if it was me? What would you do if they wanted to kill me? Would you let them?"

He exhales a shaky breath. Time passes as we enter an impasse. Finally, after what seems like ages, he reached out. He brushes my cheek with his thumb, eyes softening.

"Nothing I say or do will change your mind." It's a statement, but a question. He already knows the answer.

Leaning down, he brushes his lips along mine. A soft, chaste kiss.

As he pulls away, I can see the torment and war that he's fighting against. And yet, after taking in a deep breath, he says, "There's no way to get you down to him - not without causing a scene. You get the boy. Meet me back here."

"Thank you." Relief floods through my veins.

He gives a slight shake of his head. "Don't thank me yet. This is far from over."

27

The Cathedral can be a very creepy place in general. But tiptoeing through the barren halls in the middle of the night tops the charts. All we need is a camera and some urban legend. Wes Craven and Rob Zombie would be proud.

After Lennox got his head out of his ass and realized that I wasn't going to back down, we devised a plan. There was no way I'd be able to sneak back down that forever spiraling staircase. It'd bring too much attention. That and I didn't exactly know where Xi was being kept. Lennox would know where to go once he was down there and could use his stature to get the demon out.

In the meantime, my number one goal is to get to Meyer and get him out. He needs to be as far away from this place as possible. I put him in danger. It's only right that I get him to safety.

I follow Micah through another set of hallways. No matter

how long I've been here, this place will never seem less of a labyrinth. At any moment, a Minotaur can round it's way around the corner.

Apparently, the Angel's Child is kept in a remote wing. They don't stay in the dorms. While the other young Changelings have roommates and are able to live a semi-normal life, Meyer is secluded. Whatever is was that made him be chosen for the position, also turned him into a social leper.

As we quietly stalk through the night, Micah turns and asks, "What's the plan after all this?"

"I don't know." And that's the honest truth.

Aside from getting Xi and Meyer out, I don't have much of a plan lined up after. I know without a doubt my welcome will be worn out. Hell, if they find out I was the one that did this, I wouldn't put it passed them to put a hit out for me. I'm sure Lennox would just get a slap on the wrist. As for Micah, I have no clue how they'd react to him helping me. They've kept him alive this long, what would it hurt to keep him around a little longer? Or why not kill him to avoid any other issues?

Willow has been MIA or else I would have gone to her. She may know of some safe house or an exit strategy. I could go to Aggie's. She would take me up in a heartbeat. She's nursed Briggs back to his normal self. It's taken a lot longer than I thought. At first, I was worried they wouldn't get along. Obviously, that's not the case. Their forced rooming situation has turns into more than a platonic living arrangement. At least on Aggie's part.

A huge negative about going to her house is that the Death has already sent demons and Reapers to check her out. For all we know, they have someone staked out front every hour of the day. I don't want to put her in more danger than she already is.

As much as I tried ignoring Micah's comment from earlier, I can't help but accept that I really have been hurting everyone I care about. In one way or another, I have either gotten them killed, tortured, or interrogated. It's as if I've put their names on a dead pool the moment I started caring. I should've know better.

Biting back the intrusive thoughts, I keep close to Micah. I try remember how many turns we've taken or what doors we've passed. It's useless though. I'm beyond lost. But as we reach the end of another hall, Micah slows. Grabbing hold of his upper arm, I cling to him as if he might get blown away. He peeks around the corner. It's a quick, subtle movement. And when he pulls back, he turns and makes his back flush with the wall.

"What is it?" I whisper.

I look for myself, crossing my fingers that no one sees a head of red hair peeking around the corner. Two Changelings stand on either side of the doorway. I never thought I'd see the day when a child would need a whole security detail to sleep. Then again, it could be from the alarms going off. Or that's just how paranoid the Deacons are.

Grabbing Micah's arm again, I slip back down the way we came. I don't want to risk them overhearing us.

He lets out a deep sigh. "I don't think we'll be able to get to him. It'll make too big of a scene."

"It's the middle of the night."

"Yeah," he rolls his eyes, "and that's Francis and Leo. They're huge - more muscle than brain. But there's no way we can walk up and they'll let us through. They're dumb, but not that dumb."

He's right. The Changelings are more like soldiers than anything else. They're given an order and they stick to it.

Closing my eyes, I run through a list of possible options.

Previous experiences has marked me off the ninja list. And I know damn well I can't hold my own against the two of them. A few hours from now, Meyer will be waking up. We could wait. But, then again, it may be too late at that point.

Sighing, I look at Micah. "I need you to find an empty room and stay in it." His brows knit together. "There's only one way to get him out of there. I don't want to hurt you in the process."

Realization takes a moment, but it finally dawns on him. His eyes widen. "Are you sure?"

"No. But I can't think of anything else. It's now or never."

"Okay." He nods. Wrapping his arms around me, he gives me a tight squeeze before walking further back down the hall.

I hoped that I would never have to do this. The death of the Reaper in the warehouse didn't bother me. It should have. I should have been distraught for weeks. But it didn't – I wasn't. Whether it was because he attacked me or if Kane's death just hit me harder, I will never know.

Pulling in a deep breath, I clench and unclench my fists. Now's not a time for nerves. It has to be done. It's them or Meyer. And I'll be damned if I let it be that little boy.

When I step out, both guards are taken by surprise. They share a look, as if making sure they weren't seeing things.

"Excuse me, boys," I say, creeping closer. "I need Meyer."

The one on the left clears his throat and pulls his shoulders back. "That won't happen. Council's orders."

No, it's the Minor Council that gave them that order. There's no way for them to know what the *real* Council said. Even then, I doubt Meyer would want to be locked away every night - he'd leave that little tidbit out.

"I could give a fuck less what they said. I'm taking him.

Now."

Before either of them could answer, I grabbed onto the cord tingling up my spine. There are no words. I can't find them. None would fit the situation. A hum begins deep in my chest, rising up and up. Their hazy auras fight against the Banshee's song.

"Silence," the one belts out.

I bite down and push harder. They go to move, but quickly falter after a couple of steps. In a normal circumstance, I'd begin to see flashes of their life. Things that they've done wrong; sins that they've committed. But not with Changelings. They may be servants to Heaven, but I know damn well they've done bad things. And yet, I can't see them. Not that I'm going to complain. The visions usually come with a mind splitting headache.

The louder I hum, the stronger the Banshee becomes and both guards drop to their knees. I push away every ounce of guilt and hesitation. If I give in, even for a slight second, all will be lost. I won't be able to regain control, let alone do what needs to be done.

A cry erupts from my throat as a wave of energy rushes past me. And with it, the Changelings, Francis and Leo, lay face down on the stone floor. Their bodies, now lifeless, are sprawled out just feet away. They tried to reach me, walked until they could only crawl.

As the wail fades, I'm left breathless. My lungs heave as if I just ran for miles. Tears prick my eyes, threatening to fall. I pull in steady breaths and look up. I can't look at them - at the bodies of the men that I killed. It will only make matters worse.

"Nora!"

I hear Micah call my name, but I can't turn around. Not

now. And yet, I feel the way his arms wrap around me from behind. The touch - the embrace - grounds me away from my thoughts. A sob wretched from my chest and tears falls.

He squeezes me tighter and he shushes me. "I know. I know you didn't want to do that. But we can get to him now. We can get Meyer and get out of here."

Nodding, I try and calm my nerves. My chest aches with the knowledge of what I just did. I wipe at my cheeks and open my eyes. I don't look down, but straight ahead.

The door opens with a gentle turn of the handle and the door hinges creak as it swings wide. Light cascades in the room, standing stark against the dark. Meyer's bed is in the middle of one of the walls. He lays on his stomach with his cheek pressed into the pillow. His lips are separated and his blonde hair is mess. He's the pinnacle of innocence.

Reaching out, I gentle shake his shoulder. "Meyer." He doesn't stir. I brush hair away from his forehead and call his name again.

This time, he wakes. Heavy eyes blink as his mind adjusts. When he sees me, he lifts his head. "What are you doing, Nora?"

"I'm going to take you on a trip." I give him the best smile I can manage.

"But it's still dark outside."

I glance up at Micah who gestures for me to hurry. "I know, Meyer, but it's the only time we can do this. We need to leave."

"Did the Deacons okay this?" Slowly, he becomes more alert. He looks over to where Micah stands in the doorway and then back to me. "Is something wrong?"

Swallowing hard, I reach out and take his hand. "Do you trust me?" He nods his head, no hesitation. "There are some people that aren't happy with what happened earlier."

"But that's what the Angels said."

"I know. And you know that," I tell him, squeezing his tiny fingers, "but there are others that don't believe either of us. And I need to get you out of here before they do something bad to you."

"You won't let that happen."

The way he says those words all but breaks my heart. It's not a question. There's no reluctance. I have a list a mile long of things that I've done wrong or people that I've hurt, but if this one boy can see my intentions, then I can be okay with that list.

"I will never let anyone hurt you," I say. "Do you understand?" Meyer nods his head and rubs his still sleepy eyes. "Then let's get you changed and get out of here."

After being woken up twice tonight, Meyer climbs out of bed. He slips his feet into slippers. As I help him into a coat, Micah goes about the room. He rummages through drawers and throws clothes into a bag.

Bending down, I tell the little boy, "We need to be quick as we can. Go ahead and climb on my back. I'll carry you. That way you can wake up a little more."

Hannah used to love when I gave her piggyback rides. She said it made her feel special. She can be so little and yet she so big. I don't know if Meyer shares the same whimsical view. But he climbs up and wraps his tiny arms around my neck. I tell him to close his eyes until I tell him to open them again. He doesn't need to see the two dead bodies at his door. He doesn't need to know that I was the one that killed them. There's a lot that he doesn't need to know. Not yet. Not ever, if I can help it.

We're to meet Lennox back at the library. The two of us all but run back through the halls, twisting and turning through the maze. Our shoes slap against the stone floor. While we kept quiet before, now we run. It's a race against time. The longer we take, the less likely we'll get out of this fucked up little church.

By the time we push open the library doors, bits of the sun begins showing. It's barely the beginning of the sunrise, but it's the signal that we need. We're running out of time.

"Where are they?" Micah questions. He paces back and forth in his small bedroom. He twists and pulls at his fingers, getting more anxious with each minute that passes.

I sit Meyer down and he curls up on the mattress. The two of us watch as the librarian keeps up his worried stride. There's no point of saying anything. We knew that there was a chance Lennox wouldn't be able to get to Xi, but he was the best bet that we had.

The irony of tonight isn't past me. I came to the Cathedral for help - for security. I needed protection from Death, but I only found more danger. A place that's supposedly revered as a safe haven and a sanctuary is far from it.

My pocket starts to vibrate. Pulling out my phone, Aggie's name flashes across the screen. She must be getting up and ready for work. Little does she know what my night's entailed. Turning my phone off, I slip it back in my pocket. I'll call her back later. All answering her would do is make her worry. I have too much of my own worrying to do.

The library doors closing sounds like a shotgun. All three of us jump, startled by the sound. Meyer scrambles over to my side and I wrap an arm around him.

Micah's face is equal part horrified and relieved as Lennox walks in. He has both arms supporting up Xi, whose almost beyond recognition. Blood and bruises. Cuts and scars. I've never seen this side of Xi. As shock as I'd been just hours ago,

I'm completely taken away now. The eccentric and lively demon is barely able to hobble along on his own. His hair, which is normally perfectly groomed, is a haphazard mess. And yet, when he looks up, his eyes shine bright at the sight of Micah.

The relief filled moment doesn't last long though. Lennox catches my gaze. He doesn't even need to say a word. The way his lips form a hard line and the scratches that are already healing tells me what I need to know. We're out of time.

I call to Micah, "Are you going to be able to take both of them with you?"

"I can walk on my own," Meyer says meekly, still tucked under my arm.

Glancing down at his slipper covered feet, I try not to grimace. His little toes will freeze. With the snow that's taken over the ground, it won't take long. Before he knows it, Meyer won't be able to feel his extremities. I didn't plan a rescue mission just so he can be plagued by hypothermia.

"My car." Xi is barely audible. He mumbles the words, which only pulls harder at my heart. "My car isn't far."

"Do you think you can walk a little ways?" I ask the little boy. He nods, putting on a brave face. "Then let's get you guys going then. It's now or never."

28

They had Micah's escape exit blocked off. An iron gate was locked and secured to the space. But with the help of my sonic waves and Lennox's running force, we were able to bust it open.

Yet another thing I never thought I'd be able to say. Like at any hicksville family reunion, I could spew, "Yeah. I done did bust that gate open with my voice."

I gave all three of them a tight hug and wished them well. I made them promise to keep me updated. It'd be the last time I'd see them until I was able to get away myself. I could've gone with them. Hell, I should've. But deep down, I kept debating. While Willow has been all but absent since we got here, I didn't want to leave without talking to her first. Plus, I wanted to grab clothes. Leaving with just the clothes on my back, not knowing when I was going to have a home again, wasn't up there on my list of things I wanted to do. Again.

"They'll be okay," Lennox reassures me.

Walking back to my dorm, he slips his hand in mine. He touch is warm, helping to thaw my freezing fingers. I look up and try my best to give him a smirk. Not that I succeed.

A sigh and lean into him. "I'm just worried. For all I know, someone's waiting for them at the car. The Deacon's could've already put a hit out on them. Tagged the car and put tracking chips under their skin."

A breathy laugh escapes past his lips. "They're a little fucked up, but they're not mad scientist."

"Pretty much are."

He doesn't say anything. With the whole holy water thing and taking dead baby souls, they're up there with the Dr. Mengele. While he might take my comment at a teasing joke, there's actually a high possibility of them doing that.

Growing up, church is viewed as this all holy place. The bible is a book to live by. God is perfection. But hidden behind the walls of the Cathedral are contradictions galore. Capturing and torturing supposed enemies. Killing children. Teaming up and entombing Hell's royalty. Never once was any of this mentioned in Sunday services. I guess that's why the Deacon's and Changelings never felt bad for anything they've done. To them, it was okay. To them, every order they were given was done by wholesome beings.

I will probably never attend a Christmas Eve service again. I don't care whose birthday it is.

"What happened down there?" I ask, needing to pull away from my racing thoughts. They were only weighing me down more.

I can practically feel the way Lennox's heart rate quickens. He clenches a little tighter around my hand. "I did what I had to."

"Did they have him locked up? Guarded?"

"Nora," he breathes, "not now."

My tongue feels like lead in my mouth. "You didn't have to go after him. I could've done it. All you had to do was walk away. No harm. No foul."

He snorts. "You act like it was such an easy choice for me."

"Wasn't it?"

Lennox slows, stopping mid-step.

The tension between us hasn't broke since the argument a few short hours ago. While he may be holding my hand and kissed me, there's still a tightly tethered cord between us.

"Nothing about this is easy, Nora. You aren't easy." His voice is low and grave. He speak each word with careful thought. "These feelings I have for you aren't easy. Standing up against everything I've known to be true isn't easy. *Nothing* is easy. Choosing to go against orders and free a demon is something I've never done."

Swallowing hard, I step closer to him. "I know. I'm sorry. That was selfish of me to ask."

He shakes his head and sighs. "Let's just get you to your room. We have a long day ahead of us. All I care about now is getting you safely out of here."

Lennox goes to move, but I pull back against him. His brow creases as he turns to me. I'm not exactly short; I'd say average height for a woman. But I still have to stand on my tiptoes to reach him. I place a kiss on his lips. I can taste the hesitation, but he finally gives in and kisses me back. His warm lips against mine, savoring just a brief moment of us.

I wish I cared more, to be honest. With as little as I know

about Lennox, honor is important to him. He wants to succeed in everything his does. And yet, here I am throwing a wrench in his plans. He's going against everything for me. I should be able to give him more of myself, but I can't. Not right now. I can't even say that I can down the line. If I do, it's going to take some time. As long as he's pacified with that, we'll be okay.

Willow isn't in the room. I'm not surprised. It doesn't even look like she's been here since I came back earlier. Nothing's been touched.

"Where is she?" Lennox asks, sitting on my bed. It's odd seeing him in here. We usually keep to his room.

Grabbing my phone out of my pocket, I turn it back on. "I have no idea."

Willow and I used to have an understanding. I had considered her to be a friend. It was her idea to come here. But once she got hold of that damn holy water, everything about her has changed. She's become standoffish. The ferocity that burned through her veins fizzled out and she's become just a roommate to me.

I watch as the screen on my phone illuminates and then brings up the lock screen. I haven't changed the image of Aggie and I from a drunken night. I probably never will. Using the pin to unlock it, it nearly falls out of hands. Notification after notification pings. Texts. Voicemails. Missed calls.

I go to my messages first. There are several from Aggie and also a different phone number, one I don't have saved.

Aggie: Nora you need to answer.

Aggie: Answer the phone.

Aggie: She's in trouble.

Unknown: Nora.

Unknown: Answer. Aggie's in trouble.

Aggie: Answer the fucking phone.

My heart races as I pull up my voicemail. There are three unheard messages waiting for me.

The first, "Nora, it's Briggs. I need you to answer the phone. It's Aggie."

The second, "Nora! Answer the damn phone. She's in trouble.

The third, "They have her. I don't know what to do."

The way Briggs' voice changes from rushed, to angry, to defeated, kills me. In each message, urgency is blatant.

Guilt seeps in, weighing down my heart. My stomach twists as bile rises in the back of my throat. I look at Lennox with tear filled eyes.

He rushes over, cupping my cheek. "What is it?"

"I don't know," I whisper, shaking my head.

Hands shaking, I pull up the list of missed calls. Aggie's name is on there, as well as that unknown number. It has to be Briggs. Selecting his number, I let the phone ring on speaker.

He answers on the second ring. "Nora!"

"Yeah."

"They have her." On the other end, there's muffled movement. He swears and then says, "You need to get here."

Lennox has the phone out of my hands before I even realize it. I wrap my arms around myself, trying to steady the shakes that take over.

Clearing his throat, he takes over the conversation. "Briggs, what happened?"

"Fucking Reapers. They came to the house. I stepped outside for ten minutes - fifteen tops."

"You left her alone?" My voice is thick and cracks at the question.

Static fills the line for a moment. "I walked down the

street. By the time I came back, she was gone."

"Send me the address," Lennox tells him. To me he says, "Get clothes. We'll get going."

I nod and grab for the duffle bag under my bed. I grab my clothes and stuff them in, wrinkles be damned. When I go to grab things out of the bathroom, my reflection makes me freeze. Red has taken over my cheeks. Shadows darken my eyes. I'm a mess - a scared shitless disaster.

What the fuck is going on? There is so much that has happened within these last couple of hours. I have to be in some type of dream. There's no way in Hell any of this is actually happening. Xi being captured and tortured. Fighting with Lennox. Meyer's murder being plotted. Saving the two of them, while also killing two Changeling guards. Aggie being kidnapped. That is all too much. Maybe if I close my eyes or even pinch myself, I'll wake up.

"Nora." Lennox's voice snaps me back to reality. "You good?"

No. I want to tell him that I'm far from okay. I'm overwhelmed and struggling to fully comprehend everything.

Zipping up my bag, I turn to him. "Let's go."

. . .

Surprisingly, there's not many people awake. Most of them are probably sleeping in, trying to make up for the time they lost during the alarm. I couldn't be more thankful for that. The few Deacons or Changelings that are up cast us sideway glances, but don't stop us. That would be the last thing I need.

Lennox reaches down and entwines his fingers through mine. "Relax. You're drawing too much attention. It's not like you killed anyone."

"Yeah," I mumble. Now might not be the best time to tell him that I actually did kill someone - two someone's, actually. For all I know, they were friends of his.

"Just breathe."

Per usual, there are two guards standing at the entrance. Their backs are straight - hands clasped behind their backs. When they see us approached, hesitation dances over their faces.

"Can we help you?" asks the one.

"We're leaving," Lennox tells them.

They share a look before moving forward. "Council has directed that no one is to leave."

My hand instinctively tightens around Lennox's. This is just the interference I wanted to avoid.

"Neither of you are in the know. Those sirens last night signaled an attack." Lennox pulls on his superior mask. He's highly respected here; one of the Minor Council's go-to men. The way the men step in line as he talks is proof of that. "We have orders to search out and interrogate those that the demon named off. Do you really want to be the ones to tell the Council that you wasted my time?"

I breathe, just like he said. I pull my shoulders back and try to act as if my insides aren't a blended mess.

The guard that's remained silent clears his throat. "Of course. Apologies."

Lennox doesn't say anything else. We stroll past them and through the front doors. I half expect more alarm to go off. That'd be our luck. But as we make it out and past the fountain, nothing goes off.

Snow covers the yard. There are several tire tracks marring the white coat. There's no wind, but it's still beyond frigid outside. I hope that the three were able to make it to Xi's car safely. No matter how close it was parked, they had to be frozen by the time they made it inside.

"How are we getting out of here?"

"My car is parked around the block."

"We still have to make it out of the front gate then?"

He nods.

Great. We may have made it out of the Cathedral itself, but we aren't in the clear. Not yet.

"Does nobody else think it's super weird that a church is this heavily guarded?" The question slips from my mouth before I even realize I was wondering it.

Lennox shrugs. "Depends on what side you're looking at it from. From the outside? Yes. From the inside? No."

I grab the hood from the back of my shirt and pull it over my head as flakes of snow start fluttering down. With my head down, I keep my eyes glued to the ground. Just a step ahead of my shoes; the snow unblemished.

Everything I once knew - *thought* I knew - about the church and it's beliefs are beyond me. The childish stories and Sunday school teachings are just that. Stories. Teachings. Hearsay. These last several weeks have proved that. The congregations and spiritual words. Fuck, if only they knew they were just walking into a branch of Dr. Frank-N-Furter's castle.

As much I want to never forgive Willow for bringing me here, I can't do that. It wasn't as if she knew this would happen. If she did and she still dragged me here, then that just makes her a bitch.

The warmth of Lennox's hand twisting into my own pulls me out of my head. "Where'd you run off to?"

His gentle eyes look over, worry shining bright.

Tears instantly flood my vision. I do my best to blink them away and regain composure.

"Six months ago," I sigh, "things would still be normal if I would've just taken a taxi home. No bar for me." His brow knits, but I just shake my head. "Long story."

"I know you don't want to hear this," he says, squeezing my hand, "but things will be-"

"Miss McKinley."

Every ounce of blood coursing through my veins freezes, drying my mouth. Lennox stumbles as I stop in my tracks.

He waits on the opposite side of the gate, just mere feet away. His black coat stands stark against the purifying snow. My instincts tell me to run, to push open the gates and launch myself at him. I'd send sonic waves in his direction and bombard him like an amazon. And yet, I can't will myself to move. My limbs are numb.

"Did you lose something?"

His teasing tone sparks a flame. I slip away from Lennox, but he only catches up. Before I can reach the gate, he blocks me, holding me at arm's length.

"Think, Nora," he tells me. I look from him to outside the gate. "Don't do something stupid. He's bating you."

"Where is she?" I growl.

The bastard smiles, pulling one corner up his mouth up and then the other. I've never liked this man. That look only makes me hate Griffin even more.

29

"Where do you think they took her?" I ask, trying to calm the racing thoughts milling around in my head.

Lennox had tossed my bag in the back of his old Cadillac. It's not the type of car I expected him to drive. Then again, you can't get much more regal than a Cadillac. He keeps a safe distance between us and the black town car. It's close enough that no one can squeeze in the middle, but not too close. Snow flutters down, making the space seem even farther.

He shrugs. "No clue. There's not much open yet."

I glance at the clock. It's just after six in the morning on a Sunday. There's not going to be any life in the world for another couple of hours.

Reaching down I update our location on the map. I called Briggs once I climbed in the passenger seat. He was in Aggie's car before we even hung up. None of us know what to expect. For all we know, a demonic barbecue could be waiting for us. Or a firing squad.

Regardless, there's only one goal: get Aggie out of there. There are far too many people that have been dragged into this mess that shouldn't be. I'll be damned if she's yet another victim.

My phone pings as a text illuminates the screen. A slight wave of relief ruffles through the tension in my muscles.

Xi: Safe and sound. Meyer is napping. I'll send you the address shortly.

"Thank you," I whisper, resting my head back. Lennox gives me a questioning look. I hold up my phone. "They're safe."

"Did you think they wouldn't be?"

I sigh. "I don't know what to think anymore, especially not right now. At least they're okay. That's all that matter."

Lennox reaches over and rests his hand on my knee. "We got this, Nora. We'll do whatever we have to and get your friend out of there."

"I'm terrified." The confession forces all the air from my lungs, gasping for some type of norm.

Slipping his hand in mine, he gives it a gentle squeeze. My palms are clammy, but he doesn't pull away. He holds on.

The black town car slows. I didn't get a chance to steal a look at who the driver is. I hope it's not Singh, the poor man that carted the trio of Reapers around. He was always sweet. He's yet another person I don't want to see tangled up in this shit show more than he already was.

I send Briggs the pinned address as we park behind the car as it pulls up to a curb. An expansive building stands overhead. I've only been here once or twice. It's a theater the local college uses for their plays. Occasionally, they'll host some band or comedian.

"What they planning?" I mutter to myself as I unbuckle.

The wind has picked up, sending flurries all around. It causes my hair to dance like red wild flames. As Lennox gets out, I cross my arms over my chest, trying to keep in any warmth. We stand on the sidewalk and wait for Griffin. Every muscle in my body tenses as his long frame unfolds from the back seat. Unlike mine, his hair is plastered to his head with gel. I'm able to get a brief look at the driver. Well... the back of his head at least. Blonde contradicts Singh's black locks.

"This way," Griffin sneers. He walks tall, bringing out every ounce of his arrogant stature.

Lennox and I share a look, but follow along. Lambs being led into a lion's den. I try and keep my breaths slow and steady, despite the way the cold and my nerves collide together.

Griffin opens both doors of a side entrance, pushing them as if he's some expected royalty finally making his presence known. The two of us have to catch both doors as they swing back to avoid getting knocked in the face.

The walls travel up for what seems like miles, dark wood running into a tiered ceiling. Chandeliers look down and cast morbid shadows everywhere. For a college theater, the interior is regal with a wicked sense of charm. I move closer to Lennox, shouldering up to him. Our pinkies graze, but neither of us loop them together. But that single touch - that reassurance - it's a slice of sanity in this war. The cold follows us inside, seeping into our bones and the marble floors.

Walking through another doorway, rows and rows of seats are lined up. All of them, even the ones in the balcony, are filled. While the room might be jam packed with people, none of them seem to awake. Heads either leaned to one side or another –

resting on their chins or leaned back onto the seat.

I look at Lennox with blatant confusion painted on my face. And then my gaze lands on the stage and blood floods away from my body. Three men in suits sit on the stage under a blinding spot light. Off to the side, two men in black stand with a petite girl in between them. Aggie.

My feet threaten to betray me. As my mouth dries, I have to force my legs to stay in line. Straying or acting out won't get me anywhere. If anything, Death will only take my eagerness and twist it on their favor. Digging my nails into my palms, I pace myself.

The closer the get to the stage, I can make out the outline of a fresh pentagram burned into the wood. Salt from the dead sea combined with ash from Mount Vesuvius being burned into the ground will create a portal that the princes can travel through. Crossing the barrier is lethal - a promise of Death.

Griffin stops in front of the brothers as a venomous smile spreads across his face. He clasps his hands behind his back and greets them, "My Lords, the Banshee is here."

As he steps to the side, Belial stands. His suit is perfect, free of an wrinkles or tears. The normally pleasant demeanor sketched on his face has hardened. His mouth is pulled in a tight line and his eyes stare blankly.

"Nora," he says. My stomach twists in a knot, "as you have come to realize, we are in need of assistance."

A bitter chuckle bubbles up. "You're seriously fucked in the head if you think I'm going to help you. Just let her go."

Despite the distance, I can see the way Aggie tenses and shakes. Hell, I can practically taste the fear seeping from her pores.

The corner of Belial's mouth quirks up. "You are

thoroughly aware how situations like this end."

"I'm done. You're not using me as a puppet."

Leviathan turns in his seat. "Feisty today, aren't we?"

Standing, Satan buttons the jacket of his three-piece. Images of the way he twirled Kane around like a prized possession floods my mind. My heart plummets to the pit of my stomach with a death-defying weight, just like it had that night.

"This is not up for discussion. It amuses me how incompetent you are. Even after everything, you are unable to grasp the power that stands before you," Satan drawls, narrowing his eyes.

Behind me, Lennox lets out a low cry and grunts. Whipping around, I turn to catch the sight of him being restrained. Two Reapers – or maybe they're demons – hold a dark blade to his throat, threatening to use it. The stone sparkles under the dim light. Those blue eyes of his are wild like a rabid animal. I go to move, but he shakes his head.

A sharp yelp pulls my focus back to the stage. One of the two guards that were standing on either side of her now have Aggie in a tight hold. Tears pour down her face as one of them poise a curved dagger at her stomach, taunting to pierce through her gut.

Satan smiles. "We've learned that it takes a significant amount of demonstration to break through that dense head of yours."

"They have nothing to do with this," I hiss. "It's between me and you. Not them."

"With the loss of your lover's life," he spits at the ground, "and the knowledge of how we could affect your younger sibling, yet you still think we are concerned with taking the life of mortals. Or *Changelings.*"

My mouth gapes, fighting for word. "Just take me. Let them go."

His top lip curls. "*You* are not what we desire."

"Your voice," Belial cuts in. "Your voice is the only thing we want."

"Then take it!" Speaking of which, my voice cracks with frustration and fear as panic begins to sink in. "Take whatever you want - whatever you need. Just *please* let them go."

In all my years, begging was never something I did. I didn't beg for friendships or lovers. I sure as Hell didn't beg for my mother to stay or for my father's attention. And yet, this year, I've found myself begging more than I ever have. To be let free. To save my sister's innocence. For a reprieve. For the life of Kane. For myself. And now, for Aggie and Lennox.

Closing his eyes, Belial shakes his head back and forth. "We cannot just take your voice. It is a blessing bestowed upon you and you alone."

"It's a curse," I correct him, "not a blessing."

Satan snarls. "Enough. Terminology and diction is not why we are here, nor why you have been summoned. We need your voice and your power. It is the only thing able to free us."

"That won't happen." Lennox croaks from under his restraint. As I turn to look at him, the guards tighten their grip. He hisses as the blade cuts into his skin, a drop of blood trails down his collarbone.

"With an overwhelming amount of souls sent to Hell, it is then that we can truly be free," Belial redirects the conversation. "Free from Hell. Free from the burden of the pentagram."

I narrow my eyes. "You receive souls every day."

"We need souls of those blessed for Heaven."

"You want me to take the lives of these people?"

Belial nods.

My chest pulls. Tears coat my eyes, blurring my vision. Of course. Why wouldn't they want me to kill a group of people? Innocent people.

There's been enough killing. Too much of it has been from my own hands. Flashes of the guards outside of Meyer's door send my mind reeling. They were doing their job. Maybe they weren't innocent. They've probably killed their fair share of people - Reapers and demons. Their deaths haven't hit me the way I thought they would. Not that I've had time to stop and think. But this? This is too much.

"There *has* to be another way," I mutter. It's a weak attempt, but the only thing that comes to my mind.

"No," Belial says.

"And they will be let go?" Gesturing to the two people I care about in the room, I avoid looking them in the eye. I don't want them to see how defeat has taken over my face. Their judgement would only break me.

Belial nods.

Pulling in a deep breath, I concede, "What do I have to do?"

Leviathan and Satan do nothing to hide their pleased expressions. Their smiles shine bright under the light of the theater.

"You'll work your magic. What else do you think you'd be doing?" Leviathan laughs from where he's seated.

Clearing his throat, Belial restates, "Once you take the stage, you will begin to sing and pull at the strings of their souls. As their souls slip, they will be collected and directed to Hell."

Satan clasps a hand on his brother's shoulder. "And if you even think of pulling something, we will remain here."

"Your new toy," Leviathan teases, "and your friend will be restrained until then."

"Isn't there another way?"

All three shake their head. Pulling in a deep breath, I try to block out all the intrusive thoughts. I glance at Aggie and mouth, "I'm sorry."

Her mouth trembles and tears steadily stream down her face, but she nods her head up and down. She mouths back, "It's okay."

It's okay.

It's far from okay. Nothing about this is okay.

30

I rip off another piece of nail, hissing as its pulled from the cuticle. My knee bounces in time with my nerves as I move to another nail. A few have formed blood in the corners as nerves overwhelm all of my senses.

Death had ordered the Reapers holding down Lennox and Aggie to take them up to the balcony. Aggie quietly sobbed as she shuffled her feet. I tried reaching out to her, but the one guard swatted my hand away with the hilt of the blade. Lennox struggled to get free. I didn't expect much else from him. He's a fighter through and through.

Another pentagram was already formed in the upper level, allowing the brothers to watch the sickly performance. Before their astral forms disappeared, they gave me a warning. No tricks. No funny business. Nothing. Or else they'd put an end to their prisoners. I got the message loud and clear.

While we waited for the Princes of Hell to return, Griffin was placed on guard duty. While I sit on the edge of the stage, he stands next to me. His body never wavers from its rigid hold.

There's probably hundreds of people unconscious in the audience. That knowledge has only makes my anxiety spike. The longer I sit, the more I keep thinking about what I have to do. Kill them - kill them all. Mothers. Fathers. Grandparents. Children. People that has no clue what was about to happen to them. They have no clue that their lives are about to be over with. They won't be returning home. The coffee that's being brewed back home will be waiting an awfully long time, turning cold and stale before someone notices that their family member never returned home. And that they never would again.

Pulling in a tight breath, I flex my fingers and try to regain a sliver of calm. Going from one mess to another doesn't help my nerves. The plan was to get the boys out safe and sound. Lennox and I would flee after, putting as much distance as we could between us and the Cathedral. Running into Griffin and being sucked into this demonic mass murder plot wasn't involved. Not in the original game plan and not in the B, nor Plan C, nor even Plan Z.

"Stop your quivering," Griffin scolds, casting a side eyed glare at my bouncing foot.

Narrowing my eyes, I spit, "Fuck off."

He turns his tall form toward me. "Don't test me."

"You're not going to do anything," I taunt. "Threatening me with words is the only move you have. You hurt me and your beloved princes will send you to the pits."

Fire blazes in his amber eyes. Both nostrils flare out, forcing out angry bits of air. I can't hide the pleased smile pulling at my lips. Well… I can, but I won't.

Behind us, doors closing startles the both of us as more Reapers file in. I sneak a glance up top. Death now sits in individual chairs near the railing of the balcony. Both Lennox and Aggie are held against their will on either side, sharpened blades poised in different areas, ready to puncture and kill.

It's almost time. I stand and turn in the direction of the bathroom, at least the door that a restroom sign hangs over. Griffin grabs my arm and spins me around to face him.

"Where do you think you're going?"

I rip away from his hold. "To the bathroom. Unless you have a pissing fetish, I'm going by myself."

"Like-"

"Griffin," Belial's voice echoes through the expansive room , "leave her be."

"She knows what is at stake," Satan follows, narrowing his eyes in my direction.

I don't wait for anyone else to add their opinion. I walk out and toward the bathroom. Once inside, I quickly shut the door and lock it. Closing my eyes, I rest my head on the wooden door and pull in slow, deep breaths.

Why, I think. *Why me? Why this?*

Running both hands through my hair, I take a few more deep breaths before I turn on the sink. I let the warm water run over and through my fingers. I cup my hands together and allow a small pool to fill between them. Splashing it on my face, I pat my cheeks and rub my eyes. I need to focus. I need this to go smoothly.

I don't even realize that I pulled my arm back and sent my hand into the mirror, shattering the glass. A pile of shards lay in the ceramic sink bowl. Water covers each piece. Red mixes in as blood drips from my hand. The tops of my knuckles and fingers are cut and bloody.

"Fuck," I bite out, running my hand under the water to wash away as much blood as possible. Pulling down a piece of paper towel, I wrap it around tightly and shut off the water.

A knock comes to the door, startling me once me.

"It's time." Griffin's voice floods in from the crack at the bottom of the door.

My hair is still wet due to the snow, making it look dull and lifeless. Shadows haunt the underside of my eyes. A hoodie and leggings. I'm a completely mess. Not what you'd picture a guest singer to look like. Grabbing another paper towel, I wrap it over my hand to hide the red leaking through and head out the door.

My gaze travels upward as I take the stags once more. In the darkness of the balcony, Death sits, attentively waiting. Aggie doesn't seem to be crying, but she's beyond frightened. That's certain.

Pulling one more deep breath and swallowing hard, I scan the room, taking in the filled seats. This is wrong. These people are innocent.

And yet, I open my mouth and begin to sing.

"Oh, misty eye of the mountain below. Keep careful watch over my brothers' souls."

It's the only song I can think of. It's nothing great Hell, it's a song about dwarves. Not even real dwarves, but one of Tolkien's creations.

"If this is to end in fire, then we should all burn together."

It fits. It honestly fucking fits. Some of the group stir, while the rest remain unaware. Satan leans forward in his seat, watching intently.

"And if we should die tonight, we should all die together."

251

White films rise up from the crowd. Some stretch out more than others. I want to close my eyes and shut out the sight, but I can't. I need to focus. If I stray, Aggie's soul will be taken along with them.

Curling my hands into fists, I hiss at the way the right one stings with the movement. Biting down, I push harder, pulling more at the souls.

"I see fire burning the trees. And I see fire hollowing souls."

Color drains from several of their faces, while others sway in their seats.

A little more. A little harder, I remind myself.

Images flood my mind. A stolen bicycle. Overlooking a neighbor sunbathing. Nothing major. Nothing like what I've seen before. And yet, as the tingling sensation spreads up my spine and out my mouth, pain begins radiating through my head.

As tears leak out the corners of my eyes, I glance up. Pride coats Death's face as they peer down below. Lennox's face is strained as he occasionally tries wiggling free. And Aggie. She keeps her eyes trained on me. I never wanted her to see this side of me. But there's not a hazy glow around her. Her soul is still intact. And right now, that's all that matters.

"And with our shadow on the ground, I hear my people screaming out."

With one more gusto, a final push, an airy wave washes over me. While the seated bodies collapse, Reapers squeeze their way out of the woodwork. They begin chanting, collecting the souls and sending them to Hell. My knees grow weak and I collapse, blurry eyed from the growing headache. As the souls are sucked down one by one, I let the tears pour from my eyes.

The ground below begins shaking, trembling through the

foundation. Not as violent as the Playground had, but it's still an unnerving feeling. Above, the brothers stand.

"Well done," Belial says.

Satan turns to his left and snaps his fingers. As the three disappear, the man holding Aggie drops the dagger. Despite the room full of dead bodies, a relieved smile takes over my face. One of the guards raises both of his hands and grips either side of her head. A spark ignites inside of me. But before I can react, he twists.

And Aggie's body falls lifeless to the ground.

"No!" I bellow out, losing all feeling in my body.

Tears pour down my face as a sob takes over. Waves rush out as a cry burst from my chest. The Reapers are thrown backwards. Lennox takes the moment to move, attacking his guards. I stumble to my feet and trample down the stage. Griffin is nowhere to be found.

I crawl up the back stairwell leading to the balcony. My arms and legs tremble. I don't let my gaze stray to the bodies in the seats. There's no hope for them now. I collapse to the ground when I finally reach Aggie. Blonde hair halos around her head. Lifting her head into my lap, I pat her cheeks.

"Wake up," I beg. Another sob sneaks out when she doesn't react. "Please, Ag, wake up."

"Nora-"

"No!" I bite out, shaking her shoulders. I feel Lennox sink down beside me. He wraps both of his arms around me, pulling me closer. "She has to wake up."

He squeezes. "Nora, we need to get out of here."

I shake my head. "We can't leave her."

He places his lip on the top of my head. "We won't. Promise." I meet his eyes, overwhelmed by the urgency coursing through them. "I need you to stand. Can you do that?"

I nod, blocking out the heavy weight of sadness trying to overtake my senses. I let him help me up, grabbing both of my hands and pulling. Bodies of the Reapers that guarded them are now scattered across the space, blending in to the corpses they helped condemn. Burning flesh caused by the glowing crystal Lennox carries mar each of them. Slices across their throats. Stabs through their chest. Lennox had been lethal, offering no mercy.

Once he has her in his arms, I lead the way down the steps, wiping at the wetness covering my face. Pushing through the front doors, the snow is still coming down. I head toward the Cadillac, not looking back, not wanting to see my lifeless friend in the arms of my lover.

"Nora!" Briggs voice grabs my attention.

In his arms, Griffin struggles to free himself. Briggs is pure muscle. While he's lacking in height, he's able to easily overpower the Reapers. Looking past me, his face falter. I bite down on my lower lip to keep it from trembling. He looks to me and I simply nod.

A rage that I've never seen in this man takes over. Throwing Griffin to the ground, he sets his targets. Hit after hit. He cries out, landing more blows, bloodying the golden man's face.

"Keep going," Lennox says, urging me forward. "We need to get her in the car."

I nod and keep moving, not letting my gaze travel to the ground. I climb in the backseat, scooting over as far as I can. Lennox carefully lowers Aggie in, resting her head on my lap.

He looks at me. "Are you okay?"

I shake my head. "I will never be okay."

He holds my gaze a moment longer before he slips away, shutting the door behind him.

Brushing away the hair that's fallen in her face, I lean down and place a kiss on Aggie's forehead. Tears fall down my face in a silent stream. This. This is what I wanted to prevent. This should never have happened to anyone, especially not her.

A bang at the rear of the car startles me. A moment later, the boys climb in the front seat. While Lennox starts the engine, Briggs looks over his shoulder to where I cradle her head. His eyes shine. Clenching his jaw, he reaches back and takes her limp hand in his.

"Give me your phone," Lennox orders.

I slip it out of my pocket and hand it to him. He pulls away from the curb and begins driving.

"I'm sorry, Nora," Briggs croaks, looking me in the eye. "I shouldn't have left. I should've stayed there."

Shaking my head, I tell him, "None of this-"

Slamming on the brakes, Lennox jostles all of us. My head bouncing off the seat in front of me.

"What is that?" Briggs asks, leaning closer to the dash.

A couple of yards from the front of the car is a gaping hole. No. Not a hole. The pavement is cracked and opened, looking more like a newborn canyon. Steam rises out of the crack. A traffic light hangs down on the ground, shook loose from the formation of the crater. Several people are gathered around, gesturing to the formation. The sound software wailing sirens grow louder the closer they get.

The Changeling mutters something too low for me to hear.

"Lennox? What is it?"

He clears his throat. "Hell. Those bastards opened a Hellmouth. It won't be long before all its creature climb their way out."

"They didn't do anything." Those brilliant blue eyes catch mine in the rearview mirror. "That was me. I did that." Guilt sours my stomach. "And because of me, there's going to be Hell on earth."

Part Two

Persephone heard him from her throne and replied, "Love was never alive."

-     Zan M

31

Fire engulfs my body, ripping apart every nerve and charring my flesh. There's no air to breathe as fiery smoke fills my lungs. All I see is a rolling darkness. Her cry pierces my ears, fading deeper into this Hell.

Nora.

The stone is warm to the touch. I'm naked, leaving my skin bare and vulnerable as I lay here. I can taste the dust and dirt that stirs with each inhale and exhale. I can't move. It's as if my limbs are infusion with stone, weighing them down.

Curling my hand, I focus every ounce of energy I have left. I peel my eyelids open, ripping them away from where they've all but dried to my eyes. Nothing but a dark cavern surrounds me. Stones and rocky earth. My brain feels like it's rolling around inside my head. Blinding pain flashes with every fraction of an inch that I move.

Hell. I'm in Hell.

I give up and let my head collapse back down to the ground as my eyes close. The pain is excruciating. I want to cry. I want to scream and then I want to cry. *Fuck*. I'm a grown ass fucking man laying here wanting to sob like a damn child.

How did I even get here? I can still feel the way that blade cut into my skin, searing the flesh. The cracking as her neck twisted in my hands. The blood in my veins burning with rage. And then the paralyzing sensation as Satan spun me around like a damn prized showcase.

I didn't expect the engulfing flames. *Fuck*, I didn't expect any of that. Serves me right though. I should've kept my head on straight. I allowed the feelings I have toward Nora to overshadow my judgement and duty. I should've known Vivian was working with Royce. I should've had some inkling as to what I was walking into - that we were being led to our slaughter. I should've known or done a lot of things, but I didn't. And now I'm here.

A muffled cry reaches me. It sounds as if it's coming from miles away. Or right next to me. I can't tell.

Pulling in deep breaths, I open my eyes once more. The ghosts of flames flicker along the wall; their shadows dancing in time. With each inhale I take, the more I begin to feel. Pain. An aching sensation barrels deep into my bones. Mentally forcing any and all energy into my arms, I push up. My muscle strains with the movement, begging me to stop. And when I finally do, my body slumps as I lean against the wall.

Rock. I'm surrounded by nothing by rock. Stone. Dirt. A cavern etched in the pits of Hell.

Bars line the entrance of the cave. Reds and burnt oranges

color the walls. As the shadows continue to flicker and dance, they highlight and shadow every inch of this prison.

Whether or not this is actually Hell or just my own, that means Nora isn't here. While she might not be locked away like a rabid animal, she's alone - unguarded. I just pray she was able to get away before Death laid their sickly hands on her.

"Fuck," I mutter, leaning my head against the wall behind me.

I'm sitting in a cell praying. *Praying.* I don't do that shit. It's a Changeling hijinks to keep the mortals in line. And yet, here I am, praying for her.

She's fierce. But there are millions of other things in the world stronger than her. More cunning. Slithering along, bending to the will of the princes. This is the exact situation I wanted to keep her away from.

The sound of rocks quietly being sifted under footsteps grabs my attention as a larger than life shadow stalks in my direction. Time moves slowly until massive feet step in view. Inky paw-like claws dig into the ground with each step. Thick, scaly skin encompasses the rest of its body.

I was never given the choice of taking up a Reaper's duties. Belial never came to me in his true form and extended his gift of a fucked up reincarnation. Stories and nightmare inducing sketches. That's how I know what to expect as my gaze travels upward. Spiraling horns will cascade down and around. Sharpened tusks will jut out and burrow into his lower lip. He's not just fearsome in his human skin. His true form is far superior and menacing.

"Satan." His name falls from my lips in a wheezy breath.

Grasping his hands around the bars, he sneers down at me. I don't move to cover myself. I can careless if he's sees my dick.

I don't have the strength to move. A smaller shrouded figure steps up beside him. It twirls a rod in its long, decrepit hands. The end of which, glows a searing red.

"What are you?"

I don't know why I thought the demonic Satan would sound anything like his human form. Down here, the words come out in a deep, echoing drawl. It's what most would picture a big bad guy sounding like.

When I don't reply, the minion extends the rod through the bars. I know what he plans on doing with it. And yet, I don't bulk away. I watch as the hot end lands on my skin. Bellowing out, I clench every muscle in my body as the branding iron sizzles against my ribs. By the time the cloaked bastard pulls it away, a sheen of sweat coats my face.

Satan asks the question once more.

"You know what I am - a fucking Reaper."

The iron lands on my calf. This time, I shy away.

"I answered your question," I bite out. "I don't know. I'm a Reaper. Nothing more."

The small figure shoves the searing end up under my arm. I cry out. My voice is quickly growing hoarse, tiring out like the rest of me.

Satan extends a long fingered hand; claws protrude from the ends fingertip. A tight pull forms in my chest. Arms. Legs. Head. All else are weightless as I'm lifted up off the ground. Like in the basement of the Playground, I'm pulled near the prince.

I always thought Hell's servants over dramatized Death's demonic features. They'd go on and on about how his tusks and other teeth are stained with blood near the gums. How his elongated ears are lined with black hairs. But they weren't wrong. No. If anything, they didn't do him justice. He's horrific.

"You do not possess a Reaper's spirit." An odd sort of lisp whistles out as he speaks with those saber teeth. "Every fiber of your being would have been desecrated. Ashes to dust. And yet, here you are. I ask again, what are you?"

Through gritted teeth, I say, "I don't know."

With a flick of his wrist, I am thrust backwards through the air. Body and skull collide with the wall, cracking against the stone. Ringing fills my ears as I collapse on the ground once more.

"You have chosen to make this difficult for yourself. So be it then." Stepping away from the bars, he raises his voice. "You have deserved your masters. And for that, I will flay open every inch of your skin. Over and over again until you reveal your true self."

Stone crunches under their feet as both retreat back to where they once came. Tension floods from my muscles as I slide down into a mass on the floor.

Hell. I'm in Hell, I think as darkness overtakes me.

. . .

I don't know how much time has passed. I slipped into a dream state for what could've been hours or mere minutes. I'll never know. At least this time, when I open my eyes, I'm able to lift my head without as much effort.

Blistered patches cover the areas that I was marked with the branding iron. They mirror that of cigarette burns.

This isn't right. Why am I here though? I shouldn't be. Like Royce, I shouldn't be here.

Or maybe…

"Royce!" I call out. My voice is rough, barely audible. I call my friend's name once more, only to slump down in defeat. There's no answer.

That explains all the questions then. I'm a Reaper. Well, I *was* a Reaper. Now I'm just a prisoner, tucked away in some layer of Hell. Something must've gone wrong. Maybe the *all-mighty* princes aren't as powerful as they thought.

A tortured cry finds its way to my cell and I cringe. The marks from the hot iron burn in memory as it was pressed to my skin.

"I will flay open every inch of your skin. Over and over again until you reveal your true self."

Only the devil knows what's happening to that poor soul. After all, this is the *real* Devil's Playground. Xi's bar is nothing more than a mirage. A twisted fantasy that's mistaken as place people would die to get into. All the drinks. The sins. Within its walls, demons flourish. Reds. Greens. Blues. All sorts of perversions exposed and accepted.

Green envy courses through the veins of those denied entry, while they have to sit on the sidelines and watch as unworthy people are let in. The color of sage as money is passed through hands, paying off debts, tipping the bartenders, adding more and more to their tabs.

The awakening sky that is opened up to them inside the dark walls, showing them just what their souls have been craving. Tears of joy. Acceptance into a crowd they once shied away from.

Rotting of teeth and blood as drugs enter the body. Empty arties, all filled with yellowing tar. Teeth break as they chew on ice, trying to calm to heat.

But the reds. Red silk water falling down generous curves.

Red - ruby red painted on tempting lips. Red curling in to gentle waves.

Red.

Nora.

My heart lurches in my chest. Even just the thought of her starts a turmoil in my body. The way those full lips pursed when her temper got the best of her. Those emerald eyes spiraling as she looked up from under thick lashes.

I should've stayed away. Things that I could've done differently - should've done differently - keep running through my mind. As much as Nora coming into my life has changed me for the better, I had the opposite effect on her. She's been beaten, bruised, tortured, and put into a twisted sort of a coma. Every step, every touch, pushed her further and further into the arms of Hell.

Our forceful bond may have gotten her out of her father's house and away from the stress of raising a child that isn't hers. I mean, people do it all the time. Stepfathers. Stepmothers. Grandparents. In-laws of all kinds. But in Nora's case, her father and stepmother lived under the same roof as her. They shared a house. And yet, they used her younger sister to chained her to the foundation.

Nora kept her complaints to a minimum. She cherished the time she spent with that mop of curly blonde hair. It mentally and emotional hurt her not being with her. The time that she did get a chance to see her was a painful reminder that she couldn't hold or talk to the little girl while in her position.

Nora doesn't belong in this world. Not with as pure of a heart that she has. She shouldn't even know about the after life. If anything, she should be on the lighter side of things - the *all holy* Changelings. Not on the damned side.

And yet, she is. And I'm no longer there to play buffer and shade her from all the darkness.

32

Several feet scuff along the ground, growing louder as they near. I've done nothing but curl up in the corner of the stone cell. It hurts. *Everything* hurts. Breathings hurts. Moving hurts. Hell, blinking fucking hurts from having to peel open my eyes. Needless to say, as whoever approaches, I don't move. Three shrouded figures stop at the entrance of the prison I've been stuffed into. One is short, much like the one that had accompanied Satan. The other two tower over it, holding cast iron chains in their bony hands.

"Piss off," I grumble, slumping down further to the ground.

None of them speak. They simply stare at me like a caged animal, naked behind bars. I didn't care the last time whether or not I had an audience, nor do I this time either. Well... I shouldn't say that I don't care. There's no strength or will left in me. If they want to get a look at my limp dick, more power to them. And yet, as they stare through the bars wordlessly, my conscience prickles its way up my spine. Their covered bodies and faces give no tell as to what's on their minds. Raising a knee, grimacing with the movement, I block the goods from view.

The shortest minion pulls a vial out of his clock. He pours it across the opening. Steam - no, smoke, begins rising up from the bars. In front of my eyes, my cage disintegrates into thin air. Magic. Sorcery. Or some fucked up metal eating acid.

Both of the taller ogres step inside and reach down, grabbing for me. I try and wiggle away, only causing rocks to burrow into my back. There's nowhere for me to go. I'm cornered. They grab hold of my upper arms and pull me to my feet. My body cries out in retort.

"Fuck off," I spit.

The chains that they carry are wrapped around each of my wrists. Metal, which is usually cool to the touch, burns my skin. I clamp down my jaw, hiding how badly they hurt. The cuffs dig in to my skin. My weak attempt to get away only makes it worse. I fight. They pull. My skin scorches under the weight.

"Stop fighting."

A haunting voice grabs my attention. But, in the brief moment of distraction, they're able to pull me along. My feet stumble bare along the heated stone. The lessened tension calms the pain to a manageable warmth. Fire to a mere flickering flame.

As the two oafs lead me on, I glance around, trying to catch sight at who told me to stop fighting against the chains. It wasn't the overbearing sound of Satan's voice. If anything, it sounded like a man - a mortal man. But as I look in through the bars of cells, I can't see anyone. Were they cowering in the back? Or are they just empty cells? For all I know, I completely imagined that voice.

Rows and rows of cells wrap around a Hellish colosseum. In the open space, it's exactly what nightmares depict Hell to be. Fire. Torture. Spinning wheels. Torture devices. Pained cries. The sight of all the sentenced sinners dries my mouth. Their cries are real. Their pain is real. And if what Satan said is true, my own cries will mingle with theirs soon enough.

"What is this?"

No answer.

I anticipate them to take me down to the center floor, adding me to the main event. Fuck, for all I know, I could be today's star attraction in their circus of dungeons and doom. But as we continue on, they don't lead me to the opened area. Instead, they take me to a hollowed out space - a red room of pain.

A solid section of metal stands in the center of the room. Spikes cover the plate, gleaming in the flickering lights. The cloaked minions pull me towards it, but I fight back. As I pull, the cuff bite into my flesh. The heat encompasses my wrists, threatening to sear straight through. While they keep pulling me toward the spiked plate, the shorter one steps up. It pulls a coiled whip from somewhere in the decrepit cloak. With a flick of his wrist, pain erupts across my back. I cry out. The whip slithers across the ground, painting the dirt red with my blood. The other two take advantage of my torture and back me up. The moment the sharpened points prick my skin, fire erupts at every point. Images of Vivian digging that damn Changeling blade into my skin flashes in my mind. The fight in me awakens. I thrash against the chains, despite how the metal at my wrists digs in deeper.

I have to get out of here.

The demented giants pull tightly against the chains. Both of my arms are spread out, practically popping my shoulders out of their sockets. I'm thrust backwards. Liquid pours down my back. More blood. I cry out as the spikes puncture through my tightly strung muscles. I pull, trying to regain even an inch of reprieve. Nothing. The chains are hooked to sections in the wall, stationing me in the same position. Agony. I'm in pure agony.

"Silence him." The deep, daunting voice of Satan is heard before he steps into view.

With the back of his hand, a minion strikes me across the face. I bite down and grimace. The beast-like paws disrupt the settled dust as Satan walks in. He's followed by two other creatures.

One is a lot shorter and plump. Algae green scales cover it from head to toe. A collar of excess skin fans out around its neck. As it steps further into the room, it's tongue slithers out, tasting the stale air. As sarcastic as Leviathan is, his demonic form is nothing short of nightmarish.

The third creature, the most level headed of the brothers, glides into the room. Belial is usually calm and collected. Always has been. He's cover in a thick, red coat of fur. His face resembles that of a ram or an elk, but lacks horns. He gives off the same vibes. Regal. Respected. Calculated. Even so, his true form is not one you'd want to pass on the street.

Leviathan opens his reptilian mouth and a deep growl emerges in an awkward grumble.

"He refuses. If he willingly gave up the information, we would not need to be wasting our time," Satan snaps, glaring from across the room.

Taking a hooved step forward, Belial looks over every inch of me. His lip pulls up, bearing a row of cracked and stained teeth. I can't help but wonder if they're like that from eating too much of is favored snack - the ribs of man. He drawls out a response in some language I've never heard of.

His brother gives a tight nod and also steps closer. The way that Leviathan moves is like that of a crocodile. Each step is slow. His whole body moves from side to side as he waddles towards me. His tongue slithers out from his sharpened teeth every few seconds, tasting the air. I wonder if he can taste the fear twisting and churning in the pit of my stomach.

The closer he gets to me, my heart rate quickens. As much as I hate the Hellish trio, their true forms are utterly repulsive. It makes being in their present so much worse. They're a terrifying sight that would scare even those that get off on horror and gore.

Leviathan reaches out, taking one of his sharpened claws and runs it along my skin. A thin line forms along my side. Blood doesn't seep out, but the area is irritated and red. Just when I think he's going to turn and leave, he reaches up once more. This time, he presses harder into my flesh. I clamp down my jaw, fighting back a yell as he cuts along my side again. Blood pours down the opened wound. He holds up his coated finger, letting it tongue lick at the dripping blood. Another low growl comes from him.

"I had already came to that conclusion." Satan rolls his eyes. "You were informed that he is not a Reaper."

The scaled jaw gnashes just mere inches from me. I flinch in defense, which only digs the spiked in deeper. I try to not let him see how much he's getting to me. But if I bite down any harder, I'll crack my teeth into pieces.

"We could," Satan muses. Turning to the plump minion,

he orders, "Get the parasites. Be sure they are hungry."

As it disappears, the brothers crowd closer together. A mixture of neighs, growls, and an inaudible language buzzes around. I try to drown them out, but it's difficult. With the spikes threatening to press further into my skin, I'm highly aware of every inch I move. Of every sound that echoes through the barren room. Of every dreadful second that passes.

As the stout figure returns, Belial mutters something in the ancient tongue and the larger oafs move in . They pull me away from the metal plate, only to have me turn and face it. My stomach recoils. Blood - *my* blood - drips down and pools on the floor.

I should've known that slight moment of reprieve was just that: a moment. Where the spikes had burrowed and cut their way into my flesh, more pain erupts. Turning my head, I catch a glimpse of Leviathan's clawed hand holding onto a bloated worm. A razor head seemed to spin round and round as it wriggling in his grasp. And then he latches it onto my back.

"Turbulent parasites," Satan drawls, "are worse than any leech in the mortal world. They are such an outdated and trivial practice. As you can feel, they create caverns into the flesh with their rotating teeth, crawling deeper and deeper into the body. They consume not only blood, but also muscle and bone. Painful bastards. But if you are not willing to hand over the information we need, then there are other ways for us to get it out of you."

Leviathan places another on me.

"Why?" I cry out as it burrows near my spine.

"Why not?" And with that, the brothers retreat, leaving me alone with the cloaked ogres and the vampire worms.

33

A smile spreads across her face, eyes bright. Her cheeks turn the slightest shade of pink. My heart lurches in my chest.

Perfection.

She nuzzles her nose against mine as I stroke her cheek. Her skin is soft and smooth, just like it always is.

"Kane," she whispers.

My name falling from her mouth is pure sin.

"Kane."

Her body tenses in my hands. Her eyes grow wide, rabid and wild with fear. She opens her mouth, ready to scream. Black smoke spews out, taking over her face - taking over everything. I reach out and try to pull her back to me, but she slips through my fingers. Smoke. Just like smoke.

"Stop fighting it. Stop fighting us."

Her words echo in my mind.

"Stop fighting."

I sit up, clutching at nothing but air. My chest heaves as I gasp for oxygen. Sweat coats every inch of my skin. A dream. It was only a dream. And yet, her touch, her voice, it was all too real.

With the leeches inching their way through my body, I've been in nothing but pain since they tossed me back in my cell. Pulling on them doesn't do anything. They merely stretch like rubber and hold on tighter, tunneling in further. The cuffs left blistering and bleeding welt around both wrists. While they ooze, the puncture wounds from the metal table sing in pain. It's a different level of torture. Having to lay here in this much pain is simply agonizing.

I need to get out of here. I need to get to her.

Holding onto the cavern wall for support, I limp to the metal bars. My knees shake and threaten to give out with every step I take. The one cloaked figure had taken a vial and dumped its contents. Liquid. Ash. I'm not certain what exactly was in it, but when it was poured over the bars, they disintegrated. In the time spent in that torture room, the bars had reformed. The cheesy magic trick had to be done once more before they could toss me back inside. At the time, stars and blackness shadowed my vision, making it so I couldn't see what was used.

I reach out and grab hold of one, only to let go instantly. The skin of my palms is burned, searing off the flesh where it made contact. I try another bar with the opposite hand. I hold on maybe a second longer, but I only end up crying out and letting go.

"You tried them both," a man comments. "You tried both

hands, did you not?"

I know that voice. It's the same one that told me to stop fighting against the guards.

"Hello?" I call out. "Who's there?"

A distant chuckle finds its way to my cell. "A prisoner. Just like you."

"Who are you?"

Another cackle. "I am you. You are me. We are all the same, you and I. Prisoners of Hell, trapped for eternity under a sinner's guilt."

The riddle like speech hits a nerve. He's toying with me. That or he's gone completely insane. Taking a deep breath, I slide down to the floor, avoiding touching anything with my hands or back. At this point, the only things unwounded are my feet and legs.

"How long have you been down here?"

"Time does not pass. Years. Months. Centuries. Decades."

The voice cracks every so often as he speaks. He forms his words slowly and they shake like an old man's. He probably could be some elderly person. He could've been here for only a few years. *Time does not pass here.* Or longer.

A low hum picks up. Nonsense and insanity fills each note. There's no rhythm or organization. The tune is a mess and one that I've never heard of.

"I'm Kane," I call out, introducing myself.

"Mhmm," he muses. "I know. I have heard them muttering of you. Your name. Your debacle."

The humming picks back up. I roll my eyes, pushing past the irritation flickering in my chest. Biting his head off won't do me any good.

"And you are?"

He lets out another awkward chuckle. "My name? It's long been forgotten."

Of course. They parked me next to a Jurassic lunatic. Nora would love it. She once told me the lunes, the ones most would steer away from, were her favorite patients. She said they were misunderstood.

"You may call me Earnest?"

"Earnest?"

"Full of seriousness and purpose. That is who I am."

The corner of my mouth quirks up. She would definitely love him. That's for sure. I rest my head on the wall behind me.

"What are you in here for, bud?"

"You, Kane, wish to know my sins - my undoing's?"

My brows crease together as regret fills my chest. I should've just kept my mouth shut. I still can. And yet, I mutter, "Sure."

Earnest picks up another tune and starts to hum that. This one seems more whimsical than the last. Happier. Much like one of those simple songs she'd always sing.

"Amuse a poor old man," he says, ending the song abruptly. "Tell me of the world. It is anew from the one I once walked the streets."

"It's not that great."

"Do not make me beg."

Wide green eyes stare up at me. Hope and promise shine brightly in them. I can almost hear her telling me to be kind and to give in to the small talk. Kindness overwhelmed her heart, while mine was free of the defect.

Sighing, I concede, "Buildings are everywhere. Sky high with busy streets running in between."

"Horses?"

I can't help the laugh that bursts out. "No. Cars and buses. Massive machines that run on fuel, traveling ten times faster than horses."

"Good. Those beasts smelled like shit."

"I bet," I say, wrinkling my nose. "No horses. Not anymore."

I couldn't even imagine what it'd be like traveling the world on foot and horse, searching for souls to reap for Hell. Just thinking about the amount of time involved in getting to the souls makes me cringe.

Luckily, we had Singh. Quiet and compliant. The Indian man knew his job and did it well. He never tried sticking his nose where it didn't belong. Nor did his loyalties stray.

"The food," Earnest continues. "And what of the food?"

Chicken with pesto sauce. Local pizza and takeout.

"Most is preserved with chemicals. It's all fried in oils and grease."

"Bleh," he blanches. "Oil. Never cared for it."

"You sure as Hell-"

The realism of the words ties up my tongue. *Sure as Hell.* Now more than ever, I know that Hell exists. Clearing my throat, I reassure him, "You wouldn't like any of this."

Silence creates a void between our cells. After a few moments have passed, a faint snore reaches through the bars. The sound mixes with the pained cries out in the arena.

Sliding down, I wince as the leeches get caught on the rough wall. I collapse on the ground, laying on my stomach. I sprawl out and keep my hands fisted together. Resting my head on my arm, dust and dirt stirs with my breath. I run an unmarked finger over the ground, the rock warm to the touch. Down and swooping around in a curl. Nora has this one lock of hair that hangs down near her face. It twists into soft curls. Her hair is just that: soft. Soft and smooth like silk.

One of the bloody bugs nicks something, causing a jolt of pain to spread through my body. I groan and close my eyes. I take a few deep breaths to try and calm myself.

Stories on top of rumors. Never once did I peg Hell to be like this. Not the slow pain and hours alone in a cage. I honestly don't know which is worse. At least on a constant spinning wheel of punishments, I wouldn't be burdened with my thoughts - my memories.

I keep up with steady pulls of breaths until the darkness of sleep comes for me. And I slip away, dreaming of red curls and waves.

34

I was never a TV watcher. Royce was. He was addicted to those Spanish soaps. He would record them. Follow the show's gossip. Go on tangents about characters and plot lines. It was rather annoying. Once I saw that Nora didn't have an escape plan up her sleeve, I got a small TV for her. She'd watch reruns of this gay man and his redheaded roommate. Occasionally, she's stream old cartoon movies - something she used to do with her sister. There's one movie in particular that's been sticking with me. Hercules is a cheap take on Greek mythology. But there's one part in the movie where the gods and goddesses are chained and pulled from their homes in Olympus. *That's* what I pictured Hell to be. Not this.

In whatever time frame I've been down here, they've gone from leeches, to flaying sections of my skin, and even draining the majority of my blood. They want me to tell them what I am. Other than a Reaper, I have no clue. As far as I'm concerned, my second life was dedicated to collecting souls for Hell. I don't know what answer they're looking for. I know nothing of what my life was like before becoming a Reaper. *Nothing.* They don't believe me though. Even if they did, I doubt they'd even care. No matter how many times I try to tell them, they deem it yet another excuse. I'm truly Hell's bitch through and through.

I've given up on trying to contain myself. Pride has flown out the window at this point. For as many times as they've inflicted torturous pain on me, I should be nothing more than a sobbing lump in the corner. Currently, my chest burns from where they stabbed me, then sealed the wounds with a branding iron. The blood and flesh has bubbled over into blisters. When I think part of my body is healing, they pursue different torture techniques. One gaping wound leads to another. And, at this rate, they'll never heal properly. I've tried keeping some composure, but that only lasted so long. Let them see me scream and cry. I'm stuck here regardless.

Earnest was right. Time is endless. There's no sign of how much has passed. Hours? Weeks? I have no clue. It seemed as if a month had passed before they dragged me out of my cell to extract those parasitic bastards. All the while, Death stood there and took in the sight of my torture with gleaming eyes. Fucking sadists.

Sliding down onto the floor, I rest my arms on my knees and lean my head back. More waiting. That's all I do. I wait for them to come back and collect me. The torture is never the same. It's always something new they have up their sleeves.

The old man next to me clears his throat. "What was it today?"

"Poke and burn," I grumble.

At first, I didn't mind Earnest. He was someone to talk to - something to not feel as lonely. I never thought I'd enjoy another person's company. All I kept thinking about was Nora and how she'd react to my cell neighbor. But then came the questions. He had an endless stream of them. He never answered any of mine. Instead, he'd throw his age into the mix to avoid answering.

"They are sticklers for consistency," he says, his voice filled with amusement.

I don't answer. Closing my eyes, I pull in a few deep breaths. As far as I'm concerned, they could be trying out new torture techniques. They weren't going to change up they ways for a lowly Reaper.

"Who is the one you call Nora?"

My eyes snap open and my body grows stiff. "How do you know that name?"

"You talk when you sleep. You say that name over and over again."

My mouth dries and my tongue grows heavy. I can't believe I said her name aloud down here. I don't want her anywhere near this place. Not now. Not ever.

"Kane?"

"She's nobody," I bite out, flinching at how defensive it sounds.

Earnest laughs. "Nobody. Nobody would not fill a dream. Nobody would not linger on your lips with you sleep."

I sigh. "She's just a girl I used to know."

"You love her. Not past. Present. You love her now."

"What's it to you?" I sneer.

"Does she know?"

Those words hit like an aimed missile. The force of the

explosion throttles my heart down to the pit of my stomach.

"Yes, she knows."

"Tell me about her."

I want to tell him no. I want to tell him to fuck off and to leave me alone. And yet, I want to tell him about the amazing woman that stole my heart. Better yet, that turned my cold heart warm.

Closing my eyes again, I picture Nora and all of her perfections. "Red hair. Not that carrot red though. Deep and thick with curls at the tips. Green eyes that I could get lost in for days. She has freckles splattered across her nose and shoulders." There's too many to count, but that doesn't mean I didn't try. "She's kind and caring. She will do anything to protect those she loves, even if it means putting herself through Hell. She's the strongest person I've ever met."

"What is she?"

"A nurse."

The old man lets out a quiet laugh. "Not a human. Not a Reaper. What blood runs through her veins?"

The sound of her cries echo through my mind. From practicing with Yvette, to waking out of the power induced coma. Each one rings in my ears.

"She's a Banshee."

Silence takes over, blanketing us in an odd tension.

Nora had no idea that what she was. Her mother left when she was young and her father was distant growing up. As far as she knew, the Banshee wasn't in her blood line. But once she pushed herself and accepted that she wasn't normal, she owned it.

"*That* is who they speak of." Earnest speaks extremely quiet, low enough that I can barely hear him.

I all but crawl over to the bars, careful not to touch them. "What are you talking about?"

"They send out Reapers and demons, all to find the Banshee. They want her and her voice."

"She hasn't even uncaged it yet."

"That is not true. The say she has taken control of her cry, wrangling in the Banshee."

Trying to contain the anger boiling inside, I ask, "What do you mean?" A low hum floats its way into my cell. "Earnest!"

"She has gone missing from their sight. Her whereabouts are unknown to Hell - to the world. They want her. They *need* her," he explains in a sing-song melody.

Missing. What does he mean missing? I knew she would get away. My girl is too strong to be taken prisoner. With both me and Royce gone, who's protecting her? Willow? Knowing Briggs, he'd just hand her to the Changelings.

"Why do they need her?"

"Hell is a penitentiary for all. Sinners. Demons. Devils. All they want is freedom to bring Hell on earth."

I shake my head. "The Changelings would put a stop to that."

"No," he teases, drawing out the words. "Lucifer was an angel once - His favorite. He knows. They know. There is no greater power."

"What does that mean for Nora?"

Her picture in my mind flickers, wavering into darkness.

"Banshees are not what they seem. Pretty hair. Pretty voice. Lethal to hear."

My blood begins to simmer, feeling anxious with his nonsensical words. Of course she's lethal. She can literally force a soul out of a body and send it straight to Hell.

"Not all keys are metal," Earnest whispers.

"What does that mean?" No answer. I give it a moment before asking again. Yet again, I don't get an answer.

A quiet snore wages its way into my cell. The old bastard fell asleep. Just my fucking luck. Collapsing again the wall again, I take in a deep breath.

This is not how any of this was supposed to happen. Not at all. She's supposed to be safe, protected from Death. No one knows where she is. For all I know, she could be dead.

35

The minions haven't come back for me. This has probably been the longest I've been in my cell. They usually come back by now, chain me up and lead me out. Then again, it could be the same amount of time and my stress is just getting the best of me.

Ever since Earnest told me about Nora, my mind's been on a constant loop. Millions of what-ifs have formulated and planted themselves in my head. It doesn't help that the old man hasn't answered me. I've called out his name more times than I can count. There's never an answer. Occasionally, I'll hear a low hum or his snoring, but he's gone radio silent other than that. There aren't any questions. He doesn't ask me to ramble on about the human world. Just silence.

The sound of footsteps causes my ears to perk up. Shadows dance along the wall as they near. I move closer to the bars, avoiding their touch. I've learned my lesson.

"...church."

I almost miss the word as it's muddled in with a cry from the coliseum's pit. But with each step towards my cell, I'm able to piece together bits of their conversation.

"Many souls..."

"Come here... in cells."

"They will walk."

"Lords and knights... fight...."

"...chaos on... land."

Two cloaked figures pass my cell, but don't give me a second glance. Their voices and footsteps fade as quickly as they came.

What did they mean by many souls? There's already a million and seven souls locked down here. Lords and knights rule under the Princes of Hell. What need would they have to fight?

"Do you know why Banshees were created?" Earnest's voice practically makes me jump out of my skin. His speaks in a slow and grave tone, forming each word carefully.

"To help funnel in more souls."

"They bring deaths," he says. "They bring Death."

I get as close as I can to the cell's entrance, careful not to burn myself on the bars, but also ensure I can hear every word that comes out of his mouth.

Banshees are a harbinger of Death. They can use their voice to separate a soul from its host. Nora had been working with Yvette to form sonic waves as a fighting mechanism. According to the witch, Banshees don't always have the same powers. Some were more powerful than others. Some were only able to lure out a human soul from its host.

"What is it that you know of Hell?"

"It's where damned souls go for the rest of eternity.

Humans are punished for their sins. And it's hot as, well… Hell."

"What of the hierarchy?"

Once upon a time, Lilith and Lucifer ruled. They had Knights and Princes to do their dirty work. With the help of witches and Changelings, they were overthrown and the King was entombed, as well as his Queen. Ever since, Death has ruled with an iron fist.

Earnest listens as I tell him all I know. He doesn't make any comments. He just listens. I should be used to doing all the talking when it comes to him. And yet, the vibe he's giving off makes me wonder if I should keep my comments to myself.

"Your knowledge is obscured."

"Excuse me?"

He sighs. "What you know is not the truth. A twisted fantasy of saints and sinners.

"Lucifer and Lilith sat in thrones of cartilage and bones. Their say was final. Others disagreed. They wanted more power than what was given to them," Earnest goes on. "They kept their enemies close, absorbing threats. With word of an uprising in the midst, our gracious King and Queen sought out protection. Lilith lured men to her chambers in the mortal realm, tainting them and their future bloodline."

"Banshees?" I ask, trying to keep up with all the information.

"Means to an end. An end to a mean. A secret ploy to stop the revolt."

"Why didn't they want anyone knowing?"

He snickers. "Humans are casualties of war. Their lives are limited and there are many to spare. They die. A child of endless and to end was to be rare and coveted power."

I shake my head, completely lost to what he's saying. "What are you saying, Ernest?"

"Princes and sons."

Goosebumps raise the hair at the back of my neck. "Death? The princes are children of Lucifer and Lilith. What does this have to do with them?"

"They are replaceable."

"Were they the ones starting this uprising?"

Ignoring my question, he simply says, "A successor was being born, far from their knowledge."

I run a hand through my hair, doing all I can not to rip it out. This man isn't making sense.

"What you're telling me," I speak each word slow and clear, "is that Lilith gave birth to Banshees and they were created to replace Death?"

"A weapon."

"They were created as a weapon?"

"Yes."

"Is that why-"

"Another was being born," he interrupts me, letting out a frustrated sigh. "Kept out of reach from the brothers. A true heir, but untainted from egocentric desires."

Death is Death. Satan, Leviathan, and Belial. It's a known fact. A fourth brother? That's something completely unheard of.

"So where is this other one?" This makes no sense. "Shouldn't he be here?"

"Like a Banshee, his is hidden by his own self. Locked away from the lack of knowledge."

"Why?"

"Lilith and Lucifer were entombed before they could baptize him in the unholy world. Until then, he is ignorant to his existence."

Of course, because nothing can be easy. They can't just pass out cards with profiles on them. Bob, you're a Reaper. Jean, you're a Banshee. But Rupert, you're a secret son of Lucifer and his bride. Hope you enjoy the promotion.

"And those from the Banshee bloodlines were supposed to kill off Death?" He lets out a high pitched hum. Sighing, I lean my head against the rock. "I take it Death doesn't know that Nora was designed to kill them?"

A humorous giggle comes from his side of the wall. The irony of the situation causes the corner of my mouth to twitch. They wanted her power, but didn't know it was designed to kill them. Bastards fucking deserve it.

"How do you know all of this?" My question puts an end to his laughter. "Earnest? Don't you dare go quiet on my now."

"You deserve any and all information." I bite my tongue, wanting to tell him that damn right I do. "I am no mortal. I did not sin and pass on from my mortal life, securing my fate in Hell. Sorcery. Blood magic. I was Lilith's most devoted servant. Any desire of hers, I made a reality. I aided the both of them in creating the Banshee bloodline. And I was also the wet nurse to her infant."

All the feelings in my body seemed to drain away. He wasn't making this up. Yeah, it's a little fucked up in the way he's going about it, but Earnest is telling the truth. That explains why he knows as much as he does. But then that means...

"You know who entombed them?"

"Their sons."

Death. Death were the ones to lock away Lilith and Lucifer. They twisted the rumors, making it seem like the witches and Changelings were the ones to entomb them.

"Why have you kept quiet about this? Why are you telling *me*? Why *now*?"

I can picture him shrugging his shoulder. "You told me things - kept me company."

"But why now?"

He sighs loud enough for me to hear. "Death is luring your Nora into their grasps. They will use her to open a gateway from Hell, allowing them to walk free."

"I don't understand. The only way for them to go up above is through the power of the pentagram."

"Not unless the mouth of Hell opens wide, allowing it's profanities to spew out."

"How's the possible?"

"If the Banshee is as strong as I have heard, she will be able to open it. She will do it all on her own. With enough souls, especially those blessed to the Heavens, the mouth will open wide for her."

Images of Nora using her voice flash through my mind. She's strong. At times she can be an unstoppable force. But I don't know if she's strong enough open a Hellmouth, let along kill a prince. That far too much.

"What is she can't?"

"Then her powers with consume her and she will die."

"I can't let that happen, Earnest."

I need to get out of here. I need to find a way to get to her and save her before she does something that will be the end of her.

"I know how you can free yourself from those chains."

It's as if he took a bucket of cold water and splashed it on my face. "You know? You've known all this time and haven't told me."

"It wasn't the time."

"So when is the time?!" I bellow out, letting go of the string I tied around my temper.

Earnest hums. His random tune turns up the heat, sending my blood from a simmer to a full steaming boil.

"Earnest!"

He hums louder, ignoring me. I go to open my mouth and yell once more, but he stops just as quick as he started.

"Now. Now is the perfect time. But," he says, "you must take me with you."

"Tell me what I have to do."

36

"Is there a sharp rock in your cell?"

I glance around the space, looking for a divot in the walls. There's nothing really. I scramble around, patting the dirt floor. Near the back is an odd shape stone. I grab it and start slamming it against a bar. At this point, I don't care if I'm heard. If I can escape and get to Nora, I'll do whatever I have to. After a few tries, it breaks in half, leaving the one side jagged.

"Sorry to tell you, Earnest," I say, inspecting the rock, "but this isn't going to saw through these bars."

That sends him into a laughing fit. Chuckling, he says, "It is not for the bars, but for you. There is only one thing that's able to get these bars to dissolve. Use the rock to slice your hand. Then run slide your hand down a bar. Keep doing it until you have made enough room to get out."

I don't see how this is going to work. Last time I tried touching these damn things, the flesh on the palms of my hands seared off. The pain was immense and I'm not too keen on trying again. But, the old man seems to know more than he lets on.

Taking the jagged part, I cut into my palm. A pained hiss slips out, despite how hard I clench my jaw down. Blood starts pooling. I grab hold of the one bar. My fingers instantly burn, but I push past it and slide my hand down the length of the bar. Almost instantly, the bar dissolves.

"You've got to be shitting me," I mutter, amazed by the simplicity of it.

I slide my hand down another bar and it reacts just like the other. By the time I get to the third one, there's not as much blood. I cut a little deeper and let more blood coat my hand. Again and again I do this until there's enough room for me to slip out.

Peeking my head out, I look to make sure there aren't any guards lurking around. Thankfully, there's not. Just a long empty hall lined with prison cells.

Every time that I was taken out and dragged to a new form of punishment, I tried looking into the cells, especially that of my elderly neighbor. If it weren't for the merciless cries of torture, I'd swear that I'm alone down here.

As I near his cell, anxiety washes over me. I've gotten over the whole having my dick out 24/7. But finally meeting my neighbor has me feeling self-conscious. He knows a fuck ton more than he let on. He knows everything about Lilith and Lucifer being entombed, and about the Banshees. Shaking my head, I knock out any and all fleeting thoughts from my head.

Earnest waits near the bars of his cell. He's a short man with a square head and a bulbous nose. A scraggly beard falls down to his chest. He flashes me a smile, barring gaps in between his teeth.

"Kane!" He bounces back and forth on the balls of his feet.

"Do the same?" I ask, holding up the rock.

Earnest nods his head. Switching palms, I dig into my flesh and rip downward. I bite down the back of teeth. While I've given up trying to hold in my pride with Death, I don't want to make a scene. That'd be the worst thing to do right now. I slide my hand down three bars, creating just enough room for him to slip through.

"I don't get it," I blurt out, staring at where the bars are starting to reform in my cell. "Why hasn't anyone tried this before?"

He rolls his eyes. "It won't work for just anybody." Seeing the dazed and confused expression on my face, he continues, "Only those made in Hell can wield its power."

"I wasn't made-"

"No, no," he cuts in, "wrong word. Only those born from Hell itself can wield its power."

I sigh, running my hands through my hair despite them being covered in blood. "I'm a Reaper, Earnest. I wasn't born here."

"You are not a Reaper that reaps." Before I can open my mouth, he lifts a long boney finger and places it on my lips. "You know nothing of your past, because you do not have one. Your existence was desecrated, because you do not live a Reaper life. You were born to rule."

A sardonic laugh bubbles up from my chest. "You're mistaken."

The old man's face falls. His brow knits together as his gaze narrows. "A scar lies along your right rib cage."

His words make me flinch. Reaching to my side, I run my blistered fingers along my ribs. A long slice of a scar runs all the way across.

A gleam shines bright in his eyes. "As a son of Lucifer and Lilith, you were given the rib of your father and the blood of your mother."

"Why don't I remember any of this?"

"She begged - the queen begged for the knowledge of your existence to remain a secret until the day you were baptized. Death caught onto plans of deceit and formed a way to idle their predecessors power. They were entombed before you could take hold of your throne. And so I ran, keeping my word to keep you safe. With the reincarnations of Reapers, that was the only way any of this would work."

"Fuck," I bite out.

My heads is spinning a million miles a minute. Everything I once knew of this place is a lie. *I'm* a lie. I was never a Reaper to begin with. That would explain why I didn't remember anything of my past life. As Earnest said, I have no past.

"I don't know what your plan is," I say, still overwhelmed by the information bomb. "But if the brothers can only be summoned through some twisted blood magic, then we're screwed. No one will be looking for me, let alone trying to reach to me." I gesture to the ceiling of cavernous rocks. "They think I'm dead."

Earnest reaches out and pats my arm. "Once the Hellmouth is opened, we can flee."

"We don't even know when it'll open or if she can even do it."

He shrugs. "You trust in me."

I can't believe he talked me into this. It's a mistake. He's got to be off his rocker. There's no way in Hell that he's telling the truth.

I let out a sigh. "Earnest-"

"Come, come." He grabs hold of my arm and pulls me down the hall.

I should put a stop to this. It's ridiculous. We're going to get caught and end up in another round of sadistic torture. Then again, what if he's telling the truth? That would mean I could get back to Nora.

Nora. I have to get to her.

Pushing aside all my reservations, I follow along, letting the old man lead the way.

. . .

It's far too quiet. There are usually hundreds of cries mixing together, creating a twisted sort of white noise. But not right now. An eerie silence has taken over. Every creak is amplified. Each whisper of sound echoes through the cavernous halls.

"Where are we going?" I ask, keeping close behind him.

Earnest is about a foot and a half shorter than me. Despite my pained strides, I have to force my legs to slow.

"We need to get to the river."

"I don't know how long you've been down here, but I can assure you there's no river. Water doesn't flow. It's too hot," I point out.

Earnest flashes me a toothy grin. "Not all rivers are fire."

He slows his steps, making me run into him. Your naked dick running into an old man's ass is that last thing I ever wanted to do. It doesn't help that my chest jutted into his back, causing the newly formed wounds to resonate with pain.

Earnest flexes his hand in a come hither motion and then he points a finger at two shrouded figures. "You are young. You have more strength than I have. We need their cloaks. Being noticed will not be good for us."

I glance around, making sure there's no one else that might be hanging around. Aside from the decrepit looking hands, I haven't seen what they look like. Most are stout, while the others are tall and hunched over like ogres.

Stepping out of the shadows, both figures burst into movement the moment that see me. They scuttle over and launch into attack. I should be quick to react. I should be able to take both of them in an instant. But the wounds and experiments they've inflicted on me, I'm sluggish. When one moves to grab hold of me, it takes a moment for me to react. That gives other enough time and leeway to jab the branding iron into my side.

By the time I'm able to get them both down and out, I'm worn. My arms hang limp at my sides. Earnest hobbles his way over.

"Well done."

The old man gets right to work. He pulls at their cloaks to get them off. As he exposes them, my stomach knots. I taste in the back of my throat. They're covered in rotting flesh. Grey matter with maggots coming out. They're faces - well, they aren't faces. The eye sockets are black pits, along with their noses and mouths.

"Here, put this on," he instructs, tossing one my way. I make the mistake of bringing it to my nose. It smells like literal death. Earnest raises a brow when he catches it still in my hands. "Well, go ahead. Put it on."

I don't want to do this. This is the last thing I want to do, to be honest. But I've got nothing else to lose.

"Here we go," I mutter, pulling the damp threadbare material over my head.

37

The cloak smells like twenty different kinds of shit. I want to fucking vomit. I have to force myself to breathe through my mouth to help with the stench, but even that leaves a taste in my mouth.

"What's going on?"

Earnest shushes me over his shoulder. Motherfucker. I wish I didn't need him. I wish there were some type of exit or detour sign. But without them, I unfortunately need the old man. I don't trust him as far as I could throw him. He could drown me in this damn river. But he's the key to my escape. So while I don't trust him, I need him.

He abruptly stops and flattens himself against the wall. I do the same, not sure what he saw. A few seconds later, I have my answer.

A group of creatures walk by. Where we're standing in the shadows, they can't see us. But it does give us a prime spot to see them. They aren't in shrouds. They walk freely without chains. Monsters in every shape and size. Fur. Scales. Short. Tall. Long limbs. Tails. Are they knights? Guards? Whoever they are, they don't speak English. If anything, it sounds like they're talking in whatever dialect Belial speaks in.

"What are they saying?" Impatience creeps its way up my spine.

He takes a few steps deeper into the cave, adding more distance between us and them. "Portals are being christened. Not old ones. New ones. The Banshee is to be drawn out from hiding with a mortal bribe."

The cracking of my knuckles as I fist my hands sounds like shotguns in my ears. This isn't right. She wasn't supposed to get this far into it. Death knows Nora will do anything for the people she loves. *Anything.* All they would have to do is threaten her little sister and she'd comply. That's what happens when you care. You grow weak and vulnerable.

I have to get to her. I have to get to her before-

"You knew."

Earnest looks up at me. There's no trace of a smile on his face, but his eyes gleam. "I know many things."

Without thinking, I grab hold of his cloak and force him up against the wall. He's much lighter than I anticipated. "You were waiting around all this time and you didn't tell me?"

"No."

"This is bullshit. You're fucking insane."

"Patience and will," he says. "With those, anything will happen."

I let go and the old man slides to the ground. Looking down the cave, the monsters have moved on. They're shadows no longer block the opening. I move, trudging down the way. There has to be another way out - another way to get to her. Without him.

"Truth can be revealed." Earnest's words stop me in my tracks. I turn as he hobbles down the distance I've added between us. "Would you like to see?"

I clench down my jaw, wanting nothing more than to free myself from his antics. They're getting me nowhere. Earnest motions for me to come closer. He reaches out and places a hand on my forehead. His lips move, muttering words that make no sense to me.

And then darkness fades in.

"Take him," a woman pleas.

Pieces of her thick dark hair is matted to her sweating face. Her eyes are rabid; they're not quite green and they're not quite blue. She lays on the floor, surrounded by dirt and rocks. The linen dress she wears is drenched with blood along the bottom.

A man steps into view. He holds a baby in his arms. It's still covered in a mess from birth and the umbilical cord hangs down. Blood coats the man's hands.

He shakes his head. "He will be damned if they learn of his birth."

"He is damned either way," another man barks.

He walks over, folding his long frame down to wipe the hair off of the woman's face. He places a kiss on her forehead and then helps her up. She's weak and leans on him for support.

"Do whatever needs to be done," she says. She reaches her hand out, but only for a hesitant moment. "He cannot know until the times has come. Be it tomorrow or three hundreds of years from now, he must not know."

The first man nods his head. "Yes, my Lady Lilith." He turns to walk away.

Pieces of the image break away, pulling me back to reality. Earnest looks at me. He slowly bring his hand to his side.

"That was you," I mutter, recognizing his face. It was much younger in the vision, but it was most definitely him.

He nods. "Lilith entrusted me in securing your fate. Blood magic can do wonders."

"What does that mean? For me?"

Earnest takes hold of my wrist and pulls me to follow him. "Once baptized, you may take hold of your true form and powers."

"If I'm one of them, I can't walk around in the mortal world."

"Do you have a hard time comprehending what has been said to you?"

"No."

"They will use the Banshee and create a Hellmouth, allowing those strong enough to climb their way out," he rambles, pulling me down another tunnel. "Now hurry. We must take our leave before we are spotted. If not, then you have sealed both of our fates and that girl of yours will be dead before a new sun rises."

I can't keep track of where we're going. He takes me through turns and tunnels. There are no real markings to tell us where we're at or what direction we're headed, but that doesn't seem to bother him though. He knows where he's going. Or at least I hope he does.

Surely enough, he does. The air grows thick and hot as we near the end of a hall. Oranges and reds flicker along the walls, more than I've ever seen. The further we step, the closer we get to an opening not much bigger than our cells.

"What is that?"

Ernest spits. "You are filled with questions. Don't talk. Just move."

I roll my eyes, reigning in what little control I have left.

A roaring sound fills my ears the closer we get to the opening. The air is practically unbearable to breathe. It's too thick. Trying to inhale foam would be easier to do.

Bracing ourselves at the edge of the opening, the both of us peer down. Massive amounts of fire move in a steady stream. He was right. There is a river - a river of fire.

A massive lump forms in my throat. "You want me to go in there." Ernest glances up at me with a wicked smirk on his face. "Fuck that."

"It is the only way."

I shake my head and step back. "No. There has to be somewhere - something - else."

"The last son of the Lord and Lady must be baptized."

I can't help the way my head tosses backwards, laughing at his comment. Stepping forward, I gesture down to where the river burns hundreds of feet below.

Loathing and contempt laces their way into my voice. "It's a river of damn fire! From what you've been babbling on about, no one's been in there for decades. There's no way to survive that."

The fire dances in his eyes as he stares at me. The sneaky smile falls from his face, taken over by somethings much more sinister. "We will know."

"What-"

One moment I was standing, ready to knock some sense into the old man. The next, the pressure of him ramming his whole body into me send me flying. I lost my balance and tipped over the edge. I bellow out as I fall. Further and further into Hell's river.

38

Air breezed past me as I tumble further and further down. My arms and legs flail, hoping to grab of something - anything. It was useless. There was nothing. Nothing but the inevitability of landing it's the burning pit.

On my way day, I keep my eyes locked onto Ernest's face as he looks over the edge, watching with a coveted interest. Not only did he seal my fate, but he placed a wax stamp on his own as well. If I survive this, he's going to pay. He'll wish it was one of Hell's demons torturing before I'm through with him.

The simplicity of freefalling to my death... well, third death, brings every damn thought front and center. Anything I've been keeping swept under a rug is lit up with neon flashing lights.

The guilt I felt standing of Nora after I placed her in the spare bedroom. Her hair a tousled mess, but her face serene and worn.

Debating calling it quits and handing her over to Death. Or worse, Griffin.

The wave on contradictions as my body reacted to hearing her voice - seeing her in that sinful red dress. All the while, being petted by Vivian. The pent up tension I took out on her so that I didn't snap.

Jealousy tainted my veins at the sight of her speaking to Baz.

The death I wished upon myself as she stared up at me with fear blazing in her eyes.

Everything. Every damn thing that I kept hidden from others. Some things I cloaked from even myself.

The closer I grew to the river, the louder it became. The crackling popped in my ears, while the roaring overtook my thoughts. The way it rushed, running along the bottom of the cavern.

The flames the engulfed my body were excruciating at first. The way they burnt every inch of skin from my body. Feeling as the flames slid down my throat and filled my lungs.

But then... numb.

I felt nothing once I was completely submerged by the river. I kept my eyes shut, not wanting to witness my own flesh burning to a crisp.

And just as quick as the numb came, pain spread throughout my body. My shoulders, spine, head, all bursting with an unbelievable force. A scream, shameless and barren, ripped from deep in my chest. My body twisted one way and then another.

Burning.

Pain.

Stabbing.

Gouging.

Everything all at once.

It was too much - whatever the Hell was happening.

If I thought any torture I've experienced thus far was bad, it held nothing to this.

A stabbing flooded my veins and I snapped open my eyes. Flames, that were once wild and untameable, calmed. Their arches and dances ceased. They died down as my body was brought closer to the surface. Reaching out, I grabbed hold of a rock that rest at the edge of the river. Despite the lethal sensation encasing each of my nerve endings, I pull myself up. I focus any trace of energy that might be lingering in my bones.

But as I collapse onto the red rocky shore, something isn't right. I can breathe easier, but my lungs pull in more air. My body feels larger than it should. Sitting up, I glance down. While the olive tone of my skin is still there, inky black veins have taken over. Any blueish hue is lost. It's all just stained black. The outer side of forearms fade into ebony spikes, jutting out in a row. Reaching up, I feel similar shapes formed at the top of my head like devil horns.

What the fuck?

I inch closer to the river and peer over the edge. In the flickering flames, I'm met with the reflection of a stranger - a monster. Copper eyes have faded to black, shadowed in ink colored veins. The horns protrude through the oiled mess of hair on top of my head. Two fangs have taken over my canines, protruding into my bottom lip.

"What is this?" I say, the voice not of my own. It's deeper, rumbling with each word that lips from my lips.

Footsteps near, causing me to startle. The old man carefully climbs over a row of boulders. He stares at me, eyes wide and awestruck. Before I can say anything, he falls to his knee, bowing before me.

"Your majesty," he breathes, peering from under his brow to stare at me.

"What is this?"

He stands slowly, knees fighting to bend. "It is you, Prince. Your true form."

I glance back down to the fiery river. No. This can't be true. And yet, as I run a hand over my face, the beast continues to stare back.

Rocks fall from the ceiling above. They crash into the fiery river, splashing the flames several feet in the air. The ground shakes.

"What's going on?" I yell over the roaring sound of the quakes.

Ernest nears and sets a bony, aged hand on my arm. "The Hellmouth. Your destiny."

Acknowledgments

I'd love to say that A Tainted Light came just as easy for me as A Hollow Cry did. I honestly wish I could, but I can't. I struggled. Despite jump right into the second book, there was a major disconnection there. I yearned to write Kane. He's a character that I loved to write. Lennox is a very important part of Nora's tale, but I still craved portraying Kane and his broody Reaper self.

Eventually, I was able to find the diamond in the rough with this story. However, I wouldn't have been able to tucker down and finish this manuscript without my support system.

First of all, Clarise Tan did an amazing job at creating the gorgeous cover for this installment. Switching designers can be extremely terrifying, but she made the process easy. She answered any and all questions I had. I could not be more proud to share her work on this book.

To my critique partner, I honestly wouldn't have been able to do this without you. I didn't matter how many emails I sent you, you read every single one. You gave your honest opinion. And that means more than you'll ever know. You understand the books I love to read, which translate over to the books I want to write.

To my rock, the one who I dedicated this book to, if words could describe how much your support means to me, this little bit would be a seven book series. Your love knows no bounds, mirroring your support. Through the teenage drawn up vampire stories, to my second published book, you've stuck by me through everything. And for that, I owe you it all.

To my heart, you poor bastard. Who knew you'd wind up with a writer in your life, driving you crazy with all her fears and doubts. I know I'm not the easiest to handle and when my anxiety kicks in, I can be unbearable. Thank you for it all, for believing in me, even when I didn't even want to look at a notebook or my computer.

And while each of these people hold a special place in my heart, my readers take over the rest. Without you all, I wouldn't be able to do what I love best. Without all of your kind words and encouragement, I wouldn't have had the strength to write this book. And I sure as Hell wouldn't have the guts to keep the wording rolling.

I hope you all enjoyed A Tainted Light! This book was rough to get out, but I'm finally proud to show it off. I have plenty more in store, so be sure to keep a look out!

-Bee

About the Author

Bee Douglas resides with her family in a small town in Ohio. She is known for being a professional book hoarder. That's how most writers start out, right? Wanting to see their own name on the cover of a best seller next to their favorite authors? That's where her dream of becoming an author all began. In between writing and planning her next project, she enjoys binging Netflix and game nights.

Contact Information:
Email: *beedouglasbooks@gmail.com*
Website: *https://beedouglasbooks.wixsite.com/beedouglas*
        (link in book section to order personalized copies)

Social Media:
Instagram: *@beedouglasbooks*
Facebook: *Bee Douglas*
Twitter: *@beedouglasbooks*

www.ingramcontent.com/pod-product-compliance
Lightning Source LLC
Chambersburg PA
CBHW020405260626
47156CB00007B/2243